"I want *you*, Kitty Grant."

Tack leaned down and kissed her, the slide of his lips against hers not as devouring as his expression, but far from chaste. His tongue sampled her flavor, but didn't dwell there. Moving his mouth down her neck, he pressed, tasting kisses along the path, leaving a trail of sparking nerve endings in his wake.

"Tack! What are you doing?"

He looked up at her, his expression wicked. "Playing."

His answer was so unexpected, she gaped at him for several seconds. "I thought we were going to make love."

"We are. Haven't you played in bed before?"

"No."

His smile was one hundred percent wicked. "I told you, I'm going to rock your world."

"Consider it rocked."

He shook his head. "Not even close, Kitty. We've got a long way to go…"

WILD HEAT

BY

LUCY MONROE

FOREVER

NEW YORK   BOSTON

Forever
Hachette Book Group
1290 Avenue of the Americas
New York, NY 10104

www.HachetteBookGroup.com

Printed in the United States of America

First Edition: April 2015
10 9 8 7 6 5 4 3 2 1

OPM

Forever is an imprint of Grand Central Publishing.
The Forever name and logo are trademarks of Hachette Book Group, Inc.

The Hachette Speakers Bureau provides a wide range of authors for speaking events. To find out more, go to www.hachettespeakersbureau.com or call (866) 376-6591.

The publisher is not responsible for websites (or their content) that are not owned by the publisher.

For my sister Katy. Thank you for pushing me to push myself and believing in me even when I'm not sure I do. I love you so much and am so grateful God made you my big sister!

WILD HEAT

CHAPTER ONE

We're all going to die."

Caitlin Grant's head snapped up at the high-pitched tone of the small boy in the seat beside her.

He looked at her with an earnest brown gaze that dared her to disagree. The urge to hug him and tell him everything was going to be all right like Caitlin's gran used to do for her was strong. Children should not be afraid.

"Shhh, sweetheart," his mother comforted from his other side, though she sounded more worried than confident. Still, she rubbed his short nappy hair in a tender gesture. "It's going to be fine, Joey. You heard the captain. It's just turbulence."

"The plane is *shaking*, Mom. This can't be good." Joey sounded so adult and so childish at the same time.

Caitlin felt her lips curving into her first smile in months as she laid a hand on his forearm. "We're coming into Anchorage. It's usually choppy on these flights, but it'll be fine."

"You've been on a shaky plane before?" the boy demanded.

Caitlin nodded, one bright red curl slipping from its clip to brush her cheek. She pushed it back impatiently. "Many times."

She should have used more hair product this morning. Taming her wild red curls was a science. Fighting the near irresistible urge to go to the bathroom so she could smooth her hair uniformly back into the clip, despite the captain's instructions to remain seated, Caitlin tucked the errant strands more firmly behind her ear.

"This is really bad." Joey's tone indicated disbelief for her calm assurances.

Doubt in her judgment was something Caitlin was very familiar with. Whether it was the way she chose to wear her hair or the orchestra she hired to play at their annual outdoor fete, her ex-husband had frequently expressed *concerns* about Caitlin's *questionable* choices, opinions, and taste. She'd learned not to defend herself because arguing always made it worse.

But Joey wasn't her ex and Caitlin couldn't ignore his worry.

Taking a deep breath, Caitlin forced further reassurance from a tight throat. "I've been on planes that shook worse than a baby's rattle and made a lot more noise."

How ridiculous for it to be so difficult for her to add support to her own assertions.

"Really?" Joey asked hopefully.

Caitlin managed another smile. "Really."

"And you didn't die?"

She actually had to suppress the urge to grin at that. Schooling her expression into lines of seriousness, she said, "No."

His mother wasn't as adept at hiding her reaction, doing a poor job of hiding her chuckle with a cough.

Joey didn't seem to notice. "Cool."

A burst of raucous laughter from the rows behind them surprised Caitlin enough to draw her gaze. She knew that voice, though for a second she couldn't place it. It was just a reminder of Cailkirn, a sound that brought forth feelings of safety and regret in competing measure.

She turned and tried to get a good look at the man whose laugh had drawn her attention. Stylishly cut dark hair topped a handsome face, and surprised recognition mixed with the other emotions his voice had engendered. Rock Jepsom's younger brother.

The last Caitlin had heard, Carey had taken off for Hollywood with his inheritance and no intention of returning. Ever. Just like Caitlin, except her inheritance had barely covered the cost of university.

Carey had had a couple million to support his dreams. He sure didn't look like he was coming back broken like she was. In fact, he was surrounded by a group who were clearly in *the industry*.

Caitlin had spent eight years living the life in LA, and she could recognize actors and production people as easily as she could a knockoff Chanel bag.

What were they all doing heading into Anchorage? It was unlikely they were here for a shoot, because even though a lot of movies purported to be set in Alaska, few actually were. It was something of a joke among residents how seriously wrong the media usually portrayed America's largest state. But who knew, maybe they were here for a shoot. Stranger things had happened. She certainly never thought she'd be moving back to Alaska.

Not that she had any intention of asking. Caitlin wasn't the extrovert she'd been when she left Cailkirn. She was a lot more judicious about who she spoke to and why. The fact that she'd chosen to interact with the small boy beside her was as surprising as Carey's presence on the plane.

"They're all laughing. They're not afraid," Joey said, sounding like he was trying to process what that might mean.

"I imagine they are used to flying, sugar," his mother said.

Caitlin nodded. "I'm sure they are and they know just like I do that we're all going to be okay."

Joey's smile was worth her foray out of her self-imposed shell.

His mother's silently mouthed, "Thank you," caused an unfamiliar furl of warmth inside her as well.

Maybe Joey wasn't the only one who needed to know they were going to be okay. Maybe Caitlin needed to remember she was okay too. That she'd taken the steps she needed to get her life back. She wasn't running away from anything now, just returning to safety and the one place maybe she really belonged.

* * *

Tack MacKinnon finished nailing down the new stair riser on the back porch steps of the Knit & Pearl Bed-and-Breakfast.

It was a rare morning off for him during tourist season. Even though it was early May, he still had plenty to do getting his business ready for the busier months to come. Whether he was out blueprinting a new tour, navigating old ones and looking for changes in the land over the past year, or taking out some of the early-season clients, Tack's long hours had already started.

He'd planned a trip into Kenai for this morning, but when the eldest Grant sister had phoned to ask for his help, he hadn't even considered saying no.

He might be a MacKinnon, but everyone pitched in to help the Grant sisters. The Grant sisters were the last of that particular founding family still living in Cailkirn, and Alma, Moya, and Elspeth were as close to town royalty as anyone was ever going to get.

Even though Miz Alma was technically a Winter by marriage and Miz Moya, her sister-in-law, was a Grant because she'd married the only brother, most folks didn't distinguish between them. They were still "Grant sisters." Sadly, both women had lost their husbands before Tack had even been born. The final sister, Elspeth Grant, had never married.

And was one of the most vigilant matchmakers in all of Alaska, along with her sisters. Though few questioned the claim that Miss Elspeth was the most romantic of the lot.

"Oh, thank you, Tack. You're such a good boy." Miss Elspeth smiled at him from the wide porch. "You'll stay for some tea, won't you?"

"Of course, Miss Elspeth." It was getting too late to make the trip into Kenai and be back in time for his afternoon tour anyway. "A man would have to be a fool to turn down your shortbread cookies."

Miss Elspeth went pink with pleasure. "Maggie Grant brought the recipe from the Old Country and it hasn't changed in nearly two centuries. Our dear grandmother passed it down to me even though Alma is the oldest."

"My da won't admit it, but they're even better than my

gran's shortbread." Tack grinned up at the elderly spinster. "I'd appreciate it if you didn't mention that to Gran MacKinnon, though."

Miss Elspeth laughed, the sound soft and youthful despite her being closer to seventy than sixty. "Your secret is safe with me. I've got a secret of my own, you know."

"Really?"

"Yes. I haven't even told Moya," she finished in a conspiratorial whisper.

"Oh?" he asked, indulging the sweet elderly woman.

"Nope."

That surprised him. The two women had been best friends before they became sisters via marriage and were extremely close. Usually, what one knew, so did the other— and both delighted in knowing something Miz Alma did not.

The childlike delight in Miss Elspeth's faded blue eyes made him smile. "Are you going to tell me?"

"You know, I think I just might." She nodded, her straight red hair fluttering in the breeze. "Yes. You deserve it; you take such good care of us."

* * *

Some might think the Grant sisters were a few crayons shy of a full box. What with all three of them still dying their hair red, claiming to be a good twenty years younger than they were, and wearing fancy hats to church every Sunday. Then there was the way Miz Moya talked to the ghost of her deceased husband, in company. And all three of the sisters were convinced their home-turned-bed-and-breakfast was haunted by the first Maggie Grant.

Still, Tack liked them.

No one in the town loved Cailkirn more or was more dedicated to the town's thriving.

None of them wanted it to turn into another Anchorage, or even Fairbanks, but Cailkirn was less than a decade shy of its two hundredth birthday. He and the Grant sisters shared the need to know that it would celebrate that centennial and many more.

Miss Elspeth had fussed Tack's muscular six-and-a-half-foot frame into a sturdy wooden chair at her kitchen table and put the kettle on before she returned to her *secret*. "Someone's coming home."

Tack didn't want to steal Miss Elspeth's thunder. So he didn't tell her that he'd heard rumors of Rock Jepsom's younger brother coming home. Carey and a bunch of his friends had booked into the Northern Lights Lodge. With twenty guest rooms, it was the only thing resembling a hotel in or around Cailkirn.

The vast majority of Cailkirn's tourist income came from the half a million guests of the cruise ships that docked daily in their ports May through September. Day-only visitors, they had no need for local lodgings.

In a bid for town harmony, Tack did his best to share the MacKinnon Bros. Tours clients with the lodge run by the Sutherlands and the Grant sisters' B&B. Thankfully the different types of accommodations appealed to different types of his "Enjoy the Real Alaska Experience" clients.

"Who's coming for a visit, Miss Elspeth?"

"Oh, she's not coming for a visit. She's coming home to stay."

"She?" he asked in thunderstruck tones, disbelief causing a major disruption in the synapses of his brain.

"I always knew she would, no matter what Alma said.

Sean would have, too, if he and Gina hadn't been in that ter-
rible accident."

A frisson of foreboding spun through Tack, sliding right
into *no-the-hell-way*.

Miss Elspeth could not mean who he thought she did.
She hadn't stepped foot in Alaska since dropping out of college to marry Nevin Barston eight years ago. No way was
she coming home to Cailkirn. Unlike Tack, her former best
friend and the fool who'd loved her too much and too long,
the petite redhead hated Alaska. She especially despised life
in the small town that her parents had fought so hard to leave
behind.

"Yes, my niece." Miss Elspeth put her hands together as
if in prayer. "Kitty's coming home."

Tack took a big gulp of tea and then choked as he tried
not to spit it out in shock at its scalding heat.

Kitty—*call me Caitlin, please*—was coming home.

Miss Elspeth was up patting his back before he realized
she'd crossed the kitchen. "Are you all right, Tack? You
work too hard. You need to take a day off."

He didn't mention that today, or at least that morning,
was supposed to be exactly that. Doing so would be churlish
and there was something truly wrong about being grumpy
with a Grant sister. Even after she announced the woman
who had broken Tack's heart and abandoned their friendship
for the acceptance of people like Nevin Barston was coming
home.

Moving home.

"What about Barston?"

"She divorced him." There was something in Miss Elspeth's tone.

Grief. Anger. Satisfaction.

It was all there.

"I didn't realize they were having problems."

"Well, it's not as if you listen to anything said about her. You practically run from the room when Kitty is mentioned."

"I do not." Though probably? He did.

She'd been the love of his life and she'd never seen him as more than a disposable friend.

"Well, that is neither here nor there. Kitty always said everything was fine, but we could see there were difficulties. She lost her spark, our Kitty. She also lost so much weight she looked like a skeleton." Miss Elspeth had maintained the trim figure of her Miss Alaska days, but she'd never been rail thin like so many of the women he'd met in Los Angeles.

"That's not all that abnormal for LA, Miss Elspeth." He didn't like the thought that Kitty's blue eyes had lost their shine, though.

Her summer-sky gaze, so different from his dark one, had been the first thing his six-year-old self had noticed about the new girl in school. Pale with tiny freckles, she was so different from the boy who took his coloring from his Inuit mother. He'd been mesmerized by that difference and she'd never lost her fascination for him.

Which was why he'd never allowed himself to stick around when people were talking about her. The only way to sever his Kitty addiction had been to cut off all ties to her, just like she'd cut off all ties to him.

"If you'd seen her, you wouldn't say that. When she called from the hospital, she weighed ninety-three pounds."

Pain pierced Tack's heart, though he'd never acknowledge it. "That can't be right."

Sure Kitty had lost some weight once they moved to California to attend USC, but she'd been healthy the last time Tack saw her. She might have been a little thin for his taste, but she still had curves in all the right places. And she'd still turned him on like no other woman ever had. Kitty hadn't been bone-protruding skinny by any stretch.

Miss Elspeth sat down with her own cup of tea, her expression somber. "Our Kitty almost died and we weren't there. Moya went, though, after our girl called. She stayed with Kitty for six weeks. You remember?"

"Yes." It had been the previous winter.

Despite her lifelong and very vocal lack of desire to ever visit the Lower 48, Miz Moya had said she was going south for the sunshine. Tack had thought it odd but chalked it up to the elderly woman missing her only grandchild.

"Kitty said that's why she'd had so many broken bones over the last couple of years. They'd gotten brittle she said." Miss Elspeth frowned. "Grant bones don't go brittle. We're hardy stock. My grandfather lived to be ninety and Gran another twelve years after that. Neither had a single bone break in all those years."

"Kitty broke something?" Tack asked in disbelief.

She'd gotten into more scrapes as a kid, always taking risks. He could remember the tumble she'd taken when they'd been hiking on Resurrection Pass when they were twelve. It had about stopped his heart, but she hadn't so much as gotten a hairline fracture.

"More than one something. She didn't break her wrist, crack two of her ribs, and break her clavicle bumping into walls, no matter how brittle her bones."

Bile rose in Tack's throat. "Nevin Barston beat her?"

That son of a bitch! The primal urge to protect rose in Tack. Images of beating Barston until Tack had broken every bone that Miss Elspeth had listed, plus a few more, flashed through the red haze in his mind.

Elspeth's lips thinned in a sad line. "Kitty never said so, but that man destroyed our girl."

"She's coming home now, though." Tack just didn't understand why, if it had been that bad, Kitty hadn't come back a long time ago.

Or at the very least last spring when a pretty subdued Miz Moya had returned to Cailkirn. She'd stayed in California another full year by his reckoning.

Was her dislike for their small-town life so strong she'd rather live with a monster than come back to it?

Miss Elspeth reached out and patted Tack's hand, her smile belied by the tears sparkling in her faded blue eyes. "You're right. She *is* moving home. And it's going to be all right."

Tack rose from the table and gave the older woman a gentle but firm hug. "Of course it will."

Tack had more doubts on that front than he'd had since bringing his broken heart home to Cailkirn seven years ago, but he wouldn't voice them.

* * *

Keyed up by the idea of returning to Cailkirn for the first time in almost a decade, Caitlin walked behind Joey and his mother toward baggage claim.

When they arrived, a huge man stepped forward, stopping the mother and son's progress. Like a lot of Alaskan men, particularly those who lived outside of the major cities, he had facial hair. Before she could stop it, an image of the close-cropped beard and mustache Tack MacKinnon wore popped into her head. It was the perfect, perpetual five o'clock shadow and the only beard Caitlin had ever found appealing.

It didn't bode well that she'd been on Alaskan soil for less than an hour and she'd already started thinking about Tack. Moisture slicked her palms at the prospect of seeing the man again, nerves superseding the anticipation she shouldn't be feeling. She'd callously jettisoned him from her life, betraying years of friendship. She doubted Tack would have the time of day for her anymore, much less be interested in renewing their acquaintance.

There would be no healing of that particular self-inflicted wound in her heart. Considering how stomped on and shredded that organ had been over the past years, Caitlin was surprised at the level of regret that thought elicited in her.

She'd pretty much decided her heart was beyond fixing. She'd erected a steel wall around her emotions a long time ago, and it had been tempered in the fire of pain that burned through her life. There should be no room for regret at a loss that had already happened. The last thing she needed was the vulnerability of any kind of relationship, even friendship.

Pushing aside her own disturbed thoughts, Caitlin couldn't help noticing the way Joey and his mother reacted to the man who was so clearly there to meet them. Joey was staring up at the man in rapt fascination, but his mother appeared as nauseated as she had on the plane, her gaze shadowed by trepidation.

"Is this my new daddy?" Joey asked with the keen interest and innocence of a small boy.

Shock coursed through Caitlin at the question and her brain spun with explanations of where it could come from.

Daddy? They were a family of strangers, or a family in the making?

The man had the looks of a modern-day Cossack, the mother had the accent and delicate pale features of a Southern belle, and the little boy had short nappy hair and skin the color of coffee with just a dash of cream—they embodied the diversity so much a part of her home state.

The man stared down at the boy for several seconds of tense silence. Then he addressed the woman. "Savannah Marie?"

"Yes."

"You didn't say you had a child."

"You didn't ask."

Caitlin recognized Savannah's tense stance all too well. The Southern woman didn't know how her Cossack was going to react to her words, but she wasn't dissolving into apologetic explanations either and Caitlin couldn't help admiring that strength.

The tall Alaskan man turned abruptly and started walking away.

Savannah's shoulders slumped, the defeat in her posture too familiar for Caitlin to ignore.

Not that she'd ever let her own sense of despondency show, but Caitlin had felt it too long and too deeply not to recognize it in another human being. She might have learned to stifle concern for herself, but Caitlin had never been able to turn it off completely in regard to others. Since marrying Nevin, she'd done her best to protect her grandmother and aunts from the sharp edges of Caitlin's life, but this overwhelming need to react to a stranger's situation wasn't something she'd experienced in a long time.

Caitlin wasn't looking for a friend, or complications to

her barely pulled together life, but her feet moved of their own volition, drawing her nearer the other woman.

She reached out to touch Savannah's shoulder and offer help, though heaven knew Caitlin wasn't anyone's idea of a hero.

However, before her hand connected, the man turned back with a brusque, "Aren't you coming? You'll need to point out your bags for me. We've got to get on the road. The drive to Cailkirn from here isn't short."

The Southern woman's sigh of relief and whispered, "Thank God," got to Caitlin in a way that nothing else had in a long time.

Before she could talk herself out of it, she let her hand fall on Savannah's shoulder, causing the other woman to stop and turn to face Caitlin. "Pardon?"

"You're going to Cailkirn?" Caitlin forced herself to ask.

The woman's gray gaze reflected the mix of emotions Caitlin had heard in her voice a moment ago as well as confusion. "I think so?"

Caitlin nodded. "Come on, then. Let's get our bags. We're going to the same place and I'm going to talk your...friend"—she was uncertain what the relationship was at this point—"into giving me a ride."

Her original intention had been to rent a car and make the drive herself. Her brain was telling her that's exactly what Caitlin should do. But she couldn't help remembering all the times in the last few years she'd wished someone else had stepped in as a buffer between her and Nevin. She wasn't sure Savannah needed one, not really, but Caitlin wasn't walking away until she was sure the other woman didn't.

"Oh, I don't know..."

"Don't worry. I won't take up a lot of room." Caitlin winked, proud of herself for making the comment without feeling the shame that still sometimes accompanied any reference to her body.

"But—"

"He won't mind. It's an Alaskan thing. Neighbors help neighbors. Especially in the small towns, but nowhere more than in Cailkirn."

They reached the luggage carousel and the bearded man.

"Caitlin Grant." She put her hand out to him. "I'm headed to the Knit and Pearl B and B. I would really appreciate a ride if you've got room."

"Nikolai Vasov." He shook Caitlin's hand. "I know the Grant sisters."

Caitlin gave Nikolai the polite expression that she'd perfected in her years with Nevin. "I'm not surprised. Most people in Cailkirn do. Moya is my grandmother."

Her grandmother and great-aunts had lived in the small town on the Kenai Peninsula their entire lives. With her grandfather and great-uncle Teddy gone, the three elderly ladies shared the spacious Victorian house that had been built on the original Grant homestead more than a hundred years before.

As far as Caitlin knew, her aunt Elspeth had never lived anywhere else and her grandmother had lived in the Grant home since her marriage to Grandfather Ardal forty years ago. Aunt Alma had moved back into the big house after Teddy Winter's death a few years after the turn of the century.

It was a couple of years after the oldest Grant sister moved in that the sisters decided to turn the house into a bed-and-breakfast. Caitlin had been preparing to go away to college and her grandmother and aunts claimed they needed something to keep them busy.

Caitlin realized Nikolai looked more than a little like the Vasov boy who had been a couple of years ahead of her and Tack in school. "Are you related to Alexi Vasov?"

"He's my cousin."

She nodded, vaguely remembering talk about Alexi's uncle. Peder Vasov had left Cailkirn right after high school just like Caitlin's parents. Somehow, both their children had ended up back in the town settled by Scots and Russians, integrating a small Inuit village along the way to incorporated town status.

Nikolai nodded his head abruptly. "We'll make room for you."

He didn't ask how much luggage she had. It wasn't the Cailkirn way.

Caitlin turned to Savannah and her son. "I should introduce myself to you too. I'm Caitlin Grant and you can find me at the Knit and Pearl Bed-and-Breakfast. You and your son will always be welcome."

Though she was probably the last woman who should be trying to offer hope and help to someone else, Caitlin couldn't seem to stop herself.

"I'm Joseph, but everybody calls me Joey," the little dark-haired boy offered while his mother stood in apparent shock.

Caitlin shook his hand and didn't tell him she'd heard his name on the plane. "It's very nice to meet you, Joseph. I'll call you Joey if you like."

"Yes." He stared at his mom, clearly waiting for her to say something.

The other woman offered her hand. "My name is Savannah..." She cast a sidelong glance at Nikolai.

He gazed back, his expression impenetrable.

Savannah took a deep breath. "Vasov. I'm Savannah Vasov."

Caitlin schooled her features not to show her shock. She hadn't heard of a proxy marriage since she was a teenager, but what else could this be?

In a state where the male population outnumbered females of marriageable age, long-distance relationships were not uncommon. Marriages brought about through a third party weren't unheard of either.

Heck, they happened in the Lower 48 too. The dot-com matchmaking entities were an ingrained part of American life now. Entire reality shows were dedicated to the concept of matchmaking and selective pool dating with the endgame being a marriage.

Proxy marriages were a lot less common, though, to the point of being almost unheard of. Oh, they happened, but most commonly among active duty military.

They were legal in only six states, California being one of them—which explained how Savannah and Nik had managed to marry by proxy. It wasn't a legal practice for an Alaskan-based marriage ceremony.

Though foreign brides marrying American men by proxy was still an active practice. Caitlin had known more than one beautiful Eastern European or Asian woman back in LA who had married her wealthy but otherwise unremarkable middle-aged husband, by proxy. It had worked out beautifully for some and not so well for others.

Not that Caitlin was in a position to pass judgment on anyone else's marriage, hers having been its own horror story.

They retrieved their luggage and headed out to Nikolai's

truck, where the big man let Savannah, her son, and Caitlin into the vehicle before stowing the suitcases in the back. Anticipation born of loss and growth filled Caitlin as they headed back to her hometown, the one place she'd been so sure she never wanted to live again and the only place she could now imagine trying to rebuild her life.

CHAPTER TWO

Tack closed the browser on his tablet, the images of women suffering from anorexia leaving his stomach tight and hollow.

He couldn't imagine Kitty's body so emaciated. Didn't want to imagine it. Even more horrific was the possibility that in that physically and, according to what he'd read about the disease, emotionally vulnerable state, Nevin Barston had been physically abusive to Kitty.

Tack had spent nine years resenting Kitty's rejection of their friendship, even after he'd overcome the hurt of unrequited love. He'd pushed every happy memory of her deep into the darkest recesses of his psyche and had only allowed himself to remember the Kitty who was so intent on making a life for herself in California, she'd been willing to dump her best friend to do it.

He'd spent a dozen years as Kitty's staunchest friend.

Then she'd cut him off and he'd let her. It had hurt less not having to see her in love with another man.

He'd written off the more brittle personality of the LA Kitty he witnessed from a distance his final weeks at university in California. No way had he suspected it was the beginning of a self-destructive eating spiral that would land her in the hospital weighing thirty percent less than her ideal weight.

All the regret in the world at not looking closer, not being more determined to maintain their friendship, couldn't change the past, but that didn't mean Tack didn't feel it. It would take an asshole of mammoth proportions not to be moved by what Kitty had gone through in her marriage and what she'd done to herself in reaction to it.

Kitty had been funny about food sometimes when they were kids. Like when she obsessed over tests in school, she'd stop eating and start drinking coffee so she could stay up late studying. Miz Moya would have been livid if she'd known, but Tack had covered for Kitty.

He'd thought it was no big deal. And maybe it never would have been, if she hadn't married that bastard in California.

Tack had transferred to Idaho State without a single pang of conscience. He didn't regret that decision now either. Kitty *had* dumped their friendship and he had hated LA, but that didn't mean he felt *nothing* at the knowledge Kitty's life over the past years hadn't been nearly as tranquil as his.

Shit.

Tack recognized the feeling welling up inside him as inexorable as a hot spring geyser. Protectiveness toward a girl who had repaid his friendship with unswerving loyalty, honesty, and warmth for twelve years. Right up until she withdrew every bit of it, right down to the honesty, apparently.

She'd made out like everything was perfect with her Prince Charming, only maybe Nevin had been more of a demon. He'd certainly done his best to suck the soul out of Kitty.

* * *

Tension hung thick in the extended cab of Nikolai's four-by-four. Caitlin sat in the back with Joey, who had bounced and chattered nonstop for the first thirty minutes before falling asleep midsentence.

Slumped against the side panel, he slept on while the adults maintained an uncomfortable silence.

Savannah sat in front, her body as close to the door as she could get and still stay on the seat. There'd been no question she would rather have sat where Caitlin was for the drive, but Nikolai had loaded his passengers with unmistakable intent. He didn't talk a lot, but the words he used left no doubt what he expected to happen.

Caitlin had observed quietly as Savannah had tried to engage in conversation with Nikolai a couple of times, but his monosyllabic answers had not encouraged further attempts.

Having some experience with taciturn Alaskan men, Caitlin wasn't convinced of Nikolai's lack of interest in Savannah's conversation. Though it was clear the other woman was.

Her expression dazed, Savannah's focus was entirely on the passing scenery now. Therefore, she did not see the sidelong glances Nikolai cast her way every few miles.

Caitlin would be content to finish the ride in silence. She

had a lot of practice at surviving this kind of tension, but being back in Alaska was calling to her true nature, to the woman she'd buried deep and tried to forget.

The Alaskan girl with a friendly, curious nature her ex had worked hard to suppress if not destroy completely.

Caitlin wasn't going to let him win. She remembered the final bit of advice from her therapist at their last appointment: *Leaving your husband isn't going to help you, if you continue to live as if he's still looking over your shoulder.*

Every day might be an effort to reconnect to the world in a meaningful way, but Caitlin was a fighter. No matter how little that had shown in the past years of her life.

"How old is Joey?" she asked Savannah, noticing Nikolai tensing as if waiting for a reply as well.

"He's six."

"Does he like school?"

"I've...um...been homeschooling him. He's smart. Really, really smart." That at least brought some spark to the other woman's demeanor.

Nikolai barked out, "Why are you homeschooling the boy?"

"The boy has a name." From Savannah's tone, her attitude toward Nikolai was sliding from overwhelmed to irritated.

His expression unchanging, his tone showing no overt annoyance at the need to repeat his question, just the same gruff demeanor, Nikolai asked, "Why not put Joey in school?"

Nevin would have been furious if she had ever stood up to him the way Savannah held her own against Nikolai. Strangely, the other woman's response triggered gratitude in Caitlin for her own freedom. She never had to pretend to be *fine* to placate a dangerously angry husband again.

"I thought homeschooling was common in Alaska?" Savannah asked, rather than answer.

Nikolai grunted. Was he annoyed Savannah hadn't answered his question?

"In a lot of places, it is, but Cailkirn has always had its own elementary school," Caitlin hastened to assure her, continuing a patina of babble in hopes of smoothing over the growing tension inside the truck. "It's small but the community is always ready to pitch in. Once the children reach middle school, they have to bus to one of the bigger schools."

"How does that work in winter?" Savannah asked, her soft Southern drawl drawing Nikolai's attention, though she didn't seem to notice.

"It's not bad. Sometimes children miss days because of extreme conditions, whether because the carpool from Cailkirn can't make it to the bus route to drop the kids at their stop or sometimes because the buses aren't running. It really doesn't happen as often as you might expect."

"We're prepared for the weather," Nikolai inserted. "Some parents send their teens to college prep boarding schools."

Muscles that she hadn't been aware were tightening in Caitlin's neck and shoulders relaxed as it became apparent there wasn't going to be a full-blown argument.

* * *

"No," Savannah said with unexpected force and a glare for Nikolai that Caitlin wasn't sure he'd earned with his simple observation. "I'm not sending my child away to school."

Nikolai shrugged. "There are some years before we have to consider high school."

Savannah visibly deflated. Whether from relief at that fact or the man's dismissal of her concerns, Caitlin could not tell.

"My grandmother didn't send me away to boarding school and I didn't have any problems at university coming from the local high school."

In fact, her college years shone as bright beacons on the map of her life. Not least of which because her best friend, Taqukaq MacKinnon, had opted to attend USC as well. She'd loved life in California those first few years.

Panic welled at memories of Nevin's reaction when she'd told him she wanted to go to Tack's graduation a year after she'd married. She'd had some crazy idea of renewing her friendship at least enough that they could send the occasional e-mail or Christmas card. Nevin had made it very clear that was not acceptable.

Ignoring the rise and fall of stilted words coming from the truck's front seat occupants, Caitlin practiced her calming techniques. It took about twenty miles, but eventually her breathing returned to normal and the band around her chest loosened.

Her therapist said Caitlin had a form of PTSD. She'd survived her own private war, and not without internal wounds. Some of which she wasn't sure would ever heal.

Caitlin hadn't spoken to Tack in years and she hadn't seen him in even longer. But suddenly the desire to talk to her oldest friend was so strong she would have called him if she had his cell phone number.

And wouldn't that go over well? Not.

He'd probably disconnect the call the second he recognized her voice.

"Caitlin?" Savannah's expression indicated she might have tried to get Caitlin's attention more than once.

"Sorry. My mind wanders sometimes." Caitlin did her best to focus on the other woman. "What were you asking?"

"How long will you be staying in Cailkirn?"

"Permanently." Caitlin tasted the word on her tongue and it wasn't nearly as bitter as she thought it would be. "I'll be helping my grandmother and great-aunts run the bed-and-breakfast."

Savannah smiled, making her lovely face almost super-naturally beautiful. "I'm sure they'll be happy to have your help."

Nikolai grunted. Again.

* * *

The sound carried both agreement with Savannah's words and disapproval for Caitlin leaving the elderly women to handle things on their own for so long.

Typical Alaskan man.

"I'm looking forward to being back." And surprisingly, Caitlin found she wasn't lying.

She'd missed her family and had a new appreciation for the slower pace of life in Cailkirn. She was ready to start life over away from the bright lights and fast living of LA.

Savannah shot Nikolai a sidelong glance and then asked Caitlin, "Do your parents live in Cailkirn as well?"

The old, familiar pain of loss washed over Caitlin, the ache duller but no less physical today than it had been when she was six and was told her mom and dad were never coming home. Some children who have trauma in their early years forget most of it to protect their emotional well-being. But Caitlin remembered everything about her parents, from the way her mom read to her every night before bed, even after she learned to read to herself, to her dad's preference for kid's cereal for Sunday breakfast.

"Oh, so where are they now?"

Caitlin shook her head, the loss still poignant after a lifetime. "They died in a car accident."

"Oh, I am so sorry." Savannah looked stricken. "You said your grandmother raised you. It didn't click until just now why that must have been."

"It's all right. It was more than two decades ago now." She ruthlessly tamped down the urge to wrap her arms around her middle like she used to do whenever talking about her parents.

"But that kind of loss never goes away, does it?" Savannah said softly.

Caitlin wondered if the other woman had suffered a similar loss but didn't ask. She knew how little she liked people probing into her past. If Savannah wanted to tell Caitlin, she'd offer the information.

Rather than waiting for any kind of reply from Caitlin, Savannah said, "Living in Alaska is going to be really different than California."

Savannah bit her lip, clearly worried about something. Caitlin didn't blame her.

"The boy will be fine," Nikolai said.

Savannah sent him a shocked glance, showing he'd pegged her concern just right. "How…"

When Caitlin realized Nikolai was not going to bother answering, she said, "Cailkirn can be a great place to grow up."

Savannah smiled her gratitude at Caitlin. And right there, an unbreakable bond of understanding and commiseration formed between the women.

* * *

Tack was late for dinner.

The Grant sisters served it promptly at seven spring through fall and six in the winter (when the guests were few and far between). It was a quarter past seven, and Tack knew he'd be in for anything from a gentle reprimand to an acerbic tongue-lashing, depending on which of the elderly sisters took him to task.

He didn't mind. His Inuit mother and grandmother had taught him to respect his elders, especially those of the female gender.

Tack pulled into the B&B's drive and was surprised to see Nik's truck parked in front. Tack thought the man had gone into Anchorage to pick up his mail-order bride. He still couldn't believe his friend had gone ahead with the proxy wedding. He understood the pressure Nik was under from his grandfather but still couldn't see how this kind of marriage was the solution. Nik deserved a real marriage to a woman he loved. But then maybe Tack was just too traditional.

True love sure hadn't worked out for him.

As he climbed out of his truck, he realized a woman sat in the front seat of the dusty red extended cab, the top of her blond hair just visible above the back of the seat.

Was this the bride, and what in the hell was she doing in Nik's truck without Nik?

He looked beyond the truck to the open door of the bed-and-breakfast in time to see Nik coming out the door. Not the most affable of men, Tack's friend looked even more pissed off with the world than usual.

He stopped when he saw Tack. "What are you doing here?"

"Eating with the Grant sisters. Is that your bride?" Tack tilted his head toward Nik's truck.

"Yes," Nik bit off. "And the boy sleeping in the backseat is her son."

Shock coursed through Tack. "Her son?"

"Yeah, I wasn't expecting that news either." With that, Nik yanked his door open and jumped into his truck. "Good luck with the Grant sisters, man. I've got my own woman troubles to deal with tonight."

He slammed it closed and then pulled out of the drive with a spray of gravel.

Well, hell.

He might have advised Nik against the whole mail-order bride thing, but that didn't mean Tack didn't want it to work out for the other man.

Shaking his head, Tack climbed the front porch steps. From the way they squeaked, he decided they could use a little maintenance as well. He added that to his to-do list in his head. The sound of all three sisters talking at once led him to the front parlor, but his steps slowed as he heard another voice mixed in.

* * *

Soft feminine tones he would never forget still echoed in whispers as he woke from the kinds of dreams men were supposed to stop having once they'd left their teen years.

Kitty Grant was here.

Miss Elspeth had to have known Kitty was coming in today, but she hadn't said so. She'd told him her niece was coming home, but Tack had thought that meant at some point in the future. Not today.

Not right this minute when he wasn't prepared for or expecting it.

Nik's words made more sense now too. The other man knew about Tack's history with Kitty, so his words had been a warning, but damned if Tack hadn't gotten it.

He considered turning around and leaving, but his feet just kept moving forward as the sound of her voice grew more and more discernable and had its typical impact on his libido. It had been years, but hearing her voice still turned him on faster than a woman's friendly hand on his thigh when he was in the mood to scratch that itch.

His heart beating as fast as if he'd jogged a seven-mile trail uphill, he stopped in the open doorway to the parlor and got his first view of Kitty Grant.

All the air expelled from his lungs and he couldn't seem to suck any back in.

He'd expected Kitty to look emaciated; after the research he'd done, he'd rehearsed in his mind how he wouldn't react outwardly to her appearance when he finally saw her. He hadn't prepared himself for the woman who stood before him. No, she didn't have the same curvaceous allure she had six years ago, but even from the back, Kitty was still breath-stealing.

She was thin, but her limbs didn't have the fragile skeletal appearance from the previous winter that had so concerned Miss Elspeth, and her clothes fit over obvious feminine curves. Gratitude that he hadn't had to come face-to-face with signs of her illness gave him the wherewithal to finally take in another breath.

He didn't ever have to admit it to anyone else (or acknowledge it to himself again if he could help it), but it would have destroyed something inside Tack to see her as sick as Miss Elspeth said Kitty had been.

The female form he had always considered perfect was encased in a pastel pink suit that highlighted her understated curves. No doubt by some big-name designer, the jacket had a ruffle thing around her hips that accented the gentle slope of her ass. He liked it. The skirt hugged her hips, its hem a few inches above her knees, giving him a view of her toned legs.

Her heels had to be at least three inches high. They looked neither comfortable nor suitable for life in Cailkirn, Alaska. But hell if they didn't make her calves look delicious and spark his imagination about what she'd look like from the back walking in them.

Undeniable arousal hit him hard and without provocation. Worse than the sound of her voice, the sight of her had him craving things he knew damn well no good could come from wanting. Renewed sexual attraction to the woman who'd decimated his heart was not in Tack's list of approved scenarios.

He once again considered turning around and leaving before anyone noticed him. What were the chances Miss Elspeth would remember inviting him to dinner?

Who was he kidding? That woman remembered everything. Including how many times she'd changed Tack's diaper when he was a baby.

Besides, his feet weren't listening to his brain. He'd kept moving and now he stood right behind Kitty, her subtle floral perfume mixing with her natural scent and reaching out to tug at his senses.

The urge to touch her nearly overwhelmed him. He had to squelch it, and fast.

"I would have expected you to arrive in a limo, Miss Barston." His words acted like an anvil on the feminine chatter.

Kitty's back went rigid, her head jerking, like the sound of his voice had shocked her even worse than hearing hers had shocked him moments ago. There went his chance of leaving undetected. Shit. Why hadn't he kept his mouth shut?

All three of the older women turned to face him with varying expressions. Miss Elspeth glowed with delight. Miz Moya's eyes were suspiciously moist, her smile a little wobbly. Miz Alma's usual dour expression was lightened enough for an almost smile to curve her precisely painted lips.

Kitty turned too. Slowly, as if cautious about what she was going to find. Her eyes locked with Tack's, their blue depths filled with a hell of a lot of emotion. None of which he could, or wanted to, interpret.

And you keep telling yourself that, boyo. Ignoring the sarcastic inner voice, he drank in the sight of Kitty full-on.

Her wild red curls, longer than they had been the last time he'd seen her, were mostly tamed with a clip behind her head. Though one curl had slipped forward to lay in a ringlet over her ear. Her cheeks were not as full or rosy as he remembered, but she looked nothing like the pictures of dangerously underweight anorexic women he'd looked up online after leaving the Knit & Pearl earlier that day.

Her breasts were still rounded, the mint-green top she wore under her suit jacket cut low enough to hint at cleavage that fed the desire he was doing his best to ignore.

And she was still more beautiful than any other woman he'd ever known.

Her blue eyes were just as vivid as they'd always been, but the sparkle of laughter, of perpetual mischief...of *life* that was such a part of the Kitty Grant he'd grown up with was missing.

Even without it, or maybe because of that single difference, he couldn't look away.

He stood, trapped in her gaze, memories he thought
buried bombarding him. Feelings he would never acknowledge crashed through him. A man had his pride, though.

Tack's wouldn't allow any of that to show on his face, but
he wouldn't look away.

Kitty didn't seem any more capable of breaking eye contact. Her own lovely features were smooth, devoid of the
maelstrom swirling in her blue depths.

A mere foot separated them, but it might as well have
been the width of Bristol Bay.

But their gazes held.

CHAPTER THREE

It's Grant," she said after a prolonged silence no one else seemed ready to break, her soft voice going straight to his dick. "I asked for my name back from the courts as part of the divorce."

"Erasing Barston from your life?" Like she'd erased Tack so completely, though he'd no doubt the other man deserved it.

He deserved a hell of a lot more, but if Tack got to thinking on that, things could get dicey. He didn't lose his temper often, but when he did, it was ugly.

And he couldn't afford to hop a plane for California to hunt down Kitty's ex-husband to give him a well-earned beatdown he would never forget and might not walk away from.

"If I could cleanse him from my memories, I would." Kitty's expression defied him to judge her for that.

Like he would. Still, the bitterness lacing her tone was

new. Kitty had never been bitter. Not even about her parents' untimely deaths.

Fury at the absent man bubbled under Tack's fixed expression, his temper stirring dangerously again. "He must have been a piss-poor husband for you to feel that way."

Kitty flinched a little, as if Tack's anger bothered her, but then her eyes narrowed, and for just a second he saw a reflection of the inner fire that used to fascinate him. "He was."

"He was a monster," Miss Elspeth said with conviction.

"Clearly damaged in the head to treat our Kitty the way he did," Miz Alma opined. As the eldest, she expected her opinion to be taken as gospel too.

Tack wasn't going to disagree, though. He thought the sisters' assessment of Barston was damn accurate.

"Oh, Kitty," Miz Moya said in a tear-filled voice.

If he didn't do something fast, the older women were going to drown Kitty in pity, and from the expression on her face, he didn't think that was going to be beneficial for anyone concerned.

"I thought dinner was at seven?" he asked with as much innocence as a twenty-eight-year-old man could muster.

Miz Moya's hands flew to her pink, round cheeks. "Oh my. With Kitty's arrival, I forgot the roast."

She rushed off to the kitchen, Miss Elspeth following, saying she still needed to set the table, her hands all aflutter.

It was early May and the first cruise ship hadn't hit the harbor yet. There was only one guest room occupied, as Tack had been told that morning while he worked on the step. However, the fact that they only had two guests instead of eight wouldn't diminish the sisters' mortification at serving dinner late.

The older couple might well be in the dining room, but

they were conspicuous in their absence from the front parlor.

Miz Alma gave Kitty and Tack a measuring look. "I had best make sure Elspeth doesn't drop Grandmother Grant's china in her dither. I'm stunned she was able to keep your upcoming arrival a secret, Kitty."

Everyone knew Miss Elspeth was not good at keeping secrets. Tack had to wonder why she'd been so committed to keeping this one.

"She likes knowing something you don't," Kitty offered with a shrug that bothered Tack more than it should.

Back in the day, she would have said the same thing with a sly smile and a wink. The lack of animation was not acceptable, but he wasn't exactly sure what to do about it.

Do something he would, though.

It wasn't in Tack's nature to leave something broken that needed fixing. Not even people.

"Yes, well... we'll have dinner on the table in about five minutes." With that, Miz Alma left the room.

Tack didn't bother to hide his continued perusal of Kitty. He would never admit to anyone else how hungry he was for the sight of the one woman he was determined never to give another chance at his heart.

Color climbed her cheeks and she turned away, her hand reaching for one of the many photos on the fireplace mantel. It was of her and Tack before they left for USC, their arms around each other.

She stared at it for several long seconds. "I know I look different."

"I'm glad you grew your hair out again." He'd always loved how it tumbled wildly around her head.

She spun back to him, like his words surprised her. "That's all you see?"

He grinned. "You've stopped wearing all that black goop around your eyes too."

She laughed. It was barely a puff of sound, but it seemed to startle her. "That's the second time today."

"What?"

"That I've laughed. I don't laugh anymore. I guess coming home is going to be good for me after all."

Stunned at her words, he stared at her. Kitty Grant not laughing? He couldn't imagine it. "You belong here."

"I didn't used to think so."

She would probably decide she didn't again, but it wasn't his place to remark on it. She'd been wrong back then and she'd be wrong when she left again, but one thing he was sure of. Kitty would leave.

Her parents had left a legacy of more than money to their only daughter. They'd left how much they despised living in the wild north to her as well.

"It's good to see you," Kitty said when the silence had stretched a little.

"Is it?"

"Yes. I missed you." Deeper emotion than he would ever allow himself to trust from her seemed to infuse those four little words.

"There was no place for me in your life."

"No. Not when I was with Nevin."

Because back then there'd been no room for someone who happened to be both her best friend and a man who loved her. He'd become an awkward problem she didn't want to deal with anymore.

He didn't love her now, that was for damn sure, but desire was making itself known in the swollen flesh pressing against the button fly of his jeans.

"No place for the little people when you were married to LA elite." The words might be bitter, but his tone wasn't.

He'd been hurt back then at her rejection, but he wasn't naïve to the ways of the world. Even if he was from a small Alaskan town.

He hadn't fit in with the Los Angeles glitterati, even when he'd been a student at USC.

Her perfect bow-shaped lips twisted in a grimace. "You won't understand, but Nevin handpicked the people in my life, from my yoga instructor to the woman who called herself my best friend. He saw you as a threat, though I didn't realize it until much later, so..."

"I got kicked to the curb."

Her head dipped, as if that shamed her. "Yes."

She was partially right about him not understanding. He couldn't imagine allowing anyone to have that kind of power in his life; however, there had been a time he'd left behind the life he loved because that was what this woman wanted.

"You must have loved him very much."

"I don't know." Kitty's blue eyes clouded with confusion and pain he didn't want to see. "Maybe I loved him once."

She'd given up her education, her family... She'd given up Tack for Nevin Barston. Of course she'd loved him. And Tack didn't like dwelling on that truth any more today than he had eight years ago.

She shrugged, a move he was quickly learning to dislike. It was way too noncommittal for the Kitty Grant he'd known. No way he could be sure when Kitty had started changing, but change she had. When they'd been friends, she would have argued her point of view, even in the face of irrefutable evidence.

The woman standing in front of him wasn't about to do that.

The truth of the difference between Kitty then and Kitty now hit him hard and right between the eyes. Shit. Piss. Damn.

That urge to take a little trip south and beat the ever-loving shit out Nevin Barston washed over Tack again.

"It's complicated, Tack." Kitty made an aborted move with her hand. "And I've had a really long day."

Oh, he believed it was complicated all right. However, Tack knew the flames of her nature might be doused, but he refused to accept that an ember didn't still burn somewhere deep inside her.

"Kitty, I know you've been through hell—"

Kitty interrupted before he could go any further. "I go by Caitlin now."

"Well, maybe you need to find Kitty again."

"And you think I'm going to just because you use that name?" She might not realize it, but there was a tinge of the old Kitty snark in that tone.

He grinned. "I don't know, but I'm not calling you Caitlin."

"*You* haven't changed."

"You're wrong about that too."

"Too? What else am I wrong about?"

"You're stronger than you think."

"Because I finally divorced the monster who claimed to love me?" She laughed, the sound hollow, no amusement in it at all. "That was an act of desperation, not some grand stand."

"You still did it."

"He was out of the country. If he hadn't been, I would never have had the courage to take the first step and walk out."

At first Tack didn't know how to respond to that. Kitty so afraid of her husband she wouldn't have left him while he was near enough to do something about it? The idea boggled Tack's mind, but it pissed him off even more. His hands curled into tight fists, but he did his best to keep his anger from his face after Kitty's earlier reaction.

Nevin Barston was one lucky son of a bitch that he was in LA right now.

"Why didn't you call?" She'd needed help; she had to know Tack would have been there.

"Would you have answered?" she asked, with an apparently genuine desire to know the answer.

Because she didn't already.

Had she forgotten everything they were to each other?

"How could you doubt it? Even if you hadn't been my best friend for most of my life, you were from Cailkirn. Anyone in this town would have helped you." But him most of all.

"You were the last real friend I had and I treated you like crap." Remorse infused her words and her self-disgust was clear.

He couldn't argue with her, though, even if he felt like he should. She was just so damn fragile right now.

Thankfully Miz Alma called them to the table, her tone impatient, before Tack found himself saying things he shouldn't.

* * *

Careful to separate the roast, potatoes, and vegetables evenly, Caitlin pushed half of the food her aunt had put on her plate to one side. She was concentrating so hard it took her a moment to realize her aunts had bowed their heads for a blessing. His head bowed but his eyes open, Tack stared at her, whether in reproach or confusion at Caitlin's eating ritual she couldn't tell.

Heat shooting into her cheeks, she quickly dropped her hands into her lap and dipped her head.

The simple phrases Aunt Alma spoke washed over Caitlin with the comfort of forgotten familiarity. She couldn't remember the last time she'd engaged in something so homey as blessing her food.

There had been a time when such activities had embarrassed her; then she'd come to long for them, and now she engaged with a gratitude few would understand.

Just as with her food rituals, there was safety in these comfortable customs that had been passed from one generation to the next.

"It is so good to have our girl home, isn't it, Tack?" Aunt Elspeth asked after they'd begun eating.

He smiled at her aunt, the expression lending warmth to the hard angles of his face. He'd had the features of a boy the last time she'd seen him, but now he was a man. A very good-looking man, who wore confidence like the new sexy.

Not looking at Caitlin to include her in the warm expression, he said, "Sure."

Her aunt was appeased, but Caitlin knew his single-word answer had hardly been a ringing endorsement. She didn't blame him. In fact, Caitlin was kind of glad he didn't look at her just then.

She was finding it unexpectedly difficult to control her reaction to him. Getting the best of the genes from both sides of his family, the Scots and the Inuits, Tack had always been attractive. However, now he was hotter than anything

LA had to offer. His chocolate-brown eyes were set under a raven's brow, and his nose was perfectly proportioned for a man's face above his square jaw.

He'd been muscular before, but now his six-and-a-half-foot frame was as solid as a rock.

She'd never seen Tack as being sexy in the past.

No, that wasn't true, and Caitlin's healing required self-honesty now. She hadn't *allowed herself* to be attracted to her best friend. Falling in love with Taqukaq MacKinnon would have meant staying in Cailkirn, and that was something Kitty Grant had been determined not to do. Funny the difference eight years could make. Because nowadays, Caitlin looked at Cailkirn as the one place of safety in the whole wide world. The only home her heart would ever long for.

Even so, she didn't welcome her reaction to Tack's twenty-eight-year-old self. And she didn't think he would either.

The biggest surprise *wasn't* that Tack was the object of her fluttering sexual desire; it was the fact that she was feeling that kind of craving at all. She couldn't remember the last time she'd felt desire. But her body was reacting to Tack like he'd been bathed in aphrodisiacs. She wanted to touch him, taste his salty skin, and inhale his scent. It was such an unfamiliar sensation that Caitlin struggled with following through on her food ritual.

She had to eat the portion of food she'd assigned herself. Her head knew that. The rest of her did not want to co-operate.

Forcing herself to take a bite, Caitlin let the conversation go on around her.

But her reaction to Tack didn't get any more comprehensible or easy to handle, and every bite was an effort in a way eating hadn't been for a while.

It took all of her self-possession to stay at the table when what she really wanted was to get up and leave. As happy as she was to be with her family again, she felt them watching her, gauging her mood and her health. Their concern was a balm, but it overwhelmed her, too, pressing in on her, making her feel the need to keep repeating that she was all right. That they didn't need to worry about her anymore.

Even if she wasn't entirely sure that was true.

She couldn't help but feel nauseated just looking at the plate of food in front of her. The half she'd portioned to eat looked like a mountain of meat and vegetables now.

That combined with Caitlin's unexpected sexual reaction to Tack and the desire to find her old room and hide behind a closed door just got bigger.

But hiding hadn't done her any favors in the past and she was doing her best not to revert to what had ultimately become a self-destructive defense mechanism.

So, she ate. Very little and very slowly, but she kept at it and did her best to ignore her response to Tack.

Even if he didn't hate her for the past, she was never putting herself at the mercy of a man again. Not even Tack. Caitlin was going to die a Grant now that she'd reclaimed her maiden name.

Besides, of all men, Tack deserved a woman who wasn't glued together like a shattered vase.

CHAPTER FOUR

Tack shifted his tall frame restlessly, kicking off the blankets in the dark. Thoughts of Kitty would not let him sleep.

Even though his father and grandfather had built the bed for Tack's comfort, he couldn't settle tonight.

He was pretty sure the size of his bed had been a not-so-subtle hint from the older generations. It was the width of a king and had an extra six inches in length, definitely more than big enough for two people.

No one else had shared it with him in the two years since he'd moved into his custom-designed log cabin.

Tack didn't have time for a relationship and kept his sex life to tourists or trips to Anchorage in the winter. A healthy adult male with a strong sex drive, if not inclination toward commitment, Tack had been a temporary visitor on a helluva lot of cruise ships moored in the Cailkirn harbor.

He didn't bring casual sex partners to his cabin. Tack had every intention of sharing his home with a wife and family someday, but until then it was his sanctuary—the way it should be.

It didn't sound like Kitty's place in California had been a sanctuary for her. Not even a little bit.

Tack had spent eight years resenting her for ejecting him from her life the minute she got engaged to that bastard Nevin Barston.

Tack had never once considered that Kitty might have caused herself more emotional damage with that decision than she'd done to him. He sure couldn't ignore that possibility now.

There was no damn question that she'd needed him the past eight years. No matter what Kitty had convinced herself to be true.

Her LA friends hadn't had her back. That was for sure. If Tack and Kitty had still been friends, no way would Nevin have managed to crush her indomitable will and spirit.

It was a fair bet the man realized it, too, or he would not have pushed her into giving up her friendship with Tack. Assuming that was what happened.

Kitty had implied as much. And maybe eight years ago Tack would have said no one could force her to give up friends she wanted to keep. However, the Kitty he'd seen this evening was a far cry from the stubborn girl who had punched Benji Sutherland on the playground when the older boy had called Tack *chief*.

A smile twitched at his lips as he remembered. It hadn't mattered to her that she was pint-sized compared to both boys or that Benji hadn't had a clue he was being insulting. Kitty had laid into the older boy with impressive fervor and vocabulary for a six-year-old.

They'd all become fast friends by the second week of

school, but Kitty's actions had set a precedent. The feisty redhead had never stood by and allowed anyone to get bullied, not even the best friend that was near twice her size by the time they hit middle school.

Not once.

How in the hell had the girl who had stood up for the world stopped standing up for herself? One thing was for sure—Kitty needed a friend, and no matter how she'd treated him in the past, she needed him now. She'd made one devastating mistake, both for herself and for their friendship. He was man enough to admit to himself that in a way, Kitty had done him a favor.

He would never have stopped loving and lusting after his best friend if she had remained a big part of his life. Years of trying attested to that. Tack hadn't been able to really let her go until she did it for him.

So, maybe he could forgive her for pushing him away. Didn't mean he was going to give her another crack at his heart, but that woman was still way too close to broken for him to turn away from her now.

She needed to be reminded of who Kitty Grant was at the core of her soul, of the fearless woman who had talked him into attending university twenty-five hundred miles away.

Tack was just the man for the job.

No, he would not love her again, but damned if he'd stand by and watch Kitty Grant live like a wraith among the people of Cailkirn.

* * *

Tack cursed as he realized the new guide he and Egan hired hadn't completely filled out the paperwork for his first solo tour. Both Egan and Tack had taken Bobby out on an excursion with clients to train him in the process.

Yesterday, he'd taken out his first small group of tourists from Anchorage on his own.

There was no excuse for forgetting the most important form of all: the personal indemnity release. Tourists did stupid stuff and no way was MacKinnon Bros. Tours taking responsibility for the results.

"What did that paper do to you?" a feminine voice asked from his doorway.

He didn't have to look up to know it was Kitty. Her voice was unmistakable, even if it lacked the lacing of humor it always used to have.

"It's not the paperwork. It's who is filling it out—or *isn't*, and that's the problem." He let his gaze slide up Kitty's body on the way to meeting her eyes.

Couldn't help himself or the stirrings of arousal it caused.

Her designer jeans were stressed in all the right places and the green top she wore with them clung to the curve of her breasts, its scoop neck cut low enough to reveal the top swells.

The quilted cream vest she wore open on top looked like silk and the zipper was gold.

It was the kind of thing tourists wore. Cailkirn residents? Not so much.

"Fancy for Cailkirn, don't you think, wildcat?" The old nickname just slipped out, but he didn't regret it.

He'd been careful not to use it before, needing to maintain distance from their past, but it was part of reminding her who she used to be, even if it hadn't been on purpose. He'd given her the nickname when they were still in elementary school because she was always taking chances. She might have looked sweet as a kitten, but she was more full-grown mountain lion inside.

A small gust of air released from Kitty's bow-shaped lips, glossed a tempting pink. "No one has called me that in years."

"Considering that was *my* name for you, I'm not surprised." It had always surprised him how few people realized who the real Kitty Grant—town sweetheart—was.

"It doesn't really fit anymore."

"Come on a hike with me. Don't try to take the hardest trail or climb the highest point and I might believe you."

She dropped into the chair he kept in his office for visitors. Which mostly meant his mom, who had a habit of coming by for short chats between his scheduled tours.

Kitty crossed her jean-clad legs and dropped a purse covered in *C*s—probably some kind of designer brand—to the floor beside the chair. "I never wanted you to think I couldn't keep up."

"Hell, Kitty, you pushed beyond my comfort limits more times than I can count." He leaned back in his chair, stretching his legs out to make room for the inevitable growing erection between them.

His dick hadn't gotten the message that the petite redhead was off-limits sexually and had been for a long time. Hell, last night when he'd finally fallen asleep, he'd had his first wet dream in years. Starring Kitty Grant.

It wouldn't be so disturbing if it had been the girl he'd gone to college with. He'd had a few of those over the years—they hadn't ended in nocturnal emissions, but he'd accepted a long time ago that his libido and his subconscious were always going to find fodder in her youthful beauty.

Last night's dream had starred the new Kitty Grant, his imagination filling in the changes in her body. His need to toss his sheets in the wash before coming into work proved his sex drive responded just as viscerally to the older, thinner version of this woman.

A smile reminiscent of the old Kitty revealed even white teeth. "You never said."

"Like I was going to admit I couldn't do anything you could do."

Her smile turned into a full-on grin and he felt like he'd won the caber toss at the Highland Games. "Good to know I kept you on your toes."

"You did that."

The smile slipped and then disappeared altogether as her expression turned introspective. "I don't push boundaries any longer."

It didn't sound like the thoughts going on inside her head were happy ones. "Let's take that hike and we'll see."

He quirked his brow but kept his expression serious to let her know he meant the invitation to be real.

"Um…" She looked tempted, but something around her pretty blue eyes told him she was going to turn him down.

Before she could do it, he changed the subject. "So, not that I'm not happy to see you, but what are you doing here?"

They'd come back to the hike later. She couldn't hold out for long. Kitty might not have liked living in Alaska, but she'd loved exploring in the wild.

In fact, there had always been so few individual aspects to living here that she'd claimed to dislike that Tack and the Grant sisters could be forgiven for believing Kitty would go to California and realize how much she missed home.

Not one of them had expected Nevin Barston.

Kitty shook her head. "Happy to see me, right." She winked but it wasn't accompanied by the flirty expression it used to be...more cynicism now. "Aunt Elspeth sent me over with a currant cake."

He jumped up from his desk. "And you left it out there with the hungry hordes?"

"I only saw Egan and some blond teenager." Her tone implied she thought he was overdramatizing.

"Our newest guide, Bobby. Don't you realize my brother plus an eighteen-year-old can go through one of Miss Elspeth's cakes in about five minutes?"

Kitty's small disbelieving shake of her head said she didn't buy it.

"You'll see," he tossed over his shoulder as he hot-footed it into the main reception area for MacKinnon Bros. Tours.

"We saved you some," Egan said, like he'd done Tack a huge favor.

Tack would be more appreciative if there was more than a small sliver of cake and crumbs on Miss Elspeth's china plate.

He glared at his brother. "I see you left a piece for Kitty, asshole, and crumbs for me."

Egan shrugged. "Well, if you don't want the crumbs."

Tack grabbed the cake plate with a smack to the back of Egan's head.

His brother just laughed, showing he'd known exactly what he was doing and was proud of himself for pulling it off. Bobby almost looked guilty, but the way he licked his lips belied any depth to that emotion.

"Oh, I don't need a piece," Kitty insisted.

"Of course you do." And Tack wasn't the only one who insisted she take the last small slice.

Egan was already putting it on a small plate and Bobby had grabbed a fork and napkin for her. The two men had clearly devoured theirs holding the slices in their hands.

Looking overwhelmed and like she wished she could refuse, Kitty accepted the offering.

"*Aana* would have our hides if we neglected to provide you a portion of the food gift you provided," Egan said, his Inuit heritage more evident than their Scots ancestry.

"Oh, I'd like to see your mother," Kitty said, then grimaced. "If she'd like to see me, I mean."

"Why wouldn't she?" Egan demanded. "You were practically part of the family when you and Tack were kids."

Kitty looked at Tack as if waiting for his opinion. The fact that she was so aware of the disservice she did their friendship touched him in a way that he wished it didn't.

It was obvious she didn't expect him to take up where they'd left off.

"*Aana* has already informed me she expects to see you for dinner soon," Tack assured Kitty as he maneuvered her into a seat. "*Emaa* offered to bake a salmon in the old way to welcome you home."

His grandmother had made sure that Tack and his siblings stayed in touch with their Inuit heritage. He loved her for it, and for how delicious food was prepared in the ways of her forebearers.

"She knows I'm back in town?" Kitty asked after taking a small bite, chewing it slowly and then swallowing delicately.

Bobby laughed. "This is Cailkirn, Miss Grant. The whole year-round population knew you were back in town within twenty-four hours of your arrival. It would have been even faster if you'd come in with someone who talks a little more than Nik Vasov."

Bobby's use of "Miss Grant" rather than "Mrs." showed that the town knew about Kitty's divorce and her return to the use of her maiden name as well as her return. And he was sure Kitty realized that too.

Kitty frowned up at Tack. "You didn't used to be a gossip."

"I'm still not, but it takes a braver man than me to withhold information like that from my mom. She was on the phone to *Emaa* before I even left the kitchen."

One of the things Kitty had never pretended to like was how everyone in town knew everyone else's business.

With just a little over two thousand year-round inhabitants, that wasn't true in the strictest sense, but it always felt like it. And certain families *would* always be more aware of other families and their activities.

The rivalry between the Sutherlands and MacKinnons wasn't just about the Highland Games in summer. Along with the Grants, families from the other two clans had traveled together from the Old Country to Alaska nearly two hundred years ago. They'd settled Cailkirn, aided by a couple of Russian trappers and a local Inuit village.

Later, a couple of key families from the Gold Rush had stayed to influence the development of the town. His mother's Inuit tribe had eventually assimilated into the town, only establishing a separate village again about sixty years ago.

Through all of it, the Scots clans had maintained a friendly rivalry. It didn't matter that they intermarried; each child was raised to be fiercely proud of their clan's affiliation. Maybe because the original families had fled Scotland after the unsuccessful Insurrection of 1820.

They were rebels, determined to keep their clan identities and provide a better life for their children than they could have back in Scotland.

Kitty was a Grant. The townspeople would always be interested in her.

Surprisingly, she didn't look annoyed about that particular truth right now, just resigned as she continued to eat her cake.

Egan and Bobby talked to Kitty about her plans now that she was back in Cailkirn. She reaffirmed that she planned to work at the B&B with her aunts.

Tack had a hard time seeing the designer-clad former California golden girl making beds and cleaning bathrooms at the big Victorian house.

Something must have shown on his face because Kitty said, "Aunt Alma is teaching me how to keep the books and I'll be working with someone to get the reservations computerized."

"That makes sense."

"I'll also be helping with the housekeeping when their full-time help needs it. Gran should have someone to do kitchen prep, too, though she insists she doesn't." Kitty sighed, clearly thinking over the issues at the Knit & Pearl. "There's some maintenance that needs doing too."

"We'll take care of that for Miz Moya and her sisters," Egan offered before Tack had the chance.

Kitty shrugged. "There was a time when I was a dab hand with a hammer. I don't think it's a skill that goes rusty."

It bothered Tack that her tone lacked confidence, regardless of her words.

It also sounded like she was biting off more than she could chew and he didn't like that either, but at least it was typical Kitty Grant. Just as he had back in the day, Tack kept that opinion to himself.

He and Egan would help out with maintenance, whatever she thought.

Kitty had eaten exactly half of the piece of cake before she offered the plate to Tack. "Would you like the rest?"

Then, before he could answer, she paled, dismay covering her lovely face. She jerked the plate back before he could take it. "I'm so sorry. That was extremely impolite of me. Of course you wouldn't want to eat after me."

Tack reached out and pulled the dessert from her. "I'm not that fastidious, Kitty. I can remember sharing food from the same plate with you more times than I can count."

"We aren't children anymore. I should know better."

Those weren't his wildcat's words. They were straight from that bastard who'd kept her in LA; Tack was sure of it.

"Forget it. You're not getting this cake back." He took a big bite to prove how unconcerned he was about eating after her.

"Don't you at least want your own fork?" she asked, moisture glistening at her temples, her pupils dilated so wide her irises were no more than two thin blue rings.

Hell if she hadn't had a panic attack right in front of him. And done a damn professional job of hiding it.

"Nope." He finished the cake in two more bites.

Egan and Bobby were looking at Kitty like she was a tourist. Tack cleared his throat and gave the two men a warning glare before she noticed.

Something told him their reaction would only add to her distress.

Bobby took the hint immediately. "I'd better get the paperwork filled out for my afternoon tour."

"Yes. And if there's one blank line on it when it reaches my office, you'll do all the filing for the rest of the season. You fail to get another release form signed and I'll drop you in an ice hole this winter."

Bobby winced. "Sorry about that, boss. Some of the tourists don't want to sign. They act like needing to do it means we aren't properly trained and equipped."

"No signed release form, no tour. No exceptions. The clients can take it up with me if they don't like it."

Bobby nodded, and Egan said, "I still think we need a re- ceptionist."

"I know." And Tack didn't disagree.

Having someone to handle tour reservations, liaise with cruise ships, and take care of the paperwork would be great. If they could afford it.

"If we didn't have to share time manning the phones and doing all our own paperwork, between the three of us, we could add four or five short tours and maybe even another one of your full-day wild Alaska excursions to the week's schedule. The cruise directors would love it."

Tack knew all of that was true. With some office help, he and Egan might even get home before midnight during cruise season.

"I've looked at the numbers," Tack reminded Egan. "We could only hire someone for about fifteen hours a week."

Which would help but wouldn't really be the solution they needed. Summer wages in Alaska were at a premium, even among the full-time residents of Cailkirn. There were more jobs than townspeople to fill them.

"No one is going to give up the chance at a high-paying full-time job for a few hours a week." It was the truth, no matter how unpalatable.

"What if we hired another guide and expanded our schedule?" Egan asked. "Could we hire someone full-time then?"

"You're assuming we could find anyone at this late date, for either the guide or office position." Tack squeezed the bridge of his nose between his thumb and forefinger. "Besides, if we knew of another guide we could trust, we would have hired him, or her, already."

They had agreements with other guides on the peninsula for overflow tours when it couldn't be helped, but Tack was against taking any of them on full-time.

Egan frowned. "I'm not going to argue." He looked at Kitty and rolled his eyes. "It wouldn't do any good and I know it. It took me two years to convince big brother here to hire another guide. I swear he only agreed because Bobby's family."

"Family takes care of family." And despite Bobby's youth, their cousin could be trusted to keep their clients safe. Once he got the paperwork right, Bobby was going to make a strong addition to the business.

Even so, Tack assigned the eighteen-year-old the most basic tours with the easiest trails. Some of the tours Tack and Egan led didn't follow trails at all.

"He's a good kid," Egan said, echoing Tack's thoughts. "But if we limit our hires to family, we're screwed for another guide."

"It doesn't have to be family, just someone who is as committed to safe and environmentally responsible wilderness exploration as we are."

"You can't be the only conservationist guide on the peninsula," Kitty said with a mocking tilt to her full lips.

"Don't get him started on that," Egan whined. "There's eco-friendly and then there's Tack. He's so green, when he finally does get married, his wife is going to get grass stains sleeping with him."

"So your receptionist has to be an environmental activist?" Kitty teased.

"We'll expect our clerical staff to reduce, reuse, recycle, of course, but that's not the issue." He gave his brother a quelling look. "You know I'd like to hire someone as much as you, but it's not going to work this year."

Tack didn't like paperwork and answering the phones any more than Egan did, but they weren't putting their business at financial risk in order to avoid it either.

"How much would you pay a part-time receptionist?" Kitty asked, a calculating gleam in her blue eyes.

Knowing it was about twice what he'd pay for the same clerical position in the Lower 48, Tack told her what he'd figured out they could afford.

Kitty's expression reflected an almost cautious excitement. "I'll give you three hours a day six days a week for that."

Which was three more hours than Tack had expected to get for the money, but it would mean seeing Kitty almost every day. Considering his dream last night, he wasn't sure that was the best idea regardless of how much paperwork it would save him.

CHAPTER FIVE

"What? You want to work for us? Really?" Egan demanded, sounding too hopeful. "But you're working at the Knit and Pearl."

Kitty looked around the office as if trying to picture working here and then looked back at Egan. "I'm helping my grandmother and great-aunts. I'm not going on the payroll."

"So?" Tack asked.

She couldn't need money. She'd just divorced a very wealthy man.

Tucking some wild red curls behind her ears, Kitty flipped the rest over her shoulders. "You know Mom and Dad left me just about enough to pay for college and not much more."

"But you didn't finish." And that still didn't answer the issue of her divorce settlement.

"Not back then, no, I didn't."

"Are you saying you finished your BA in business?"

Her features set in familiar stubbornness. "Yes."

Yes, his Kitty was definitely still in there. Pride in her accomplishment made him smile. "Good job."

"Thank you. Nevin paid for it, though he would have been furious to know I'd used my saved up allowance for that." There was definite satisfaction in her tone.

Oh, yeah. That was the Kitty Grant he remembered.

"Good," Egan said with approval.

"When did you do it?" Tack asked.

"This last year, waiting for the divorce to finalize. I needed to do something that made me feel like I could still be a person, that my dreams still mattered, even if they'd changed beyond recognition."

"Your dreams have always mattered." And Tack had supported her pursuing them, even when it meant leaving his beloved Alaska to watch over her at USC.

Kitty grimaced, like she was sure she agreed. "I would have finished my degree eight years ago. I never meant to be a trophy wife, but I used the last of my inheritance for the wedding. There was no money for my senior year."

That was why she'd dropped out of school? Tack regretted judging her the way he had, but then she hadn't shared any of this with him.

She hadn't considered him her friend anymore.

"You paid for your wedding?" he asked, finding that hard to comprehend when Barston was such a rich man.

"Mostly. Nevin lent me the rest after what I had left in my account from Mom and Dad was gone."

Egan made a choking sound. "He *loaned* it to you?"

"I was the bride, so it was my family's responsibility to

pay for the wedding and reception, but Nevin expected high-end everything. I wasn't about to ask Gran to foot the bill for such a lavish event."

Kitty hadn't changed as much as he'd thought back then.

Though her consideration for Miz Moya's finances didn't make up for the fact that she'd been refused the opportunity to invite any of her friends to the wedding. Her only grand-child had gotten married and Miz Moya had only been al-lowed to attend with her sisters; no other guests from Cailkirn or even Kitty's distant family in the Lower 48 were allowed.

"So you *borrowed* money from your fiancé for a party he insisted on?" Tack asked, finding that even harder to accept than her paying for the wedding to begin with.

"Yes."

"You didn't work after you married, did you?"

"No."

"Then how did he expect you to pay him back?"

"Out of my personal allowance." Bright flags of embar-rassment reddened Kitty's cheeks. "It took me five years and a lot of careful maneuvering and shopping so I could still present the image Nevin expected of his wife."

Something about the way she said that made Tack think that Nevin hadn't been as appreciative of Kitty's efforts as they no doubt deserved.

"Nevin wasn't the one who set up the repayment sched-ule, though, was he?" Tack knew her—Kitty would have tried to pay off her *debt* as quickly as possible.

That it took five years just showed what a miserly jerk she'd been married to.

"No." Kitty sighed. "And he didn't like that I was so de-termined to erase the obligation as quickly as possible. I don't know, maybe that's partly why he was so critical of my attempts to fit in his world on a budget."

Tack shook his head. He didn't think so. "Or maybe he saw the financial liability as a way to maintain control over you. The longer you took to pay it off, the longer he had that particular anvil to hold over your head."

"Asshole," Egan spit.

Kitty didn't shrug, but her expression didn't share either Egan's or Tack's outrage. "It is what it is, right?"

"Let me guess," Tack said with a narrow-eyed glare. "His lawyers kept your divorce settlement to a minimum."

"He fought the divorce, Tack. He didn't want it. He wasn't offering any settlement at all. I didn't even ask for lawyer's fees. I just wanted out."

"Even if he didn't want to give you anything, didn't the judge order *something*?" Egan asked, sounding confused.

"I signed a very strict prenup. Filing for divorce negated any and all claims I had on Nevin's assets."

"You should have sued him for the cost of that *lavish* wedding," Egan opined.

Kitty almost smiled. "I thought about it, but getting away was more important than getting anything out of him."

Egan grimaced, but he didn't say anything else. He gave Tack a pointed look that couldn't be misinterpreted, though.

"Are you sure you can work here and at the B and B?" Tack asked, wishing she'd reconsider but knowing she wouldn't.

"Definitely." Kitty's face glowed with hope for the first time since he'd seen her back in Cailkirn. "I've lost a lot, but not my ability to put my shoulder to it."

"More like your fingertips. It's a lot of paperwork," Tack warned. "And talking on the phone."

Not one of his favorite things to do.

"I can do it, Tack." She swallowed and stood, giving both him and Egan an earnest look. "I'm not useless."

Hell. Tack sighed, lost. "I know that."

"You're smart enough to keep us both in line and Bobby out of trouble," Egan offered teasingly.

And still sexy enough to challenge Tack's determination to keep her at arm's length. "I'll make a deal with you."

"What do you want in exchange?" she asked in a tone he'd never heard from Kitty Grant, her voice flat and wary at the same time.

"Go on a hike with me. You should see what we do if you're going to take reservations and liaise with the cruise ships."

She bit her lip. "I don't have any boots."

Kitty was wearing boots right now, but he knew what she meant. Something suitable for hiking. "I imagine Miz Moya has a pair of your old ones stored somewhere in that big house."

Kitty gave a barely-there nod. "I'll do it."

"Would you feel better if Egan came with us?" Tack asked, not liking that idea one bit.

He wasn't the one who had proven himself untrustworthy. Not in their relationship and not in Kitty's life.

Her blue eyes widened and she shook her head vehemently. "No. I...it's just...it's been a while. I probably can't keep up with you."

"We'll see, wildcat."

"Don't go feeling bad about it if you can't," Egan offered. "No one can keep up with Tack. I've had more than one tourist come back from his excursions asking if he's even human."

"I'm not that bad."

"You've got about as much stamina as the bear you're named for, Taqukaq." Egan shook his head. "And the tourists still request you because their friends tell them how *amazing* your excursions are."

Tack frowned at his brother. "I'm not a grizzly bear."

"You're about as big as one," Kitty teased.

He was too happy she was showing some spunk to take umbrage at her words. "Bears have a few hundred pounds on me."

"You sure about that, brother?" Egan smacked Tack's tight abs with the back of his hand.

"That was muscle you hit, little boy." At six-foot-four, his brother might be taller than average, but he was still two inches shorter than Tack.

And he never let Egan forget it.

Egan glared, looking like he was getting ready to deliver something harder than an easy backhand:

"Are you saying he has the muscles of a grizzly bear?" Kitty asked, smoothing things between the brothers just that fast.

Just like she used to when they were kids.

"No way." Egan looked properly horrified. "That might be a compliment."

Kitty looked Tack over like a musher buying a new dog for her sled. "But not too far off the mark. You've grown into an impressive man, Tack."

She wasn't trying to be sexy—her tone was too matter-of-fact—but damn if having her eyes on him wasn't making his jeans too tight at the fly again.

"*Aana* can't get him married off, so I'm not sure the women around here agree with you," Egan suggested. The little shit.

Kitty brushed past Tack, heading back to his office. "Marriage isn't all it's cracked up to be."

Egan gave Tack a look.

Tack didn't bother to answer it. He was too busy trying to mask his reaction to that very brief, very casual touch.

Kitty came out of his office with her purse. "I need to get back to the Knit and Pearl."

Tack nodded, his throat dry.

"Do I have the job?" she asked.

"Yes, but I don't want you wearing yourself out. You work the hours out with Miz Alma."

"Of course I will." The words were right, but somehow Tack didn't think Kitty meant them the way he wanted her to.

She wasn't going to give herself a break. It wasn't her way. Miz Moya had raised her granddaughter to be independent and strong. Those traits were still there inside of Kitty, even if she didn't realize it.

He would just have to watch for signs of fatigue. He'd call Miz Alma himself if he needed to.

* * *

"She needs a friend," Egan said quietly from beside Tack after Kitty left, carrying a now empty cake plate.

"I know."

"Do you?"

Tack turned to face his brother. "What do you mean?"

"You loved her, when you went down to college together in the Lower Forty-Eight."

"Do you have a point?" He wouldn't deny the truth, but he'd never said it out loud and sure wasn't going to do it today.

"She broke your heart once; don't give her a chance to do it again." Egan's dark eyes were shadowed with concern, his mouth set in a serious line.

"I've got no plans to let her at my heart." Again.

"Hey, guys, why so serious?" Bobby came out of the room with a copy machine and the table he and Egan used for doing paperwork.

Choosing not to comment on Bobby's question, Tack asked, "Do we need to get a desk or something in here for Kitty?"

"Wait. What?" Bobby asked. "Why would Miss Grant need a desk?"

"We're hiring her as a part-time receptionist. Lucky you, she'll be helping with phones and paperwork."

"That's great," Bobby said with all the enthusiasm of a teenager who just found out he didn't have homework.

"So, a desk?" Tack asked again.

Egan shrugged. "Maybe. Probably."

Bobby nodded his agreement. "Women like their own space. Just ask Jenna."

Bobby's older sister was a force to be reckoned with. If she said women liked their own space, then Tack was inclined to believe it.

"Think we can get a desk in Kenai?" He had commissioned the one in his office from his father. They didn't have the six months minimum it would take to commission another one.

"I think so, if we're not worried about getting real wood. There's that office supply store by the airport," Egan said. "They've got some desks."

Bobby whistled. "Granddad is going to have a fit if you two bring prefab furniture in here."

"We can't wait until next year for it." But Tack was pretty sure his cousin was right.

Egan frowned. "We should at least tell him what we need."

"So, call him." Granddad would know if someone in the family had an extra desk they'd be willing to get rid of too.

"Why can't you call him?" Egan whined.

"Man up. You're a MacKinnon."

"Yeah, and according to Granddad, that means I should be married and providing the next generation to Cailkirn because of it."

"Sucks turning twenty-four, doesn't it?"

"What is up with that anyway?" Bobby asked. "It's not some magic number. I could understand twenty-one, but what's so special about twenty-four?"

Tack headed to his office. "That's how old Granddad was when he married Gran MacKinnon."

"So? Your dad was only twenty and mine was twenty-two."

"Yeah, and Da reminds me of that if I complain about Granddad haranguing me about my responsibilities to the town," Egan muttered.

Tack didn't have any sympathy for his brother. He'd been getting the lecture from Granddad for four solid years. Frankly, he appreciated having someone take a little of the heat off.

He wanted Cailkirn to thrive and planned to marry one day, but right now Tack was focused on building his business.

And controlling his physical reaction to Kitty Grant, who had nothing to do with his continued single state. No matter what both of his grandmothers thought.

* * *

Caitlin heard the low masculine tones of Tack's voice float up from downstairs.

Anxiety that she'd dithered too long over what to wear on the hike warred with an inexplicable impatience to see him. She hadn't even had time to eat breakfast, which was so not good.

She should definitely be feeling more anxious about that than the idea of seeing the gorgeous Alaskan man again.

Neither reaction was helping her decide what to wear.

He'd been right that her gran had an old pair of Caitlin's hiking boots in storage. However, after he called what she had considered a casual outfit too fancy for Cailkirn yesterday, Caitlin hadn't known what to wear with them.

She only had two pairs of jeans, both designer. Her sweaters were all lightweight, appropriate for Southern California winters, which was to say no real winter at all. Even in the coldest part of the year, the temperatures rarely dropped to spring temperatures in Cailkirn.

It might be the sunniest city in Alaska, but it wasn't the warmest. This far north, the sun didn't usually mean hot. Not by the definition of anyone living south of the fifty-fourth parallel.

Certainly not like the smog-hazed sunny days in Los Angeles.

Which meant if Caitlin didn't want to spend the day shivering until she cracked a tooth clacking them together, she had to layer. Like yesterday. Too bad her layers weren't any more small-town Alaska than what she'd worn yesterday.

Caitlin had thought that with all the tourists off the cruise ships, her California style wouldn't stand out so much. She'd been more concerned about how few clothes she had than how they were going to look. She'd sold most of her wardrobe through consignment shops to help pay for her schooling, keeping only the ones two years old or older.

They were also the only ones that still fit now that she'd brought her weight up to non-dangerous levels. Her doctor had suggested she gain another ten pounds minimum, fifteen ideally.

Caitlin was trying, but then she wasn't sure what she'd do about clothes. None of the ones she'd brought with her would fit her then. At least she had a job and personal income to look forward to now.

But the ships weren't in port yet and Caitlin wasn't sure which of her clothes would garner Tack's approval.

That thought pulled her up short.

She was falling back on old behaviors, worrying about what someone else would think of her appearance to the point of paralysis. Seriously, so what if Tack thought her clothes "too fancy"? If she was comfortable and warm, that was all that mattered, right?

She'd been working very hard for more than a year to convince herself of this.

Caitlin *liked* to dress fashionably; she always had. She *didn't* like being told she'd fallen short in some way. That was too reminiscent of Nevin.

No way was she putting Tack in that role, though. He wasn't Nevin, wasn't even remotely like her ex-husband in any of the ways that counted.

If he was still anything like the boy she'd grown up with, Taqukaq MacKinnon would be appalled to think Caitlin was using his opinion as the yardstick to measure her clothing choices by. He might well make another comment today, but he wouldn't expect it to result in Caitlin modifying the way she dressed.

Frustrated with herself, especially allowing her morning routine to suffer, Caitlin pulled on a snug white T-shirt for an added layer of warmth. Her body didn't hold heat as well as it had when she'd lived in Cailkirn before.

Hopefully that would get better with time. Mindful of the time, she slipped into a form-fitting white button-down top with long sleeves and then pulled her favorite Carolina Herrera sweater over it.

The shade of the thin blue cotton was almost an exact match for her eyes. She left the shirt untucked so the tails hung below the hem of the sweater.

She donned the same quilted silk Chanel vest she'd been wearing the day before and grabbed the old ski jacket Gran had put away with Caitlin's hiking boots.

Tack wouldn't accuse her of being too stylish in the nearly ten-year-old jacket, but chances were she wouldn't need the coat today.

It was best to be prepared, though. Weather was unpredictable on the Kenai Peninsula.

She found Tack drinking coffee and eating one of Aunt Elspeth's cinnamon rolls in the kitchen. Thankful that it looked like she'd get a chance to eat, Caitlin pulled cereal from the cupboard.

She'd discovered that skipping meals wreaked havoc with her hard-won healthier eating habits. It was too easy to just keep on skipping until she'd gone a couple of days without actually eating anything.

Never again.

Her therapist said relapses happened, but Caitlin had promised herself one thing: she wasn't *ever* going to reach the point where she fainted from lack of nutrition again.

"You're not going to eat that for breakfast are you, Kitty-love?" Aunt Elspeth asked in that gentle way she had. "I've made fresh cinnamon rolls. So much nicer than dry cereal."

Caitlin eyed the gooey pastries, oozing with melted butter, cinnamon, and caramelized sugar and tried not to let the nausea building inside her show. "My stomach doesn't do well with heavy food first thing in the morning."

Or ever really, but she wasn't going to mention that. Like a lot of anorexics, Caitlin had spiraled into bulimia as well. And not always by choice. A stomach that didn't get fed very often had a hard time digesting rich foods, no matter her intentions when she ate it.

She was much better about fueling her body at regular intervals now, but she still struggled with high-fat foods, and too much sugar might as well be tequila shots.

"But—" Aunt Elspeth started.

"I packed snacks and a lunch. She'll be fine," Tack interrupted.

Which sort of shocked Caitlin. He was far too polite to interrupt her aunt, but it was almost as if he realized how difficult the simple conversation was for Caitlin.

Aunt Elspeth looked as gobsmacked as Caitlin felt, but after a look between them that Caitlin couldn't decipher, her great-aunt subsided.

"Eat your cereal," Tack told her.

Caitlin nodded and set about measuring an exact portion of the cereal and adding a level half cup of unsweetened almond milk and exactly twelve berries.

She joined Tack at the table and began to eat, jealous of his cup of coffee.

It had been years since she'd been able to have the true Colombian gold with impunity.

Tack smiled, one eyebrow quirked. "No coffee?"

Caitlin gave a negative jerk of her head, not wanting to explain how at twenty-eight, she couldn't handle the high acid content in her favorite beverage.

Aunt Elspeth put a mug of steaming yellow-tinted liquid in front of Caitlin. "I've made you some chamomile tea, dear."

"Thank you, Aunt Elspeth. You're so thoughtful."

"Think nothing of it." The older woman patted Caitlin's arm.

Guilt that her aunt had to make special efforts on her behalf washed over Caitlin. Just as quickly, she tried to let it go.

Her therapist would have reminded Caitlin that she hadn't asked for the tea. Aunt Elspeth had offered.

"Where are you two off today, then?" Gran asked, coming into the kitchen, her bright blue eyes lit with curiosity.

Aunt Alma never joined them for breakfast. She'd come down early for coffee and toast, which she'd take back to her bedroom for what she called her *quiet time*.

"We're going hiking," Tack offered.

"Yes, so our Kitty said."

Tack didn't take the silent invitation to expand on his plans and Caitlin didn't know them.

Gran nodded, seemingly unperturbed by Tack's reticence to share. "Well, I'm sure you'll have a lovely time."

"Don't forget a warm coat," Aunt Elspeth admonished.

"She's a grown woman, Elspeth," Gran said with a shake of her head. "She isn't going to forget her coat."

Aunt Elspeth didn't look convinced of Caitlin's skills at self-preservation.

Considering she was spending the day with the first man to flip her switch of sexual desire in years, Caitlin had to wonder if the older woman wasn't right to doubt her.

CHAPTER SIX

They been heading north on Sterling Highway for about twenty minutes when Caitlin said, "Thank you for running interference for me in the kitchen."

She'd spent the drive thinking about the exchange and decided that was exactly what Tack had done.

"No problem. Miss Elspeth wants to help."

"Her intentions are the best." Which made it that much harder to tell the elder woman no.

"They are, but she doesn't understand just how delicate your digestive system has become."

"And you do?"

"I read up on it."

"On…" She still had a difficult time saying the word aloud.

He said it for her. "Anorexia."

"How did you know?"

"Your aunt told me you'd dropped down to just over ninety pounds. I couldn't figure another reason for that." He sighed, his expression reflecting something she didn't understand. Guilt? "You always stopped eating when you were stressed."

"That was how it started."

"But it turned into something else."

"I couldn't always control what food was placed before me, but I controlled how much of it I took into my body."

"Or kept there," he guessed.

"Yes."

"How is that now?"

She decided he meant the bulimia. "Better."

"Good."

"You're not disgusted by me, by my weakness?"

His brows drew together as he flicked her a quick glance before putting his full attention back onto the road. "Why would you ask that?"

"I spent enough time repulsed by myself," she admitted. Some days she still was, but she fought the feelings now. "I wouldn't blame you if you were too."

Tack swore and then yanked the steering wheel to the right and pulled the truck to the side of the highway. He turned off the engine and took several breaths in silence, not looking at her.

"Are we here?" She looked around but didn't see the start of a trail anywhere nearby.

She knew he liked to explore on his own but didn't think he'd take her on that kind of hike first thing back. Tack wasn't like Nevin. He didn't revel in showing up other people.

Finally, Tack shook his head and unbuckled his seat belt

so he could slide his body toward her on the bench seat, shifting so he faced her. "Listen very carefully to me, Kitty. I want you to really hear what I'm saying, okay?"

She nodded slowly, not understanding what was happening but knowing it was important to him from the expression on the face she'd missed more than any other in the last eight years.

"You do not disgust me. I'm proud of you. Overcoming the need to starve yourself is as hard as breaking any other addiction, worse than a lot of them."

Her therapist and the doctors had all said that, too, but Nevin had always insisted the problem was her weakness.

Part of her still agreed with him.

"But I started it." No one, not even Nevin, had held a gun to her head and told her to stop eating.

Tack's hand twitched, like he was going to reach for her, but then he didn't. "And you stopped it. One in two who suffer from the disease can't completely."

"You really did read up on it."

He nodded, his dark eyes demanding she believe him. He reached out to cup her face with both his hands, shrinking her awareness of everything down to the inches between them. "You are a fighter, Kitty. You won't let this disease take your life."

"That's almost exactly what I told my therapist." Caitlin hadn't necessarily believed her own words, but she'd desperately wanted them to be true.

"Good girl. That's my wildcat."

She knew the possessive *my* had been unconscious and didn't believe for a second he meant it the way it had sounded. Still, it made her heart skip a beat and she couldn't be sure if it was from fear or joy.

"I don't think I'm her anymore."

"So you've said, but I'll let you in on a little secret."

"What?" she asked in a near whisper, her eyes focused on his lips.

"I think you are and I plan to prove it to you."

"I'll disappoint you."

"No, you won't."

"You don't know me anymore, Tack."

"I know you better than you think I do." He dropped his hands but did not move back. "That whole size zero culture down there in LA, it fed the disease. We aren't going to do that here in Cailkirn."

She missed the warmth of his fingers immediately, wanting nothing more than to have them against her cheeks again. Caitlin was starting to see how dangerous Tack touching her could be for her peace of mind. She could learn to need it and that scared her.

She couldn't afford to need anything from another person, not touch, not approval, and most especially not love. Needing gave others leverage over her and she was determined never to be in that place again.

Caitlin forced herself to ignore the craving for more of his touch and focus on their discussion.

She wasn't actually entirely sure *why* they were having it, though, why her disease mattered to Tack. "Trying to encourage me to eat too much or the wrong food can be just as bad as the subtle suggestions to eat less."

Nevin had been excellent at those, but he'd refused to take any responsibility for how difficult it had become for her to make herself eat at all.

"I know. You need to tell your family that. It's natural for them to try to feed you."

"Yeah, food is the language of love for the Grant sisters."

"If you tell your gran and aunts how physically challenging it is for you to eat rich foods, they'll channel that love into providing for your needs."

"I'm sure they would." Not only did she find it nearly impossible to talk about her disease and its effects on her, but she also didn't want people making special efforts on her behalf.

Partly because putting them out made her uncomfortable and partly because allowing it put her in their debt.

"That doesn't sound like you plan to talk to them." And *he* didn't sound like he approved of that.

She shrugged.

"I'm learning to really dislike when you shrug."

"Why?"

"Because it implies you don't care and I know you do, Kitty."

"You're so sure. I'm not the same woman you left behind in California."

"No, you're stronger. That Kitty gave up her best friend on the say-so of her boyfriend. She wanted approval too much maybe and she wouldn't have been able to fight back from anorexia and bulimia. That Kitty chose an MRS over her degree. You're winning against the eating disorder *and* you managed to finish your degree."

Maybe he was right and he *did* know her better than she thought he did, both in the past and today. "You make me sound like someone to respect."

"That's because I do respect you." He sounded so sincere.

"How can you? After I betrayed our friendship the way I did." He still had to be bothered by it, or he wouldn't have mentioned it.

"You were just twenty, still a baby. Clearly too young to choose a good husband," he said with a wink, taking the sting from the words. "So, you were just as bad at choosing what friends to keep and the ones to let go of."

"I never got to choose them."

"You said that."

She nodded, pain at her own weakness filling her. "I hate looking back at how much control I gave him over me and my life. I mean, I just handed it away, convinced I loved him and that love offered that kind of loyalty."

"If you're going to hate something, hate what that son of a bitch did to you. I do."

Laughter rolled out of her and it felt good as much as it surprised her. "His mother would not like being called a bitch."

"Are they peas in a pod, or did he drop and roll far from the tree?"

"She never let me forget that I wasn't good enough for her son. I never once called her by her first name. It was either Mrs. Barston or ma'am."

"Bitch."

"Yeah."

He smiled and something she hadn't felt in a long time stirred inside of Caitlin. A warm tendril of real friendship.

"I took way too long choosing my clothes today," she admitted, wondering if she could tell him all of it.

Tack's ultra-masculine features, a perfect mix of Inuit and Scots, creased in confusion. "Why?"

"You told me I looked too fancy yesterday. I didn't want you to disapprove of my outfit today."

"Why the hell would you care what I think of how you dress?"

Man, Tack was just so self-possessed, he really couldn't imagine worrying about what someone else thought.

"I don't. At least I don't want to. I made myself get dressed in what *I* wanted to wear."

"Good." He frowned. "Do you need me to measure what I say to you?"

"Maybe, but I *don't* want you to. I really don't. I'm not sure I could stand it if you of all people got all stiff with me."

"Not going to happen."

She felt a rare genuine smile curve her lips. "I'm not sure I can see it either. You're not a walking-on-eggshells kind of guy."

"No."

"I was."

He just looked at her.

"I spent years tiptoeing on eggshells, terrified of every crack and break I could hear under my feet."

"Tell me."

"Not all of it."

"Eventually."

"You're pushier than you were when we were kids."

It was his turn to shrug.

"Because you don't adore me like you did back then," she teased. Though for her, that affection wasn't really something she laughed about.

Not deep down inside where it mattered.

She'd taken his adoration for granted once, but now memories of their childhood and young adult lives glowed golden in her mind, helping to wash away the pain of the past eight years in its light.

"Yeah. You got away with way too much back then."

"Like you didn't get your way at all."

"We were friends," he said, like that said it all.

"I don't have friends now."

He looked at her, his face set in implacable lines. "Yes, Kitty, you do."

"Are you saying you still want to be my friend?"

"Why do you think we're out here?"

"I didn't really know."

"You need real friends, Kitty. I am your friend."

"I don't like that word."

"Friend?" he asked, looking more confused than angry.

"*Need*. It's not safe to need people or things."

"Maybe it wasn't back in LA, but you're safe enough needing me, needing your gran and aunts. We're good Alaskan stock. We won't let you down."

"What if I let you down?"

"I won't let you."

And she almost believed him.

"In the first year or so, I convinced myself that Nevin didn't *really* intend to dictate my personal choices. Not about clothes, or any of the other things he'd expressed what I *thought* was mild displeasure in regard to my selections."

"But controlling you was exactly what he wanted."

"Oh yes. He got off on control, especially when that control made it possible to hurt me." That was probably the worst thing she'd had to come to terms with: the man she'd married was an emotional and physical sadist. "He demanded full and complete dictatorship without ever once in our marriage coming out and saying so in words I could point to."

"Manipulative."

"He defined the word. Refusing to acknowledge his true nature was a huge mistake on my part." Hiding hadn't protected her; it had just made it possible for her torment to go on longer.

"I'll say."

She almost laughed, though it would probably have been more a gallows sound. Tack didn't even have a passing acquaintance with tact. There was something not just refreshing, but also safe in the pure honesty that prompted knee-jerk comments like that.

"The longer I took to learn that those seemingly throwaway comments were more in the order of commands, the worse things got." Her throat tightened as if trying to hold the words in, but she pressed on. "The harsher Nevin's criticisms, the more frequent his gestures carefully calculated to humiliate me."

"And then he got physical."

She turned away, looking out the window to the snow-covered mountains in the distance. "I never told anyone about that, not even the therapist."

"But it did happen. He hurt you physically. He broke your bones."

Caitlin had insisted to every emergency room doctor and nurse that she was just clumsy. She'd even refused to admit to her gran and therapist how her injuries had occurred, but she couldn't lie to Tack. "Yes."

"*Shit.*"

"It could have been worse. A lot worse." She'd met women in the support group her lawyer had insisted Caitlin attend in exchange for a reduction in her fees. Some of them had permanent injuries or disfigurement. Some couldn't talk without a stutter; others weren't able to meet anyone's eyes.

"By some standards, I got off pretty easy."

He gritted out another expletive, bursting into movement.

Suddenly Tack had her seat belt unbuckled and Caitlin pulled into his arms, right into his lap. She'd almost forgotten what it was like to be held this intimately by someone she wanted to touch her.

Glorious heat surrounded her, his muscles solid against her, his thighs hard and strong under hers, his scent achingly familiar and subtly different at the same time. He rubbed her back, crooning something above her head. The words didn't register, but the tone did.

Only then did she realize tears were tracking silently down her cheeks. She couldn't remember the last time she'd cried. It hadn't been safe to cry for so long.

It was safe now. He made her feel that way. Really, truly safe for the first time since she'd ejected this man from her life.

She didn't deserve the friendship he offered, but oh she didn't have the strength to reject it, not even for his own good.

Tack didn't need someone like her in his life, a woman who'd stayed in an abusive relationship until it almost killed her. She'd believed every threat Nevin made. Why shouldn't she? He'd already proven hurting her was something he enjoyed.

But she'd also believed him when he told her it was her fault, that she was stupid, useless, that no one would want her, that even her gran would be disgusted by the walking skeleton she'd become.

She'd bought into all of his lies.

Nevin hadn't been the one to put her in the hospital, a hairsbreadth from her kidneys shutting down either. Ultimately, that had been on Caitlin and the disease she'd let rule her life.

She didn't realize she'd spoken her troubled thoughts aloud until Tack went stiff against her.

He tilted her head up so she had to meet his dark, compelling gaze. "Listen to me, Kitty."

"I am."

"You didn't give into your disease any more than a woman with a broken leg *gave into* her bone's fragility. You pushed out of the abyss, fighting every step of the way just like that same woman would go to physical therapy to reclaim full mobility."

"But I knew I was losing too much weight. I couldn't make myself eat."

"And yet you did."

She stared up at him, the twin strands of guilt and shame braided so tightly together inside her beginning to loosen. "I did."

"Just like *you* ate breakfast this morning and dinner last night."

"Yes." Someone who hadn't suffered an eating disorder shouldn't be able to understand what a feat that was, that every day she ate her caloric goal was a triumph.

Yet Tack did.

"See? Not weak. Not useless."

She was determined not to be either of those things. "You're kind of amazing, you know that?"

He grinned and winked. "You go right ahead and tell my family. See if they believe you."

"Oh, they already know. They just don't say anything so you don't get a swollen head."

"That's not the only swollen head you're giving me," he muttered, sounding disgruntled. He shifted under her and she felt a hard bulge against her thigh.

She gasped. He wanted her?

Tack's eyes closed and he dropped his head back, breathing in deep. "Forget I said that."

"What if I don't want to?" Why would she?

The very idea she could turn him on was unbelievable, except for the undeniable evidence of Tack's erection.

Nevin had spent the last two years of their marriage telling her how disgusting he found her emaciated body, not that it had stopped him from demanding conjugal rights. But he'd made sure she understood how unfulfilling he found sex with her.

Tack moved her from his lap and back onto her side of the bench seat with careful but firm hands. "Friends, Kitty."

What did that mean? He wanted to be friends, but nothing else?

"What if I want more?" Had she really asked that?

Kitty had been dead certain she never wanted sex again. She was still trying to reconnect in a meaningful way with her body. She wanted to *feel* like the woman she saw in the mirror. She wasn't entirely sure she wanted it now, but she wasn't positive she didn't either.

She didn't want love or a relationship. No emotional entanglements that could destroy what was left of her heart, but what if she could have sex? Something to bring a little pleasure into the new life she was building for herself?

"That's all I'm offering." He started the engine with a vicious twist of the key.

CHAPTER SEVEN

Cringing back into the seat and away from the barely leashed power in the huge man sharing the cab with her, Caitlin nodded reflexively. "Whatever you say."

"Do your seat belt." Tack put the truck in gear.

Shaking, her hands fumbled as she tried to do the buckle, but it didn't want to cooperate. She tried harder, her efforts growing more frantic.

He cursed and shoved the lever, putting the four-by-four back into park.

Turning to face her, Tack gently brushed her hands away from the buckle. "Let me do it."

She acquiesced without a word, focusing on the dashboard so she wouldn't look at him.

He took a deep breath and let it out in a sigh, several seconds of silence following. "I'm not going to hurt you, wildcat. Not ever."

"I believe you." She *wanted* to believe him.

"No, you don't, but you're trying." He kissed her temple, his hand tangling in the kinky red strands of her hair to turn her head so they were once again eye to eye. "That impresses the hell out of me, to tell you the truth."

"It does?" she whispered. "Why?"

Wouldn't it be more impressive if she already believed him?

"Because, after what you've been through, that takes courage. Something you've never had in short supply."

She shook her head, knowing better.

He pressed their foreheads together, his breath washing over her face, the scent of cinnamon and coffee oddly appealing. "Ah, wildcat, what am I going to do with you?"

"Not have sex," she blurted out.

Tack lifted his head, his expression just strange. "Kitty, even if you weren't already off-limits, you're afraid of me."

"I am not."

"You just cringed away from me."

"Reflex. You didn't have anything to do with it."

"Reflex, my ass. I'll bet you didn't show fear to Nevin."

"Not if I could help it." She'd learned fast to hide as much emotion from her ex-husband as possible.

Then he couldn't use it against her.

"Sweetheart, even if sex between us wasn't permanently off the table, you're too fragile right now. You have to see that having sex right now would not be a good idea for you."

"Yes, of course," she said, despite the pricks of pain to her heart from his gentle but blunt rejection.

He said he admired her, but Tack thought she was broken. Too broken for physical intimacy. So damaged he *never* wanted to have sex with her.

He frowned. "I'm not sure I trust such easy agreement from you."

"Do you want the truth?"

"Always."

Right. That sounded nice, but she doubted very much Tack really wanted all of her truth.

Pushing that reality away, she said, "Until five minutes ago, I was convinced I never wanted sex again."

Tack winced. "He hurt you with that too?"

Kitty didn't bother to answer. If Tack hadn't already figured out that Nevin had used whatever he could to control and demoralize her, she wasn't going to explain it in further detail.

The man who had built his own business and a life anyone would be proud of already thought she was damaged and pitiable.

"Tell me about MacKinnon Bros. Tours," Caitlin said as Tack pulled back onto the highway.

She was done dwelling on her past and wasn't particularly keen to delve further into the present between them. What was left of her pride had taken enough hits for today.

"It's my world right now, much to Granddad MacKinnon's dismay."

"Let me guess, he wishes you would get married and have lots of Cailkirn baby residents." Tack's grandfather was a card-carrying member of the Northern Lights Service Club of Cailkirn.

Ostensibly, it was a service organization for men who were permanent residents of the town and over the age of forty. In reality, it was a lot like the Knit & Pearl (which had no age requirement). In practice, both were social clubs dedicated to gossip and the longevity of Cailkirn.

A woman didn't have to be interested in knitting, or even own a skein of yarn, in order to join the Knit & Pearl. And a man didn't have to participate in any of the yearly service projects to maintain membership in NLSC.

The organizations co-hosted monthly gatherings in the winter to which all the single residents were strongly encouraged to attend. In a word, they were a bunch of matchmakers.

She refused to consider why the thought of Tack succumbing to their machinations at some point caused her heart to squeeze so tight in her chest.

"Has your gran started in on you yet?" Tack asked.

"About what?"

"Getting married again. Giving her great-grandchildren," he said, as if it should be obvious.

Horror rushed through Caitlin, washing away any reaction to the thought of him with a wife and children. "I'm *not* getting married again. Gran understands that."

"So she says."

"Yes, she does." And no matter how much her grandmother and aunts enjoyed matchmaking, they would find out quickly there was no point directing their attempts at Caitlin.

She was not interested. At all.

Besides, while the damage she'd done to her reproductive system had been recoverable, Caitlin still wasn't the best bet for motherhood. She'd have to gain those ten pounds the doctors wanted her to before it was even a good idea to try.

And she'd have to eat another three to eight hundred calories a day during the pregnancy.

Caitlin's stomach went queasy at the very thought.

"When did you open the guide business?" she asked, determined to change the subject.

"Right after I graduated from Idaho State."

"You liked school better there, didn't you?"

He snorted. "You could say that."

"California never fit you." He'd only gone to USC because she'd begged him not to make her go alone.

And then she'd abandoned him.

"Nope."

"So, you came back from Idaho and started a business?"

"It's what I always wanted to do. Dad and Granddad helped me and Egan get it going with a small investment loan. We paid them back in the first two seasons." Tack sounded proud of that and he should be.

But there was something in his voice that said it was more than a point of pride for him.

"Good for you. It's doing well if you hired another guide, too, not to mention me."

"Our tours are popular."

"Do you offer winter guide trips?"

"Snowshoeing over most of the trails we hike in the spring and summer. Licensed hunting and ice fishing."

"So, you're busy year-round?"

"Yep, though it's crazy during the summer season. I'm lucky if I get a morning off a week, much less a full day. That's why it took me so long to get my cabin done."

He'd always been a hard worker, but that was insane. There was a time when she would have said so, but not right now. Still, what was driving him to work so hard and put in such long hours?

"You built your log cabin?" He'd always dreamed of living in an open timber log cabin and had designed it right down to the plumbing by the time they were seniors in high school.

"Yep." There was no mistaking the deep satisfaction in that single word. "It's exactly like I wanted it, including the dining table and chairs built by my dad and granddad."

"Their furniture is amazing. I'm surprised neither you nor Egan went into the family business." Though their uncle hadn't either.

"I made my own way." His tone said that was really important to him. "Bobby's older brother, Cian, works with Da and Granddad. You remember him?"

"He was a couple years behind us in school, right?" Bobby had to have been a surprise baby.

"That's the one. He apprenticed right out of high school. They've got another carpenter working for them too. He came home from Iraq with a bum leg and an intolerance for crowds. He moved to Cailkirn a couple of years ago when life in the Lower Forty-Eight got too congested."

"He must not come into town during tourist season."

"No, he sure doesn't. His cabin is farther out than mine."

"You built on the land your grandfather left you?"

Tack's Inuit grandfather had never reconciled to his daughter's marriage to a MacKinnon. His relationships with Tack, Egan, and their sister Shila had been different than with his other full-blood Inuit grandchildren, but he'd still left the MacKinnon siblings tracts of land on the outskirts of Cailkirn just as he had the others.

"Yes. Egan is going to build a home on his land next to mine. Sooner rather than later I expect now that Granddad has decided he's old enough to marry and produce offspring."

Caitlin laughed. "Your grandfather has a one-track mind."

"Tell me about it. He's driving Egan nuts."

"You don't sound particularly sympathetic."

"He can suck it up. I've been getting the lectures for years now."

Tack was twenty-eight, just like Caitlin, but he'd never married. Because of his business.

Caitlin would exchange years of building her dreams for having them torn to pieces in a heartbeat.

"By the way, I wanted to thank you for the job. I talked to Aunt Alma and she thinks it's a good idea too."

"Does she?" Tack sounded surprised.

"She's not as eager to give up doing the books as you'd think she would be at seventy-two."

"Oooh...you better not let her know you spilled the beans on her real age."

"What is age except a number? I swear Aunt Elspeth is younger at heart than me." Sometimes Caitlin felt like her spirit had more gray hair than her aunts and gran hid with their varying shades of red hair dye.

"She's younger than half the town, if you're talking about attitude."

"She's over the moon I'm working for you and Egan."

"Why?"

"You work too hard, according to her. You're one of her favorites, you know? She doesn't send tea cakes to all the residents of Cailkirn."

"She's a sweet lady."

Caitlin agreed.

"What about your gran? I can't see her being happy you're going to be spending a few hours a day away after just getting you home."

"She's all for it. Well, actually Granddad Ardal is, according to her, and she says he's grown wise in the afterlife."

"I've never figured out if she really thinks his ghost talks to her or if she's having us all on. Your gran has a wicked sense of humor."

Caitlin thought back to times she'd found her gran talking to the dead man's ghost when she couldn't have known she was being overheard. "I'm pretty sure it's not a show."

"Then I guess he did get smarter in the afterlife."

"Why's that?"

"He came back to Cailkirn and has had the intelligence to stick around this time," Tack teased.

"Is that a hint?"

"Your gran thinks you're staying for good this time."

"I am."

Tack's grunt was noncommittal.

"I'm surprised Shila doesn't want the job." If Caitlin remembered correctly, his sister had turned eighteen that year.

"She's been helping *Aana* in the office since she was fifteen."

"I bet your mom likes that." Malina MacKinnon had done all the paperwork for Natural Furnishing, the MacKinnon custom furniture making business, for as long as Caitlin could remember.

"They get along a lot better than some moms and daughters around town. At least they did until this last year."

"What happened then?"

"They've been arguing all year about college."

"Does your mom want her to stay here?"

"No way. *Aana* has got it in her mind that since Egan and I went to the Lower Forty-Eight for schooling, Shila should, too, and *broaden her horizons*."

"Shila doesn't want to?"

"No. She's already applied to and been accepted by Kenai Peninsula College. *Aana* hasn't spoken to her in a week."

"That's serious."

Tack gave one of those Alaskan man grunts. "They'll work it out."

"I hope Shila sticks to her guns."

"I'm surprised to hear you say that. You were so adamant about going."

"Yeah, well, Granddad Ardal wasn't the only one who got wiser after leaving Cailkirn."

Her grandfather hadn't wanted to stay in Cailkirn and had tried to talk Gran Moya into moving south. She'd refused with no chance at changing her mind. So Ardal Grant had left his wife and small son to make his fortune in the logging camps of Oregon.

Logging was an even more dangerous job forty-plus years ago than it was today. He'd been maimed in an accident. Ardal had gotten out of the hospital and gone straight to the local bar to drown his sorrows, only to be hit by a logging truck later that night when he was weaving drunkenly down the middle of the road.

"I'm sorry your sister and mom are at odds, but I'm grateful Shila doesn't want to be your receptionist. I didn't know how I was going to pay Gran back the money she lent me to hire a lawyer for the divorce."

Tack cast her a measuring glance. "Miz Moya isn't anything like your bastard of an ex."

"Of course not."

"You aren't going to convince me she *lent* you the money to get your divorce." Tack downshifted to take a tight turn on a high grade. "She gave it, no strings, or I don't know Miz Moya like I thought I did."

"Just because she didn't ask me to pay her back doesn't mean I'm not going to. My divorce wasn't her responsibility."

"Family takes care of family."

"Yes, we do and I have every intention of taking care of my grandmother." He should understand that. "I bet your dad and granddad didn't ask you to pay back their initial investment in MacKinnon Bros. Tours either."

"That's different."

"I don't see how."

"You're damn stubborn for a woman who let her husband dictate so much of her life."

"Definitely not walking on eggshells," she muttered as he turned off Sterling Highway. Suddenly she realized where they were going.

The Skilak Lookout Trail. About two and a half miles long, it was a hiking path that went through a more than twenty-year-old burn and led to an amazing lookout over Skilak Lake. There would be some gorgeous wildflowers along the way this time of year.

Delight bubbled up inside her. "I love this trail."

"I remember."

It was peaceful and not too long. One of the few easier trails that boasted as much outdoor beauty as those that were a lot longer and harder in incline. There was some raise in altitude on the trail, but nothing she couldn't manage.

Even now.

"Thank you, Tack."

"For what?"

"For giving me back a good memory."

He rolled his eyes. "Drama queen. It's just a hike."

"You're carrying the food."

"Damn right I am. You think I'm going to let you withhold my snacks?"

* * *

Tack had never once had difficulty controlling his breathing
or pulse while hiking the Skilak Lookout Trail.

Until today.

Watching Kitty slough off her somber nature step by step
stole his breath and increased his heart rate with more efficiency than an extreme hike in the Kenai Mountains.

The closer they got to the overlook for the lake, the more
her old joy sparkled in her pretty blue gaze. In the lightness
of her step. In the way she reached out to brush the drizzle-
wet leaves of a wild blueberry bush or the moss covering a
tree trunk like she was greeting old friends after a long absence.

It had always been like this, hiking with Kitty. The desti-
nation was never more important than the journey, and they
would take twice as long to cover the distance than he would
alone.

Unsurprisingly, she stopped to take a picture with her
camera phone of one of the many wildflowers along the
trail.

"Do you remember how you used to *gather* wildflowers
with that little digital camera your gran got you for graduat-
ing eighth grade?" he asked as she took several shots, trying
to get the perfect image.

She would print the pictures off, then trim them down to
a single bloom, which she added to a collage board she kept
on the wall of her bedroom. She called it her *wildflower bouquet* and started a new one every spring.

Kitty grinned up at him, just like she used to, the expression so unexpected and different than what he'd seen on her so far that it knocked the air right out of him. He wanted to reach out and touch her lips, curved in the innocent pleasure in her surroundings with a lack of self-consciousness he hadn't been sure she was still capable of feeling.

This was the Kitty who had captivated his young heart and lustful imagination.

Her summer sky eyes invited him to share her delight. "I wasn't about to pick them."

No. She might not be the conservationist he was, but Kitty was committed to keeping the wild beauty of Alaska right where it belonged.

"Are you going to start a new *bouquet* for this year?"

She looked startled at his suggestion, uncertainty almost pushing aside her newfound cheerful serenity.

Then the doubt disappeared and that happiness he'd once taken for granted laced her voice as she said, "You know? I think I will."

"Good." His voice sounded strange to his own ears, but she didn't seem to notice.

Kitty held out her camera so he could see the shot she'd taken. "This will make a great beginning, don't you think?"

"Yes." But he was hard-pressed to keep his eyes on the picture when the bounty of beauty that was a joyful Kitty Grant stood right there.

"Isn't it gorgeous?" she breathed, her focus on the subject of the digital picture. "It looks so delicate, but here it is, surviving trampling wildlife, frigid nighttime temperatures, and spring rainstorms."

"Not all things that look fragile can be destroyed."

She tilted her head back to look up at him, her expression still more natural than he'd seen it since she'd come home, but with a thoughtful narrowing of her eyes. "You're talking about me now, aren't you?"

"Yes."

"Two years ago, I would have argued, but here I am," she said in the same tone she'd used to refer to the wild-flower.

Out of nowhere, the desire to kiss her slammed into him with more power than a bull moose charging a rival. There was so much meaning in those words; they impacted him at a visceral level no other woman had ever touched. That place in his soul that realized Kitty Grant's survival had not always been guaranteed. Yes, *here she was*, but she might not have been.

The need to connect in a primal way, affirming the reality of her presence, nearly overcame him. He could almost feel her silky lips under his, swore he could taste the sweetness of her mouth.

She cocked her head to one side, her red curls glowing bright in the on-again-off-again spring sunshine. "Is something wrong?"

He shook his head. If he opened his mouth, he'd blurt out something better left unsaid.

He didn't do casual sex with local women and he couldn't have anything but casual with Kitty Grant. She was the one woman he refused to consider a future with.

There was as much chance that she'd leave Cailkirn for the lure of the big city again than that she'd stay. A bigger chance, if he was laying odds and being realistic.

Besides, for all her smiles now, this fragile woman had a long way to travel back from broken.

"You've got a strange expression on your face," she mused.

He could only be grateful she didn't recognize pure, un-adorned desire when she saw it. She never had back in the day, and several years of marriage had not improved her perceptivity on that score.

Which made him standing like a simpleton while she reached up to cup his cheek about as stupid as he could get in that moment.

"You always were the best this state had to offer and you still are Taqukaq MacKinnon." Her words worked where all his self-control might have failed.

He jerked back, stepping away to put some distance between them. "The best of home wasn't good enough for you, though, was it?"

There had been a time he'd been willing to offer this woman everything. But those days were long past, and he damn well better remember it if he hoped to convince her.

Kitty ducked her head without answering, her sparkle dimming just like that.

He stifled a curse, knowing he could have been kinder. Or just not replied at all, damn it.

She made a production of taking more pictures before setting off along the trail again, her silence of a completely different quality now.

Tack followed her, berating himself for the harsh words. Even if they were the truth.

She stopped every so often to take more pictures of flowers, bushes, a deer through the trees, the sad pall that had fallen over her after his words lifting bit by bit. And the regret that had been riding him for causing her to fall back to her more subdued self dissipated right along with it.

"Do you lead tours on this trail?" she asked when they were a few hundred feet from the overlook.

"It's on Bobby's schedule." Which reminded Tack that he'd need to redo the schedule of available tours now that Kitty would be working for them.

She nodded with a tilt at one corner of her lips, nothing like the grin before but a smile nonetheless. "I thought so."

"What does that mean?"

"Egan didn't make it sound like you took tourists on the easy trails, that's all."

"He doesn't mind doing a mix. But for me, the more untamed the better."

"I remember that about you. I also remember you almost getting us lost snowshoeing one winter because you claimed that since you were part Inuit, you had a spiritual connection to the land."

He laughed and shook his head at his younger self. "We would have done better if that connection was a compass."

"Good thing I'd put one in my pack."

He usually carried one, too, but he'd been going through a phase, trying to find his *instinctive link* to the earth. "I thought if I didn't give myself a backup plan, ancient instincts would come to the fore."

She laughed softly and gave him a fond look. "You were an idiot."

"So you told me then." In colorful terms her gran would have been appalled to hear.

"You acted like there were no old stories about the Inuit getting lost in the vast wilderness."

"I wanted to be special." He'd been fifteen and just realized that his feelings for Kitty were not familial or platonic.

He had thought if she saw him as her hero, she'd stop thinking of him like the brother he wasn't.

"If you'll refrain from throwing it back in my face again, I'll tell you that you always were special. You didn't need some mystical ability to navigate the snowfields."

"Damn it, Kitty. When you threw me away, I was pretty sure you didn't think there was anything good or valuable about me." And it had hurt.

So much so that he'd vowed never to let anyone's opinion matter so much again.

"Does it make it worse or better to know that I always knew how wonderful you were?" Her shoulders hunched, like she was trying to draw in on herself again. "I never doubted how lucky I was to have your friendship and I threw it away anyway. I was a real idiot."

Which just confirmed that no matter how highly she said she thought of him, Tack hadn't been important enough to Kitty for her to keep in her life. Not as a friend and not as the man in her life.

The reminder should have diminished the arousal her renewed good mood had sparked in him. But his dick didn't care about the past or even his commitment to keeping a distance between them now.

His whole body was heating with a fire nothing but drowning himself in her could put out.

CHAPTER EIGHT

They reached the overlook, and Kitty rushed forward to the edge of the rocky outcropping.

The way she turned in a slow semicircle, her hands extended as if thankful for the gift of nature, about did him in. Her soft gasp only made it worse. The sound way too much like what he imagined she'd make with his cock buried deep inside her.

"I let myself forget how beautiful this was." She shook her head. "No, that's not true. I *made* myself forget."

"I don't know if I could."

"Desperation drives us when nothing else could."

"Why did you have to forget?"

"Because I thought I was never coming back." She never looked away from the awe-inspiring view before them, like she'd never get enough of it.

"You didn't want to come back."

"You're wrong." The words were quiet.

"You hated living in Cailkirn."

She shook her head but didn't reply, just kept her focus on the lake below and the mountains in the distance.

"You always said you were going to get out of this *backwater town* and never come back." And she'd done just that.

"We were kids. I wanted life in the big city, away from the town I associated with losing my parents."

"They died in Arizona."

"And I came to live in Cailkirn right after." She sounded so lost.

He walked up behind her, forcing down the need to touch but unable to maintain the distance between them.

"I didn't have enough time in Phoenix after Mom and Dad were gone to identify it with their loss. It always felt like my grief started in Cailkirn, and somehow my life in Alaska was all mixed up in that pain. I wanted to get away from it, to get over it."

"Leaving didn't work."

She sighed. "No, it didn't work."

"You still miss them." He didn't know why that should surprise him, but he'd never even realized as a kid that she missed her dead parents.

He'd only been a small boy and in his brain, she'd always been Kitty Grant, granddaughter to nutty Miz Moya, who talked to her dead husband.

"Dr. Hart helped me understand it was a wound that would probably never heal completely and that it doesn't make me weak, or at least weaker than I already am."

"You're not weak, Kitty." He couldn't stand it anymore and put his arms around her like he used to when she stood here, looking off into the distance.

For probably the first time ever, he thought he might have an idea of what she'd thought about when they stood like this, sometimes for an hour or more.

And just like back then, she let her body relax into his keeping. "I loved Gran, but I wanted my mom and dad. I could never say, because I knew she was hurting, too, and in that way that children do, I thought it was my fault. As I got older, I became so used to hiding my hurt that sometimes even I forgot that the happy girl I showed to the world wasn't always real."

They'd been best friends, closer than he was even with his brother. How had Tack missed that underlying grief in the girl he adored?

"Your gran and aunts always said you adjusted to the loss so well." He remembered his own mother commenting on it, on how strong Kitty was.

"Gran was so proud of her little trouper." Kitty's tone made him ache deep in his chest. "And if it helped her deal with her own grief, then hiding my own pain was worth it."

Tack wasn't sure he agreed with Kitty on that one. How much of her life the last eight years was caught up in her habit of concealing her inner agony?

"But I missed my parents so bad, Tack. I cried myself to sleep every night for the first year after moving here." Kitty's voice dropped to a whisper, like she was ashamed of the admission. "I'm not even sure when I stopped. I just know that I did."

"I never knew that."

She laughed, the sound mocking but still whisper soft. "Right. Like I was going to tell my new best friend who didn't even cry when he fell off the top of the big kid's slide that I washed my pillow with tears every night."

It shook him to realize how much of her emotions Kitty had hidden from all of them over the years.

"You'll probably laugh, but for the longest time, I was really jealous of Gran being able to talk to Granddad Ardal. I tried so hard to talk like that to Mom and Dad, but it didn't work. I decided they were stuck in Phoenix while I was in Cailkirn and if I could only go home, they'd be able to hear me."

He remembered Kitty telling him she wanted to go back to Phoenix and visit her old house. One of the only times he'd seen Kitty cry had been after her gran had told the little girl that it would be impossible because the house had been sold.

Miz Moya had gotten angry and told Kitty that nothing good ever came of going to the Lower 48. After that, Kitty started talking about someday moving away from Cailkirn and not coming back.

Dismayed at what clearly had been devastating to her child's psyche, he said, "Your gran never meant to hurt you that way."

"I know." Kitty sighed. "Just like I never meant to hurt her by marrying Nevin."

Letting his arms drop away from her, he stepped back. "You know, they took that slide out of the playground five years ago."

The ten-foot-high metal monstrosity had been a child favorite and constant source of contention between the adults of the town. When one of the support poles rusted dangerously, they took out the slide rather than repair it.

"I bet the schoolchildren were disappointed."

"Yep, but my mom was thrilled." *Aana* had lobbied for its removal ever since that ignominious tumble, even though his da had insisted a few spills were no reason to take the slide out of the playground.

"She always was a woman of uncommon sense," Kitty said with a smile in her voice.

Glad their brief discussion hadn't brought back her melancholy, Tack let her soak in her fill of one of the prettiest views on the peninsula as he laid out a small tarp. Between the drive up from Cailkirn and the hike, it was past lunchtime.

"You ready to eat?" he asked as he put out sandwiches, a container of fruit, and what looked like two cups of chocolate milk.

In reality, it was a protein drink he made himself and used on his long hikes. He figured she could use the extra calories, not to mention the vitamins and protein.

She turned and took in the spread of food. "You brought chocolate milk?"

"It used to be your favorite drink," he said, sidestepping the actual question.

"It still is, but it's also empty calories."

"Not quite and this isn't, I promise."

She nodded, inexplicable trust glowing in a gaze as bright as the blue prairie flax wildflower she was so fond of. "Thank you."

Without surprise, he watched her set aside half of the sandwich and fruit he'd put on her plate. He'd noted her doing the same thing with dinner the other night and the slice of cake yesterday.

He'd taken that little quirk into account when making the sandwiches, using a denser multigrain homemade bread and adding a little extra turkey and mashed avocado disguised by the heaping portion of alfalfa sprouts on the sandwiches.

Even eating half, she would get close to a normal portion. Same with the fruit. He'd put about a third more than he usually would have on her plate.

He figured the fact that her original portions matched his would hide his intentions.

It seemed to have worked as she took a bite of the sandwich without saying anything. She made a positively indecent sound as she chewed and he had to wonder if he was going to be able to eat without laying her flat on the tarp and devouring *her*.

"You didn't put mayo on the sandwiches," she said with clear approval after chewing and swallowing a second bite.

"I hardly ever do when I'm packing food for a hike." He'd also figured there was a better chance of her eating a full half of the sandwich if he left the mayonnaise off.

"It's delicious. This is your mom's bread, isn't it?"

"You don't think I made it?"

Kitty almost looked worried she'd offended him. "Did you?"

"No." He laughed at her look of disgruntlement.

"Tease me at your peril, Taqukaq MacKinnon."

"Oh? You going to get me back?"

"Aunt Elspeth may love you, but I'm her Kitty-dear. Just think of me as the gatekeeper to her cakes and cookies and we'll get along just fine."

He laughed, liking the feisty. "I'll keep that in mind."

"See that you do."

They finished eating in silence, Tack pleased to see that not only did Kitty eat her entire half portion, but she drank the protein drink too.

"That's good. What do you put in it?" she asked as she

put the lid back on the plastic cup so it wouldn't drip remnants inside his pack.

"That's a MacKinnon family recipe. You know we don't share those, even with friends."

"Right. Your ancestors did not bring it over from the Old Country."

"Doesn't matter. A MacKinnon created it."

"You."

"Right."

"Somehow, I don't see Gran MacKinnon adding it to her jealously guarded recipe box."

"You need a better imagination, then, because it's in there, right behind the one for pecan-praline shortbread."

"I used to wonder what it would be like to have a big family like yours," Kitty said wistfully.

"You adopted me as your brother. I'd say you got close enough."

She smiled, the expression tinged with melancholy. "It's not the same."

"*Aana* and Da see you as another daughter."

"They always made me feel welcome." It sounded like agreement.

But something about the *way* Kitty said it told Tack that it wasn't. "They love you like one of their own."

"That's a sweet sentiment, but not a true one." Kitty wasn't smiling anymore, but she didn't look angry.

Just thoughtful.

"They missed you like crazy when you stayed in California." Tack had practically had to beg to get them to stop bringing her up, expecting him to close the breach between Kitty and her hometown somehow.

Their sadness at Kitty's complete defection from Cailkirn

had added to his resentment over the years. His parents and grandparents had treated her like a member of the MacKinnon clan and she'd left them all behind without a backward glance, not just him.

"For a while maybe, but I was their son's friend, not their daughter."

"That's not how they saw it." He wasn't sure why he was arguing this point so hard, or maybe he was.

The truth was, Kitty had hurt a lot of people when she abandoned Cailkirn.

"People say a lot of things they don't really mean. If you believe them, you're setting yourself up for disappointment." She sounded like she had learned that lesson painfully.

"It's not that way in Cailkirn."

"Sure it is."

"Not with me, not with my family."

"Really?" Kitty's gaze darkened with an intensity he didn't understand.

"Yes."

She could make up all the excuses she wanted for turning her back on a town full of people who had loved her, but denying their care for her wasn't going to be one of them.

"So, if Shila went to college in the Lower Forty-Eight like your mom wants her to and she met a man she thought she loved, they'd just let her disappear from their lives without so much as a phone call to see if she was doing okay?"

"Don't try to blame your years with Nevin on my parents. You're the one who turned your back on them and our town."

"I'm not blaming them," Kitty said with enough fervor he had to believe her. "I'm saying that I *didn't* have parents like Shila does, no matter how sweet the sentiment that I was another daughter to them. Your dad wouldn't let Shila's husband tell her she couldn't come back to Alaska."

"Damn right he wouldn't."

Kitty nodded. "He'd be down there in a heartbeat putting any man foolish enough to think he was coming between your sister and her family firmly in his place. Your mom would never have allowed holiday after holiday to go by without seeing her daughter. It just wouldn't have happened."

"Shila wouldn't have let it happen either."

"Maybe. Probably. No doubt she's stronger than I ever was."

"That's not what I meant."

Kitty went on as if she hadn't heard him. "All I know is that the first time Shila's husband cracked her ribs, your dad would have cracked his head."

"Because he would have known about it."

"Maybe. Probably," Kitty said again, her easy agreement bothering him instead of making Tack feel justified.

"None of us knew, Kitty." Sudden clarity hit Tack.

They hadn't known because she'd been hiding her pain for the last eight years, just like she had as a child.

"No, I know, but that's not really the point." Kitty's eyes glittered with moisture, but no tears fell. "Your parents loved me, just like a lot of other people in this town. Only *not* like they love you, Egan, or Shila."

Before he opened his mouth to argue again, Tack made himself really think about what Kitty had said, the comparison she'd made. If any one of their children had checked out of their lives like Kitty had, for whatever reason, Malina and Fergus MacKinnon would have tracked him or her down.

No question. No exceptions. And they wouldn't have let go, no matter how hard it was to hold on.

They wouldn't have let Shila hide her pain, because she was their baby girl and nothing about her escaped their notice. Not even the looks she gave Lee Bount, which went farther in explaining his mom's insistence on Shila going to college out of state than anything else.

"And I'm not saying they should have loved me like they do their own children," Kitty continued, sincerity infusing every word. "God knows they never owed me anything. I'm just saying they *didn't*."

Tack did not know how to respond. His realization that Kitty's point was valid didn't negate the truth that his parents genuinely cared about her.

However, he could not dismiss the reality that Shila would never have been as alone as Kitty found herself after Tack left for Idaho State either. He'd never regretted his decision to leave California until now. He'd given up too easily and the woman he'd loved had been hurt. It didn't matter that she'd pushed him away. Tack had been a stronger man than Nevin, even back then and despite their age differences. If he'd stayed to see what was happening, it wouldn't have happened.

He didn't ask why Kitty didn't tell her gran or aunts what was going on. Even as a child, Kitty had been fiercely protective of her only remaining family. She would never let them get twisted up in the life Nevin had sucked her into.

Her refusal to return to Cailkirn with her gran last year was starting to make sense too. "You didn't come back with Miz Moya when she came down to see you in the hospital because you didn't want Nevin coming for her."

Kitty's wince was enough of an agreement, though she didn't say anything.

"I should have checked on you." He'd been so focused on

her betrayal, it never occurred to him that Kitty needed looking after.

He'd been wrong. Damn it.

He'd promised her they would always be friends, that he
would always look after her, even though she'd staunchly
denied the need for him to do so. But she'd gotten engaged
to another man, and that had hurt more than he'd known he
could hurt.

And her little speech about needing to focus on her relationship with her fiancé and minimize the time she spent
with Tack had given him all the reason he needed to cut ties
completely. It didn't help that he'd been positive that's what
she'd wanted, but he hadn't been able to come right out and
say.

Until this very moment, he'd felt entirely justified in
giving her all the space she'd claimed to need and then
some. When she didn't return his e-mails, he stopped sending them. When she changed her phone number without
telling him, he stopped calling.

He hadn't given up without any effort, but it sure hadn't
been the fight a MacKinnon would have made to keep someone important in his life. Even if it was just a friend.

Because he'd needed the space between them to get over
his obsession with her. Because he'd been weak and that
wasn't something he'd ever considered himself.

"No," Kitty said fiercely. "Why would you? I wasn't your
responsibility. I knew what I was doing when I pushed you
out of my life."

"You didn't." Of that he was now certain.

She'd had no idea the monster Nevin Barston was, or how
much she would need someone in her corner after she married him.

. But she shook her head in denial of his words. "I knew throwing our friendship away came with a cost and I did it anyway. I *was* the one to cut off contact with your family and this town. And you. Most especially you, when you were the one I owed the most loyalty."

Hell, she blamed herself even more than he did, or had done…before today, for the choice she'd made eight years ago.

"If we'd known what was going on, we'd have come for you, Kitty, me and Da."

For the first time he could remember, the expression in her blue eyes accused him of flat out lying. And he could see that from her viewpoint, her doubt was warranted. Because they'd never checked on her. Not once.

Not one person in the town who had claimed to love Kitty Grant as one of their own had tried to find out why she never came home for a visit. They'd all assumed she'd hurt her gran and great-aunts out of pure selfishness, or at the least self-centered oblivion.

There wasn't an expletive foul enough for the feeling Tack had right then.

Cailkirn took care of its own, except when they didn't apparently.

"Stop it," Kitty ordered, her voice laced with anger for the first time since this discussion had started.

"What?"

"Thinking you or anyone else let me down. *I* let this town down and everyone who had cared for me. I let myself down. I'm not sure if that makes me stupid, weak, or both. Probably both, but I *won't* hide behind the idea that someone should have saved me from Nevin or even from myself."

"But—"

"That was *my* responsibility and it may have taken me longer than it should have, but eventually I got away and I'm *never* going back." The vehemence in her voice should have made him feel good.

Instead, it about broke his heart. "I told you that you're stronger than you give yourself credit for."

"I'm strong enough to do what I have to now." A faraway look came into Kitty's eyes. "That's what matters."

Tack felt like there was more meaning to her words than what was on the surface, but he had no idea what it was. He only knew it left him feeling unsettled.

The way she seemed to be disconnecting from the present one second to the next just made that feeling more acute. Just as she'd grown more and more content on the way to the overlook, her body language and expression changing bit by bit, now she was visibly withdrawing into herself.

The worst was how he felt like she was just disappearing. Her body was there, but he felt nothing coming from her. Something in their discussion had triggered a mental, emotional, and even physical retreat he would have denied possible if he hadn't seen it happen before his eyes.

An almost frenzied need to bring her back to the present washed over him. His instincts were telling him the best way to accomplish that, but his brain insisted it was a bad, *bad* idea.

Fighting the urge to act on his instincts, Tack cleaned up the detritus of lunch. It only took a couple of minutes to put everything back in his pack. But in that short time, Kitty maintained her distant silence and she drew further away from him.

And she couldn't afford to do that.

He couldn't say how he knew that; he just did.

Tack's certainty growing that she'd checked out mentally in a way that was dangerous for her emotions, he put his pack aside and scooted closer to Kitty. She didn't seem to notice.

"Wildcat?" he prompted, his voice as gentle as he could make it. "You okay in there?"

"Of course." The words were right, but the vacant tone was anything but.

He slid his hand under her hair, cupping her neck, giving physical contact to draw her back to him and now. She didn't react to the touch at all and that scared him.

"Damn it, Caitlin Elizabeth Grant, look at me."

Her brows furrowed. "Don't."

"What?" he asked in a tone as gentle as he'd spoken sternly before. *Come on, wildcat, tell me not to yell at you.*

Her silence changed, as if she was searching for words. "Call me Caitlin." She frowned. "I don't like it."

"I thought you wanted me to." She'd said so, hadn't she?

"No."

"Why not? Why don't you like it?"

She shrugged.

And that was it. He was done playing nice, his own misgivings not nearly as powerful as his need to stop whatever was going on inside Kitty's mind.

With careful, but inexorable pressure, he turned her head so she faced him. Her pupils were dilated like they'd been yesterday, her complexion waxy, but her lips were pink and parted invitingly.

Her breathing changed just a little bit and he took that as a victory.

"I'm going to kiss you, wildcat. Are you up for it?"

CHAPTER NINE

Tack's gut was telling him this is what he needed to do, but damned if he would kiss her without her permission.

She'd had enough choices taken away; that was becoming clearer the more he found out about her life before returning to Cailkirn.

"What?" Suddenly she was looking at him and seeing him. "You're going to kiss me? Why would you do that?"

He almost laughed. He did groan. His body was burning for her. "Because I want to."

"Why?"

"You really need to ask?"

"No?"

"You don't sound real sure there, sweetheart."

She bit her bottom lip and then released it. "I don't think I'm very good at it."

"Good thing I am, then, huh?"

"Maybe?"

"I tell you what, let's give it a try and you can let me know if you agree, okay?"

"Yes."

More relieved at her acquiescence than he should be, he tipped his head forward and slid his lips across hers in the simplest and most chaste of touches.

A small sigh shuddered out of her, the breath washing over his lips.

He kissed her again, this time molding their mouths and moving his lips against hers for long delicious moments. Her small hands came up to clutch the front of his long sleeved T-shirt, her fingers twisting in the fabric as she tried to pull him closer.

He went willingly, allowing their upper bodies to touch.

It wasn't skin-on-skin contact, but that didn't seem to matter to the electric shocks short-circuiting his nerve endings.

He flicked his tongue out to taste her. The flavor of grapes and ripe strawberries exploded on his tongue along with a sweetness that was all Kitty Grant.

Certain it would become an addiction way too easily, he still wanted more of that taste. He delved into her mouth and she welcomed him, sliding her tongue along his and pressing their lips closer together.

His reasons for initiating the kiss melted, along with everything else around them, and he reveled in the touch and feel of this woman he'd craved for too many years of his life.

He maneuvered them so she was lying on her back on the tarp and he was partially over her without once breaking his lips from hers. To do so would have been a travesty of epic proportions.

Her fingers kneaded him through his shirt like a cat. Such an innocent touch, but it felt good. So good that between that and the kiss, his erection was pressing hard enough against his fly he'd be surprised if it didn't leave an imprint on his flesh.

He wanted skin, though. Craved her skin under his fingertips and damned if common sense was going to stop him from getting exactly that.

He slid his hand under her top and ran into a barrier. A thin layer of cotton knit warmed by her body stood in the way of his caress. He pulled at the T-shirt with impatient fingers, popping the button open on the waistband and yanking down her jeans' zipper when it took too long.

The T-shirt came free and he pushed his hand up under the hem to just lay it against her stomach.

She went completely still; even her lips stopped moving and her chest barely lifted with her shallow breaths.

Reluctantly pulling his head back, he broke the kiss and opened his eyes to make sure she was okay.

Sky-blue eyes filled with wonder looked up at him. "You *are* good at this."

Pleasure zinged through him at her compliment even though he hadn't had any real doubts on that issue, but he didn't smile or acknowledge it. He couldn't. There was something too important about this moment, and if he opened his mouth, he might have to acknowledge it.

His concerns put to rest, he resumed the kiss, deliberately closing his eyes to anything beyond the sensation of touch. He spread his fingers out, expanding the contact and brushing over silky smooth skin.

A soft moan escaped from her throat but was muted by his mouth covering hers.

His pinky rested against the waistband of her panties. He rubbed it back and forth, teasing himself with how close to her feminine sex he was. The temptation to go lower too strong to resist, Tack moved his hand just enough so that two fingertips slipped past the thin elastic.

Her hand grabbed his wrist and he waited to see what she would do, knowing it would take a helluva lot of self-control to stop if that's what she wanted. Her fingers squeezed and released convulsively twice before she pushed down, offering silent permission to touch her more intimately.

He brushed the top of her mons, pleased when he encountered soft curls. Some men preferred denuded flesh down there; he wasn't one of them.

Kitty's pelvis tilted up as if asking for more, another moan pressing from her lips to his as her short fingernails dug into his wrist.

The signs of her arousal fueled his own and he gave her what she wanted, moving his hand so his middle finger slipped right between her nether lips to caress the tiny button at the top where her labia met.

Kitty's whole body went stiff and then jerked, her fingers digging more urgently into the muscles of his chest and flesh of his wrist. The small sting of pain only added to his excitement.

He pulled his head back again, this time because he wanted to see what her beautiful features looked like in passion. Dazed blue eyes stared back at him, filled with both confusion and unarguable need.

The scent of her musk mixed with moss and wet earth, headier and more potent to his libido than any perfume created in a lab ever could be. The image of her mouth wet and swollen from his kisses and her throat flushed with desire were more arousing than any airbrushed image in a skin mag could be either.

"Okay?" he asked as he moved his finger in light circles over her clitoris.

She nodded, her lips moving but no sound coming out.

"I'm going to make you come," he promised. "You're going to scream my name."

That elicited a groan and more fervent movement of her pelvis, but no words. It would have been flattering if he wasn't an inch away from coming in his shorts like a horny teenager.

He kissed her again but wasn't content with only learning the texture and flavor of her mouth. He searched out sensitive spots on her neck and behind her ears, tasting the salt of her skin and its silken smoothness with flicks of his tongue.

"Tack," she keened as he dipped his finger lower to draw her dew up to her clitoris.

He answered by biting her earlobe gently, only to be rewarded with a sweet little whimper he'd be jacking off to for weeks to come.

He was as hard as he'd ever been, but the urge to get himself off wasn't anything like the need to give her the ultimate pleasure.

That's not to say he refrained from rubbing his cock against her hip as he continued to touch her. He was only human. His every caress brought forth a sexy reaction that only increased his own sexual need and desire to please her.

She came without any warning, no stiffening of her body, no verbal babbling, no indication she was on the edge until suddenly she was over it. Her wordless cry echoed in the chill air around them, not his name but damn satisfying nonetheless.

Continuing to touch her *very* gently, he prolonged her pleasure and her sweet body convulsed and jerked in aftershocks of the ultimate pleasure. She said his name then, whispering it over and over again as her hips moved restlessly and her breath came in shuddering gasps.

All at once, it was too much and ecstasy washed over him, cum exploding out of his cock into his boxers as he came in an uncontrolled rush for the first time in years.

He dropped down beside her, content and sleepy, like he never allowed himself to be after sex. Tack MacKinnon didn't do out-of-control and he didn't do postcoital cuddling either.

But damned if he didn't want to pull her into his arms and lay together on the hard ground for the next hour or two.

His hand still in her jeans, his fingertip barely touched her swollen clitoris. "Damn. I've never done that before."

"I don't believe you," she said in a breathless voice.

He chuckled. "I meant coming in my jeans."

"You did?" She sat up, jolting and blushing like crazy as his hand moved against her sex.

"Problem there, Kitty?" he asked with a grin he knew was wicked, but couldn't help himself.

"Your hand...it's in my...you're still..." She glared at him. "Don't tease me."

"I wouldn't dream of it." He slid his hand out nice and slow.

She didn't seem to mind and made no move to push it away when he left his fingers resting against her belly, the scent of her climax floating in the air around them.

He might not cuddle, but he liked skin-to-skin contact with his lovers.

Oh shit. Tack yanked his hand away from Kitty and jumped to his feet. He backed away, looking for distance he wasn't going to find, but he had to try.

"Tack?" Kitty looked up, her expression too vulnerable for what had just happened.

"I need to clean up. I'm not hiking back two and half miles with jizz soaking my shorts."

"Um...okay. I'll just..." She looked around, clearly uncertain what *she* should do. "I'll fold up the tarp."

He nodded even as he turned away, grabbing his pack as he headed toward some brush cover for privacy.

* * *

Caitlin stared after Tack, unsure what had just happened.

He'd kissed her. He'd touched her body, making her feel like it was *her* body in a way she'd lost at some point. He'd made her come just like he promised. And then he'd vaulted away from her like she was diseased.

Or a huge disappointment.

Only he said he'd come, too, so he couldn't be mad at her for not taking care of his needs. Maybe he'd wanted her to participate more?

Nevin used to harangue her for lying like a dead fish in bed.

But with Tack, she hadn't been off in her head, just waiting for it to be over. She'd been so in the moment she'd felt like she was coming out of her skin.

Maybe he regretted kissing and touching her, only she hadn't initiated it, no matter how much she might have wanted to. He had.

Her thoughts a confusing jumble, she did what she'd told him she would and folded the tarp into a neat, tight square for his pack.

"You ready to head back?" he asked as he walked up and took the bundle from her hands a few minutes later.

She tried to look at him unobtrusively but couldn't tell if he'd taken off his shorts or just cleaned up and left them on. And she didn't know why that should matter, but when it came to Tack MacKinnon, Caitlin was discovering that her curiosity knew no bounds.

"Sure." He'd given her enough of his day.

Tack had told her how busy he was; she shouldn't be feeling disappointment that their nature sojourn was over.

She didn't know *what* to feel about what had just happened between them.

"What was that?" she asked as they started the return journey.

When she heard other hikers coming toward her and Tack, she felt a huge surge of gratitude for their timing. What had been one of most pleasurable experiences of her life could have just as easily been the most embarrassing.

Not humiliating.

She'd learned the difference between the two and Caitlin was pretty sure that nothing she and Tack did together could humiliate her. Embarrass her, yes, but not humiliate.

"A kiss," he said shortly, nodding a greeting to the other hikers as they passed each other on the trail.

She waited until they were farther away before saying, "Some kiss."

"Yeah, well."

"You regret kissing me."

"No."

Her brow furrowed. Then what? "You wish you hadn't touched me to climax?"

"Kitty! Leave it, okay?"

She would, after she told him one last thing. "I didn't know I could still come. I haven't in years. Thank you."

There, that was all she had to say.

She was wholly unprepared for Tack to spin around and crush her to him and then take her mouth in a mind-numbing kiss before pushing her away again. "We can't do this again."

"If you say so." But he was the one who still had hold of her shoulders even though they stood apart.

"I say so."

"Can I ask why?"

"I don't do casual sex with local women."

"We didn't have sex, did we?" Maybe her definition was out of date.

"No," he gritted out. "But if we'd been on a bed and not hard rock with nothing but a tarp, we would have."

He wanted her. "Oh."

"Yes, oh." He let go of her and took another step back, scrubbing his face with his hand.

"I don't mind." That kind of sex she could do. The kind that felt good.

The kind that didn't come with rules she didn't understand and consequences she couldn't guess at.

"I do."

"Why?"

"Because, Kitty, we are friends, not *lovers*," he said as if he were speaking to a small, not very bright child.

And the emphasis he put on the word *lovers*, the way his mouth twisted in a grimace when he said it. That was definitely something he did not want to be.

"So?"

"So, friends don't have sex."

"I'm pretty sure some do. It's called friends with benefits."

"I don't do that."

He wouldn't. His honor would prevent him from *using* a friend. Even if she said she didn't mind or feel used.

"Have other Cailkirn women tried to talk you into it?" There went her insatiable curiosity where he was concerned again.

She'd done her best to curb that trait during her time in Los Angeles after discovering that sometimes, the less you knew, the less you hurt.

"This is not an appropriate conversation, Kitty."

She didn't really care. And that was a pretty big revelation. "Have they?" she pressed.

"Yes."

"And you turned them down."

"Yes."

Oooh, he was growly.

"Okay."

"Good."

She didn't say anything back and he started walking again.

"So, where do you get sex?" He was too good at that stuff to be lacking in practical experience.

"Seriously, Kitty?"

"Yes. I don't think I could let anyone else touch me yet, but eventually." Which was light-years away from the never-again-in-this-lifetime she'd come to Cailkirn with. "Now that I know I can enjoy it, maybe I'll try some casual encounters."

Other women did it. And casual had the benefit of protecting a heart she was still adamantly certain she *never* wanted to put on the chopping block again.

"I'm not giving you tips on how to find casual sex." Offended exasperation dripped from every word.

If he didn't want to have it with her, why couldn't she have it with someone else? "Why not?"

"Because."

"That's a good reason," she snarked.

"Knock it off," he ground out.

She was quiet for the next ten minutes, but then some devil prompted her to say, "Well, I bet Egan will tell me."

Tack spun around, effectively stopping her too. "No, just no."

"Why not?"

Tack's face was red with outrage under his close-cropped beard. "You are not having sex with my baby brother!"

"I never said I was! Sheesh, Tack. Your brain goes weird places." That was just ick.

Egan might be twenty-four, but in her eyes, he was still a baby. Even if she was sure that *baby* had an active sex life.

"You're the one who said you'd ask him."

"About where he goes for casual sex, not to *have sex with me*. I'm sure you told him to stay away from locals too. It's the kind of thing you'd do, so he probably knows the best way to find someone to play with."

Tack looked ready to explode and she wasn't sure why. She wasn't asking him to kiss her again, or touch her, or anything.

Okay, she was poking the bear with the comment about asking Egan, but not *that* hard and her stick wasn't *that* pointed.

"Play with?" he demanded, sounding like he had rocks in his throat.

"You know what I mean."

"Unfortunately, I do. You're not thinking this through."

She really didn't get his aversion to what she was asking. "What's there to think about?"

"Would you listen to me, damn it?"

"I am listening to you." He just wasn't saying anything that made sense at the moment.

"You don't need sex."

Where did he get off telling her that? She was twenty-eight, same as him. "What?" she demanded, glaring up at him.

"You are too vulnerable. After everything you've been through, the last thing you need is to get into a sexual relationship right now."

She processed the words and their possible meanings until one stood out more than the rest. It came from that dark well inside her, the place that harbored her insecurities and pain she still struggled to deal with, or hide when she couldn't.

"You think I'm broken." He'd said as much before, but she hadn't realized how deeply his belief that she was irrevocably damaged went. "Really broken."

"Yes." He made no effort to deny it. "You said it yourself—you didn't even know you could enjoy it. Can't you see how susceptible that makes you?"

Her therapist had said something like that, when Caitlin was getting ready to leave California. Dr. Hart had been concerned that Caitlin had some distance still to go emotionally, that she was still *susceptible* to the manipulations of a man who knew how to capitalize on a woman's weaknesses.

Like Nevin.

What neither Tack nor Dr. Hart seemed to realize was that Caitlin wasn't capable of getting into another destructive relationship like that again. It required trust, and she didn't have any.

Unless she counted Tack, which he'd made very clear she shouldn't. And even with him, she didn't know how deep the conviction in his unwillingness to knowingly hurt her went. She kept surprising herself with the faith she had in him, but doubted it was an inexhaustible resource.

No matter what he and Dr. Hart might believe about her.

Kitty stepped out from under his hands. The safety in his touch was an illusion and the sooner she accepted that, the better off she would be.

Dr. Hart had said having weaknesses wasn't the same as being weak, but Caitlin had never quite believed her.

Now she was sure the therapist had been wrong.

Because Tack saw Caitlin's weaknesses and thought sex was one of them. She would have laughed if she could, but suddenly there just wasn't any laughter inside her.

Sex was the one area she *wasn't* vulnerable. In her entire life, she'd only lost her control with one man. Had only ever responded one time with such unadulterated need and desire. That was less than half an hour ago with Taqukaq MacKinnon.

She didn't say any of this, though. What was the use? Tack didn't want her and he was convinced she was too weak to have sex with a man and not get herself back into a bad relationship.

Maybe he was right. Not about the sex itself making her emotionally vulnerable to a man, but if she allowed him close enough to touch her intimately, he'd have the opportunity to hurt her in other ways.

"Kitty?" Tack prompted, sounding worried.

She put her game face on, the one she wore more and more for her gran and great-aunts these days. She'd had no idea it would be this hard being around her family again. She'd thought that was going to be the easy part in moving back to Cailkirn.

"Fine. No sex."

"Look, I—"

"Let's go. I know you have things to do."

He looked like he was going to argue, but then he turned around and started stomping down the trail.

She was back to feeling like an empty shell, but at least she'd had that brief respite from the woman she'd become to remember the girl she had been.

CHAPTER TEN

Trying her best to ignore the anxiety caused by so many calories in one place, Caitlin put the *five* bags of brown sugar Aunt Elspeth had on her list in the cart.

She knew her aunts loved food and that Aunt Elspeth had goodies to make for the B&B, but buying that much sugar at once triggered stress she could manage but not necessarily get rid of. She just kept telling herself she didn't have to eat the cookies and pastries.

The guests could.

She'd come into Kenai to shop for groceries, thinking it would give her some much needed time to herself. She hadn't counted on the contents of her aunts' grocery list.

Caitlin's shoulders jarred as her cart ran into something and the impact traveled up her arms.

She jerked her head up, an apology on her lips, only to meet vaguely familiar gray eyes. "It's Savannah Vasov, right?"

"Yes." The other woman nodded, no socially polite smile marring her face. "Caitlin, isn't it?"

Relieved at not having to pretend to be *happy* with this near stranger, Caitlin just nodded as well. "Where's Joey?"

Okay, so maybe she was a little *pensive* since Tack's rejection after that amazing kiss, but she wasn't unhappy. She just wasn't a walking fount of joy every minute of every day. Sometimes, that's the way life was. Caitlin only wished that was enough for the people she loved.

"He's back in Cailkirn with Nik. He wanted to pan for gold." Savannah was clearly trying to sound enthusiastic about that fact, but her efforts fell a little flat.

Caitlin didn't say any of the platitudes that came to mind. "It's cold and unless Nik salts the water, panning is mind-numbingly boring with little prospect at success." Caitlin adjusted the top bag of sugar to stack more neatly on the others and was proud of how well she suppressed a shudder while doing it.

Her honesty startled a small laugh out of the Southern woman. "I can stop feeling badly I didn't join them, then."

"Definitely."

"At least Nik likes Joey." The startled widening of Savannah's gray eyes indicated she hadn't intended to say that out loud.

Caitlin guessed, "And Joey likes him?"

"Yes." There was definitely gratitude infused in that single-word answer. "I thought that was going to be the hard part."

Caitlin understood that only too well. "When I was first married, I thought the most difficult thing I would have to deal with was giving up my education."

"It wasn't?"

"No."

Savannah's expression filled with understanding. "A man who would make you give up your education wouldn't think anything of making you give up other things, too, would he?"

"Like my self-respect? Yes." Whoa. Her honesty with Tack didn't surprise Caitlin, but this lack of subterfuge with a virtual stranger? Weird.

Maybe it was because the other woman had been unexpectedly open first.

There was also something about Savannah that Caitlin identified with, although she didn't have that shadowed expression of a woman who had been married to a man who hurt her. Caitlin doubted very much the other woman would have agreed to a proxy wedding, under any circumstances, if her past reflected Caitlin's either.

"You were married to a bully," Savannah stated rather than asked.

Caitlin had never put it like that, but the other woman was absolutely right. "A professional."

Savannah winced like she knew what that meant. "Nik's not like that."

"No." Tack wouldn't be his good friend if he were, and though she barely knew Savannah, Caitlin had the feeling the other woman would never expose her son to that environment either.

The love and protectiveness she felt toward the little boy had come through loud and clear on their brief acquaintance.

"I think Nik would cut off a limb rather than hurt someone weaker than him."

"You're lucky, then."

Something passed over Savannah's features. "Maybe I am at that."

They ended up finishing their shopping together, chatting about Cailkirn and what Savannah should expect once the cruise ships started coming in next week.

"It's insane. Over the course of the summer, we'll see more than half a million tourists."

"But it's such a small town."

"I know, right? It's this crazy dichotomy that you either learn to live with or avoid." Not that she'd experienced it herself much more growing up, as the ships hadn't been as frequent then.

"Nikolai seems stressed about the tourist season."

"Well, he has to run two businesses then," Caitlin said as she put her groceries on the conveyor belt. "Both the Vasov mines and the Vasov Gold Mining tourist experience."

Savannah looked surprised. "Oh, I didn't realize."

"Or he didn't think to tell you."

"He's not a big talker."

Caitlin had a feeling that was putting it mildly. "I got that impression, but Tack seems to like him."

"Tack MacKinnon? You know him?"

"You'll find that most people who have lived here longer than a year know pretty much everyone else, but Tack and I were best friends when we were kids."

She wasn't sure what they were now, but it wasn't best friends. Caitlin had begun to suspect that she was Tack's good deed for the decade and not a friend at all, no matter what he claimed.

"He's come by the house a couple of times. He and Nikolai are pretty good friends."

"There you go. Tack's the most honorable man I know." Honorable enough to feel some strange obligation to a woman who had rejected his friendship once upon a time. "He wouldn't spend time with a bad man."

"Oh, I never meant to imply—"

"Don't stress it," Caitlin interrupted. "You're in a difficult situation. I, of all people, understand how many different reasons there might be for ending up there."

Savannah nodded but didn't add any more and Caitlin didn't expect her to.

They checked out together and agreed they would try to carpool the next time they came into Kenai for shopping. Caitlin followed Nikolai Vasov's F150 onto the highway until Savannah made the turnoff to his place a little north of Cailkirn.

* * *

Tack walked into MacKinnon Bros. Tours determined to pin Kitty down to a date for dinner with his family. *Aana* was convinced that it was his fault Kitty hadn't come already.

His grandmother had gone so far as to tell him that it wasn't the Inuit way to hold grudges. Egan, that little shit, hadn't stood up for him at all, just saying he was staying out of it.

Tack didn't know what his grandmother was thinking. If he was holding a grudge, would he have given Kitty a job?

But did *Emaa* think of that? No.

When Tack got inside, Bobby was leaning on the corner of Caitlin's desk, one his granddad had in fact found in a family member's attic. The big executive desk did give the reception area a more professional feel.

And Kitty looked like she belonged there, sitting behind it. Bobby hanging off the edge not so much.

"Get your ass to work," Tack instructed his cousin as he approached her desk.

"I was working." Bobby indicated Kitty with a wave of his hand and a smile toward her. "We were going over my schedule today."

Tack felt like growling. "There's little enough on it yet."

"Yep. Next week is going to be insanity on wheels, according to Egan." Bobby sounded like he relished the prospect.

"Throw in the fires of hell and you've got it about right."

Bobby blanched. "The tourists aren't that bad, are they?"

"You've lived here your whole life. What do you think?"

Bobby went off muttering about packing antacids, pain relievers, and tranquilizer darts in his pack.

Tack laughed. "That boy is going to give the tourists a run for their money."

Kitty gave that almost-smile he'd seen a lot of since the hike. It was as fake as a "genuine Alaska gold nugget" marked with *Made in China* on the bottom. They sold those at one of the tourist shops owned by the cruise lines.

"*Aana* wants you to come to dinner tonight."

Kitty opened her mouth, no doubt to come up with some reason why she couldn't.

Tack put his hand up to forestall her. "I should warn you, I've already talked to your gran and she assures me that neither she nor her sisters need you for anything tonight."

Kitty shut her mouth with a snap.

"What the hell, Kitty? Why are you avoiding my family? You said you don't blame them."

"I don't!" She stood up, agitation clear in every line of her tiny body. "And I would appreciate you not referring to that conversation again."

Was she thinner than on their hike? He hoped his eyes were playing tricks on him. "Then why won't you come to dinner?"

"I've had things to do. I haven't lied to you."

"Well, you don't have plans tonight," he told her triumphantly.

Kitty opened and closed her mouth a couple of times before letting her face fall into that mask she probably thought looked peaceful but actually just looked empty. "Tell your mother I'll be happy to join you for dinner."

"You can tell her yourself. She's coming in this afternoon."

"I'll be leaving at one to help out at the B and B."

"Your gran said to relax this afternoon. It will probably be your last chance to have time off for a while."

"I'm sure she's not taking an afternoon for herself."

"Maybe, maybe not, but you'll hurt her feelings if you show up to work when she told you not to."

An expression of disgruntlement crossed Kitty's features, which made two honest emotions he'd seen since their hike. She'd been so free and happy on the way up to the overlook, but it had all drained away on the way down.

"Fine, I'll take the afternoon off."

"Good. *Aana* will be glad to hear it. She's hoping you'll have lunch with her."

"I'm having dinner with your family tonight."

"You know how loud and crowded that can be. She wants a chance to visit with you one-on-one."

For five full seconds, the horror she clearly felt at such a prospect washed over Kitty's lovely face, but then she schooled her expression as if the dismay had never been there.

"Why don't you want to have lunch with my mother?" he demanded.

Malina MacKinnon adored Kitty. There was nothing bad here.

"Your mom is a gossip, maybe even worse than Gran."

He couldn't deny it. In a town the size of Cailkirn, gossip was a favorite pastime of a good portion of the residents, men and women alike.

Tack shrugged. "She's harmless. She doesn't spread hurtful things." Or dig into painful situations.

She'd never once asked Nik Vasov why he didn't speak to his parents, and she'd never asked Tack for information on his friend's new proxy bride. She'd hinted at it, but never come right out and requested Tack give her the lowdown.

"*Aana* is not mean or malicious."

"I know that. You might not believe me, but I loved your mother when we were kids."

"What's your problem, then?"

"She asks a lot of questions."

"So?"

"So, maybe I don't want to answer them."

"Then don't."

"You think it's that easy?" Kitty asked, obviously feeling otherwise.

But she was wrong. "Yes, I know it is." All she had to do was ask and his mom would back off.

Kitty closed her eyes, the skin around her mouth tight, her fingers curling into fists on top of her desk. Another indication of real feeling he didn't figure would last long.

And he was right. When she opened her eyes, there was no emotion there. None at all.

"Kitty?"

She shook her head. "I'd be delighted to have lunch with your mother and dinner with the MacKinnon clan tonight."

He'd call her on the obvious lie, but there was a brittle air around her he was afraid to shatter. Besides, as much as she was prevaricating, he also felt she meant every word.

Or wanted to. "Thank you."

"Did you have something you needed?"

"We could go over my schedule."

"It's on your desk with the changes made in the last twenty-four hours highlighted in yellow."

"Okay." She went over Bobby's schedule with him personally, but Tack got a piece of paper—with highlights.

"I've also sent it to your calendar. It should be on your phone now."

"That's very efficient of you."

She inclined her head. "Organizing schedules is something I have a lot of experience with."

"Egan said you had an idea for computerizing the reservation system."

The fact that Kitty had brought it up to his brother rather than Tack bothered him, but since Egan was junior partner in the business and had said Kitty suggested he mention it to Tack, he couldn't exactly complain about it.

"Yes. The B and B's new website and online registration option got me thinking. If you had a similar feature on your website, you'd probably get more spur-of-the-moment reservations than you do now. A lot of people don't like having to call and talk to someone to make a reservation."

"How will we know their skill level or physical stamina to be sure they aren't registering for an excursion they won't be able to keep up with?"

"The same way as on the phone. Have a series of screening questions that funnels them to the pages for the tours best suited to what they can and want to do."

"It sounds complicated."

"It is, but Annie said she's designed a few similar sites for other businesses, so she could give you a discount on the base site elements."

"I don't know."

"Think about it. She'll be here in about an hour to talk it over with you and Egan."

"What?" His shock at this evidence of Kitty's former boldness coursed through him, making his heart beat faster. Yeah, that's what did that. Shock. Not her nearness. "You can't make appointments like that for me."

"Sure I can, boss-man. I checked your schedule and you don't have anything on it." The look she gave him dared him to argue that point.

No way was he going to. Since he'd been guilty of doing the same thing to her about dinner with his family, Tack wasn't going to be a hypocrite.

"An investment like this is something we have to plan for." He didn't want to squash this show of spirit and initiative, but he wasn't made of gold dust either.

Her look was wry. "Egan told me you're surgically attached to the purse strings on the business, but I crunched the numbers."

"Did you now?" He settled one hip against her desk. Not inhaling her fragrance and definitely not noticing how the subtle scent of gardenias suited her so well.

That would be counterproductive to his no-sex rule.

"Yes. That's also something I'm good at."

"Okay, I'll bite. What did your number crunching tell you?"

"If my conservative estimates are correct, the site will pay for itself in two seasons and be making a solid profit for you after that. Long-term, it will cost you less than hiring full-time office staff and make doing so unnecessary."

"That's hard to believe."

"Unless you hire more guides and take on more tours, but then the income they generate would be paying for the extra clerical hours they would necessitate."

He opened his mouth to argue again and then shut it. She was putting herself out there, using her education and intelligence to help him with his business.

She might not realize it, but he wasn't blind to how hard that must be for her. Not to mention she had some pretty good points.

"I'll meet with Annie, but I'm not promising anything."

"That's your call." Then Kitty dismissed him, going back to her computer as if he weren't still standing against her desk.

In the middle of his own damn reception area.

Hell. He'd known that kiss had been a mistake.

Not the least of which because he'd spent every night since dreaming about it and waking up with either an aching cock or jizz on his sheets.

* * *

Malina MacKinnon blew in with a burst of cold air and chatter. "Oh, Caitlin, there you are. When Tack told me you would be here so I could take you out to lunch, I thought he was putting me off. He's not fond of what he calls my nagging and has been known to avoid it via devious methods. I swear he moved into his own cabin to avoid having to come up with excuses for not attending our winter social gatherings."

"You know that's not true, *Aana*." Tack came out of his office with a smile for his mother.

Malina shook her head, her dark shiny hair cut in a flattering asymmetrical style swaying with the movement. "That's not the way I was raised, you know?" She mock pouted. "In my family, a child did not move out until they married and not always then. My sister and her family made their home with my parents until my father left us."

By *left us*, Caitlin knew Malina meant died.

"*Emaa* came to live with us then, which is what you wanted all along," Egan added from behind Tack.

The two brothers had been closeted in Tack's office discussing Annie's proposal for the website since the computer programmer had left. Caitlin didn't understand why Tack was so resistant. She was doing their books now and knew their margins had been sufficient for him to have hired full-time office help too.

His need to be a success and still entirely self-sufficient was borderline obsessive.

When they were younger, he'd desperately wanted to prove himself to the Inuit grandfather who saw Tack and his siblings as somehow *less* because their father was MacKinnon, not Inuit. Tack had faced his share of the opposite prejudice, too, especially once they started bussing to the larger schools when they got older.

But that grandfather was gone now and Caitlin sincerely doubted anyone in Cailkirn treated Tack with anything less than full respect these days. So, who was he trying to prove himself to?

"And why shouldn't I?" Malina demanded. "Not all

daughters are so quick to dismiss the value of their mother's wisdom."

"Give it a rest, Mom." Tack's use of the English word instead of *aana* was his subtle way of letting Malina know he was irritated with her.

The argument between Malina and Shila must be getting on everyone's nerves.

He'd never raise his voice to his mother, but this was the closest thing to it for both the MacKinnon boys.

Malina's indignant look said she'd noticed too.

Egan added, "Shila isn't here to appreciate the jibe and if you expect us to pass it on, you're dreaming."

"You are her older brothers. You should talk some sense into her."

"Shila's got plenty of sense," Tack said with a tinge of exasperation.

"What do you think, Caitlin?" Malina appealed to her. "Don't you think Shila should go out of state for at least one year of college?"

Tension at being put on the spot filled Caitlin, but she didn't let it filter into her voice. "I think you've raised three intelligent, independent children who are not prone to capricious decisions, Malina."

The older woman's smooth features, which did not begin to show her age, shifted into a thoughtful expression. "Are you saying I have myself to blame for my daughter's stubbornness?"

Caitlin gave Malina one of her social smiles. "Not at all. I believe you can lay your children's intransigence directly at Fergus's door."

Malina's laugh tinkled and her sons smiled, both looking decidedly relieved.

"You are as charming as ever, dear."

"Thank you." Caitlin didn't force another smile, though.

That would be too much like lying. She *wasn't* like she used to be and what Malina called charm was nothing but a well-developed sense of tact.

The older woman looked down at her watch. "It's after one. Are you ready for lunch? I'm so looking forward to a chance to talk. It's been so long."

Panic welled, but Caitlin ruthlessly pushed it down. Though she couldn't help asking Tack, "As long as there's nothing you need?"

His head shake said there would be no reprieve there.

"He and Egan don't have claim on your afternoons." Malina gave her sons a warning look that said they'd better not try to derail Caitlin's afternoon plans. "And I know your grandmother has instructed you take this one off from the Knit and Pearl."

"If the FBI recruited you, more criminals would be apprehended," Caitlin tried to tease, though her voice came out flat.

Malina laughed anyway, the musical sound infectious. Or it would be, if Caitlin could feel anything but anxiety about the coming lunch. She'd let herself forget how much socializing in Cailkirn was accompanied by a meal.

She tried to calm her racing pulse as she bent down to retrieve her purse from beneath the capacious desk. It didn't help, but she was fairly certain she'd managed to mask the stress from her expression.

There was nothing she could do about the sweat beading at the center of her back or the way her stomach rebelled at the thought of trying to eat while fielding the older woman's tenacious curiosity. Tack was right—there wasn't a malicious bone in Malina's body, but that didn't mean she wouldn't push into and well past Caitlin's comfort zone.

"Let me just grab my coat." Caitlin's voice came out a little high, but she was pretty sure Malina didn't notice.

She was busy chiding Egan for staying out until all hours the night before.

From the look on the twenty-four-year-old man's face, Caitlin thought Tack had been spot-on when he'd said his brother would be moving out on his own sooner rather than later.

She retrieved her lightweight teal and black houndstooth trench coat Aunt Elspeth had given her. The former beauty queen had told Caitlin that the coat was a mail-order item that had arrived looking much more youthful than she expected.

Caitlin didn't mention that she'd noticed the package delivered the day before or that the coat had looked and smelled like it had just come out of its plastic wrapping for shipping.

"What a lovely coat. Is it new?" Malina asked. "I thought I saw it in one of my favorite clothing catalogs for the first time this spring."

And so it began.

Caitlin finished tying the belt. "Thank you. It's new to me."

"Oh? Was it a gift?"

"Seriously, *Aana*? Does it matter?" Egan asked with a roll of his eyes in Caitlin's direction.

"I'll thank you not to take that tone with me, son," Malina admonished. She didn't raise her voice or even frown, but Egan looked suitably abashed anyway.

Tack walked up, wearing a brown leather jacket over his forest green Henley. "Are you two ready to go?"

"You're joining us?" Caitlin asked.

He hadn't said anything about doing so that morning.

"Yes," Tack said.

"No," his mother denied at the same time.

The older woman gave her oldest son a *look*. "Not that I'm not always happy for my children's company, but this is a girls-only lunch."

"You would deny sustenance when I am in need?" Tack's expression was both guileless and clearly serious, his rumbling stomach giving credence to his words.

A frown of worry creased Malina's face. "You haven't eaten lunch?"

"No, and I had a very small breakfast," he said, laying it on thick.

Another woman might tell her son to take himself off to lunch then, but not Malina MacKinnon. If her child needed feeding—perfectly capable adult or not—she would make sure he got a sufficient meal under her watchful eye.

"You don't mind him coming along, do you, Caitlin?" Malina asked.

Caitlin just shook her head, kind of amazed at how well Tack played his mother. Only she knew from the past that it went both ways. The MacKinnon boys would cross a glacier without snowshoes for their mom and not complain when it resulted in frostbite.

CHAPTER ELEVEN

They went to the only restaurant that was open year-round and was a longtime favorite of the permanent residents.

Malina had called ahead for a table. The waitress led them to a booth that was supposed to seat four but only if two of the diners were small children.

Malina and Caitlin would have fit better together on one bench seat, but Tack slid in next to her, forcing his mother to sit on the opposite side of the booth.

If Malina found that odd, she didn't say so.

Tack pressed against Caitlin from shoulder to knee and there was nowhere for her to go. Panic of an entirely different nature shot through her at the contact.

Tack might have no interest in repeating their kiss and sexual intimacies, but Caitlin wasn't so lucky. Her emotions had retreated behind old walls for safety, but this burgeoning desire was too new for her to have developed a coping mechanism to deal with it.

The restaurant did not have a menu, but a list of daily specials on the chalkboard by the front door.

Caitlin ordered a salad while Tack gave proof to his hunger by requesting a burger with the works, potato salad, and a side of the organic applesauce the diner was known for.

"Is that all you're eating?" Malina asked Caitlin, genuine concern glowing in eyes the same chocolate brown as her son's. "Don't you want some chicken or smoked salmon on your salad? Maybe half a sandwich?"

"I'm not very hungry," Caitlin said honestly. "I couldn't eat a sandwich."

She would have been happy to simply order a glass of juice but didn't think either Malina or Tack would find that acceptable. He didn't look like he approved of her salad order either. Thankfully, he didn't say anything.

Malina waved the waitress down. "Could you just have Tyler add some diced chicken to that salad?"

"Sure, Miss MacKinnon." The waitress went over to call out the order change to the cook.

Caitlin clamped down on the urge to demand they leave her salad alone. Malina meant well, as evidenced by what she said next. "I remember you used to be partial to chicken breast. You still like it, don't you?"

Caitlin could only nod.

"It's so nice to have you back in Cailkirn." Malina's thousand-watt smile warmed Caitlin but did nothing to diminish the stress churning in her belly.

"It's good to be home." Which wasn't a lie.

Not even a little one. Caitlin was very glad to be back in Cailkirn, no matter how hard she was finding it to settle in. She knew eventually she'd find her place and the peace she was searching for.

She just had to make it through the town's gauntlet of gossip and well-intended busybodies first.

"So, you'll be staying, then?" Malina asked.

"Yes."

"You haven't been back in eight years," Malina said leadingly.

Caitlin had long ago lost the inclination to defend or explain herself. "No, I haven't."

The less she said in the circles she'd moved in Los Angeles, the less likely her words could come back to bite her later.

Malina was a talented ferreter of information and she employed the silence most people would feel the need to fill.

Caitlin just took the time to smooth the edges of her thoughts. As hard as Tack's nearness was on her libido, it acted as a welcome distraction from his mother's near-palpable curiosity.

"Is Granddad still happy he hired Lee for the workshop?" Tack asked his mother.

Malina's brows drew together in an almost frown. "He's quiet, but your granddad says he's good with the wood."

"Dad and Cian seem to like him," Tack agreed before his mother could return to grilling Caitlin.

Caitlin didn't really understand why he was pursuing this line of discussion or what Malina found unpleasant about it.

But the older woman had a definite frown on her face now. "You'll see everyone tonight. Ask your dad himself if you want to know how he feels about their new carpenter."

"You know how raucous clan dinners get," Tack said with a shrug, ignoring his mother's unexpected annoyance.

Unexpected to Caitlin anyway. Maybe Tack knew talking

about the new carpenter would irritate her. Was he trying to run interference for Caitlin?

"They do, at that." Malina smiled tightly. "They all get along fine. Lee is a good addition to the workshop and he's taken some of the strain off the others."

It was clear from her tone that Tack's mom expected that to end the conversation about the newest employee for Natural Furnishings, his family's custom-built furniture business.

Malina turned a much warmer smile on Caitlin. "There's demand for their furniture from Alaska, and from Canada and the Lower Forty-Eight as well."

"I'm not surprised," Caitlin said. "They do beautiful work."

Malina nodded. "It's always a blessing when a person can do what they love and get paid for it."

"Yes, it is."

"What about you? Do you plan to take over the bed-and-breakfast one day?"

It was a question she expected to get frequently, so Caitlin had formulated an answer she could live with. "Gran and my aunts aren't anywhere near ready to give up the reins."

"No doubt. They are capable and tenacious women. We'd all do well to take a page out of their book."

"I agree."

Their food arrived and conversation stopped while the waitress arranged plates on the table. Malina regarded Caitlin's salad with disapproval.

She caught the arm of the waitress before she left. "I believe you forgot the dressing for Caitlin's salad."

"She didn't order any dressing, Miss MacKinnon."

"Well, then you should have offered it." Malina addressed

Caitlin. "They've got a lovely house dressing here. I've tried to talk Tyler out of the recipe more than once. He won't part with it, though."

Caitlin did her best to keep her voice even as she said, "I prefer my salad dry."

"Nonsense." Malina patted the waitress's arm. "Bring her some of the house dressing." The older woman told Caitlin, "Once you taste it, you'll be hooked, believe me."

Caitlin didn't bother to argue.

Tack tensed beside her. *"Aana,"* he admonished.

"What, son?" Malina asked, clearly taken aback at his tone.

"Caitlin is an adult. I doubt she appreciates you ordering for her like a child."

"But I'm just trying to make sure she enjoys her lunch," Malina said, clearly hurt by her son's criticism or the idea that she'd been overbearing.

"I know," Tack said, rubbing his temples like he always did when he was really frustrated.

Malina's eyes widened, surprise evident in their depths. She very obviously did not understand why her son would be irritated with her.

Honestly, Caitlin didn't either.

Malina wasn't doing anything different than she'd always done. She fussed over the people she cared about. It wasn't Malina's fault that fussing caused Caitlin more distress than comfort.

Another layer of stress tightened the twisted knots inside her at the thought of mother and son at odds on her behalf. "It's fine."

"There, you see?" Malina asked. "She knows I'm just looking out for her, Taqukaq."

"She's just too polite to tell you to stop," Tack said, refusing to drop it.

Which frankly surprised Caitlin. Again. Malina's children did not often disagree with their mother, and never over something trivial like this. Especially her sons.

Or at least that was the way it used to be.

"Eat your lunch, son." There was clear command in Malina's tone and it was easy to see how she'd kept three strong-minded children in line during the most challenging parts of childhood.

The table fell into silence as both Caitlin's companions began to do just that. Caitlin poured the dressing on her salad and then moved the lettuce and chicken around, coating it evenly. She did a good job of picking at it, which made it appear to the unobservant that she was eating too.

However, it was beyond her to take even a single bite. The only thing worse than skipping a meal was knowing she would not keep it down if she forced herself to eat it.

Thankfully, mother and son were too busy simmering with unaccustomed discord to notice.

Malina had eaten a good portion of her lunch before she asked, "Do you like working for the boys?"

"Very much." Despite her discomfort in Tack's presence now that she knew he saw her as permanently damaged goods in need of *help*, Caitlin enjoyed working in the tour office.

"I'm glad. They're usually very pleasant to be around."

That observation almost made Caitlin smile, because Tack could be pretty impatient and demanding and Egan didn't always know when to stop joking. Malina was right, though—they were pretty good people to work with.

"I wonder if you're going to want to pursue something

more along the lines of a career," Malina asked. "What with having your degree in business now."

Gran would have told her. Caitlin didn't mind. She was glad her family was proud of her finishing school, and she wasn't about to hide it like some dirty secret.

That didn't mean she was looking to be the next female governor of Alaska, though. "Sometimes a good job is better than a career."

Malina nodded, approval shining brightly in her dark eyes. "I couldn't agree more. I've always enjoyed running the office side of things for Natural Furnishings."

"How did you get started doing it?" Caitlin asked.

"Fergus's dad was always complaining about the paper-work. When Fergus started in on it, too, I knew something had to be done, if only to have more pleasant conversation at our dinner table. We discovered I had a knack and the rest is history."

"Da says *Aana* is more than half the reason their work-shop has grown to be in such high demand."

Pleasure at the compliment covered Malina's features. "Nonsense, but they did need organizing and that's no lie."

"I'm surprised Gran MacKinnon didn't do it to begin with," Caitlin admitted.

"Oh no, my mother-in-law is a woman who knows her own mind and she's busy enough with her garden in the summer and greenhouse year-round."

Malina finished her chicken salad sandwich and then looked at Caitlin's salad. "Have you eaten anything, dear?"

Unwilling to lie, Caitlin shrugged. "I'm not very hungry."

"But I'm sure your grandmother said you can't afford to skip meals."

Caitlin didn't have an answer for her.

Tack did apparently. He stood up, taking Caitlin by the arm. "No, she can't. Do you mind getting the check, *Aana*?"

"No, of course not, but you're leaving? I thought we could chat over coffee."

"Kitty and I have a few things to discuss. I'm sorry, but we'll see you tonight." He tugged Caitlin out of the booth as he spoke.

Not wanting to make a scene, and frankly happy to leave, Caitlin didn't balk. They stopped by the coat rack at the front door and he helped her into her trench.

When they got outside, he kept his hand on the small of her back, using it to guide her down the alley that led to the parking area behind his tour office.

"I walked from the bed-and-breakfast today." She'd been getting up forty-five minutes earlier so she could get everything done she needed to for the Knit & Pearl and still make the two-plus-mile walk between her two jobs.

The exercise was good for her.

Caitlin dismissed the small voice that reminded her that her doctor back in LA had told her walking was ideal exercise, but she needed to make sure she increased her caloric intake if she was going to walk more than two miles a day, so she didn't start losing weight again.

He'd also encouraged her strongly not to power walk.

The fact that she walked a brisk four miles per hour for a total of almost five miles a day wasn't something she dwelled on.

Tack gave her another of the probing looks she'd come to dislike so much. "I know."

She didn't ask why he was taking her to the parking area if he knew she hadn't driven to work. She wasn't walking back to the Knit & Pearl in her heels, but her tennis shoes were under her desk inside the building they were now walking around.

He stopped by his truck, pulling out his keys and pressing the unlock button. "I thought you might like to see my cabin."

"I would," she said before her brain caught up with her mouth.

She *did* want to see the results of all those teenage dreams, but she didn't understand why he was inviting her now.

"Good." He opened the passenger door and gave her a boost inside, practically lifting her, a growl she didn't understand falling from his lips as he stepped back. "Buckle up."

He didn't say another word as he got into the truck, pulled onto the main streets of town, and then headed out of Cailkirn.

"Tack?"

"What?"

"Why are we going to your cabin?"

"You have the afternoon off. Did you have something else planned?"

"You know I didn't." He'd made sure of it.

"Well, then."

"That's not an answer. Your mom wanted us to stay and visit."

"Did *you* want to stay and talk?"

"No." Eating lunch had caused a temporary lull in the inquisition, but it would have started again over coffee. Of that, Caitlin had no doubts.

"So, here we are."

"I still don't understand."

"You want to see my cabin. Let's just leave it at that."

Confused but convinced further prompting wouldn't result in any more clarity, Caitlin kept quiet on the drive to Tack's home. She enjoyed the passing scenery as she always did, the natural beauty of their area never growing old for her.

His place was farther out of town than she remembered, and not off the major highway.

"Is it hard to get out to the main roads in winter?" she asked as they traveled down a long drive.

"My truck's a four-by-four with a solid engine and frame, so it takes a lot to trap me with the weather. I've got a snow-mobile for the really big snowfalls."

"You have a snowmobile?" she asked in shock. "You always said how much you hated their noise."

"I don't use it for recreation."

"Just emergencies, huh?" Still. Wow. She guessed they'd both changed some in the past eight years.

"Exactly."

He might not want to use it for recreation, but Caitlin had no qualms about doing so. "I want to go on a ride."

"If you're still here when the snow's thick enough, I'll take you out."

"That was too easy." But then maybe he really didn't think she'd stick it out through the winter.

He'd learn. Caitlin had lost her family twice. Once by accident and the second time by design, but now that she had her gran and great-aunts back in her life, she wasn't letting them go again.

She gasped at her first sight of the cabin as they broke out of the forest. His driveway ended in a clearing big enough for a house, outbuildings (including a small greenhouse), and a garden that was at least a quarter of an acre in size.

Absolutely breathtaking, the house was made entirely of

stone and exposed logs, and it was really too big for the moniker *cabin*.

"It's huge."

"Two stories with a cellar," he said proudly.

She counted the chimneys poking up from the roof. "Two fireplaces?"

"Three, actually."

"You're using them for your main heating source?" she asked in surprise.

He'd always said he would only have more than one hearth in his home if he was using fireplaces as his primary heating source. Tack had also been adamant he didn't plan to do so.

Kitty had argued that a fire in the hearth was cozy and helped make a house into a home. She'd always said she wanted one in her bedroom and the main living area.

Nevin had derisively laughed off her suggestion they have a fireplace installed in their home. His home.

"No." Tack didn't add anything to his stark denial.

Curiosity pushed aside Caitlin's lingering anxiety. "What rooms are they in?"

"Come inside and see." He pulled the truck to a stop in front of steps leading up to the porch.

She eagerly climbed out of the cab, closing her door as he came around the hood and offered his hand.

She stared at it for several long seconds, confusion warring with desire. She wanted to take it, for this moment to be like old times, but that hadn't worked so well on the Skilak Lookout Trail.

"Come on," he urged, his hand still out there, inviting her to take a chance. "It even has the dry sauna you told me any self-respecting house in Alaska should have."

He'd never laughed at her, despite how impractical the suggestion might have seemed to some. Regardless, she wouldn't have expected him to actually install one in his home.

Tack didn't live by other people's rules, though.

Making her decision, Caitlin slid her hand into his hand and let him draw her up the steps and onto the porch. "You put up a swing."

"A family home should have a swing on its porch."

She agreed, though she felt a pang at the idea of Tack sharing this house with a family. She liked the Adirondack chairs and fat log planed smooth for a table between them sitting on the other side of the porch.

There wasn't much point in investing in more furniture for outdoor relaxation than that. Alaskans spent plenty of time outside, both summer and winter, but more often in active pursuits.

The tightly woven welcome mat she automatically wiped her feet on depicted two eagles facing each other in the traditional Inuit way. The big heavy door it stood in front of was carved with the Celtic symbol for happiness. Both sides of Taqukaq MacKinnon blessing the entrance to his home.

Tack pushed the door open without pulling out a key. "I only lock it during tourist season," he said as if she'd asked a question.

"You know, war vets aren't the only people who come to Alaska to avoid something." There was a long history of criminals fleeing to the "wild north" to avoid the consequences of their actions.

"The Kenai Peninsula is both too developed and too entrenched with small-town familiarity to make a good hiding place for someone with a dark past."

"Are you saying the interior is a safer bet?" she asked absently, taking in the beautiful great room that took up the entire width of the house.

It opened into the kitchen at the end with the dining table, making a big L-shaped living area.

"Safer? With a missing persons rate twice the national average, I don't think Alaska could be considered a safe haven for just any flatfoot looking for a place to hide," Tack scoffed.

Considering the state also had the highest percentage of missing persons in the country who *stayed* lost, she had to agree with him. "Some people don't want to be found?"

"And that works a lot better in less organized boroughs."

She nodded absently, her interest in the topic waning. She was far more intrigued by Tack's home and what it revealed about the man he'd become.

The ecru walls were finished, but exposed logs accented the lines of the huge room and the open loft above. More large traditional woven rugs were scattered over gleaming hardwood floors.

She took off her coat and hung it on one of the hooks on the wall to the left of the door, the house comfortably warm.

"It feels good." She looked but didn't see heating vents or radiators. "Radiant heat?"

"It runs under the floors. There are no cold spots in my house," he said with pride.

Well deserved, she thought. "Did you install a geothermal heat pump?" It seemed like something a man as dedicated to energy and wildlife conservation as him would do.

Tack nodded. "It was a bitch to dig, but worth it. There's a biomass gasification boiler in the cellar for when the temperatures drop too low too fast."

"I have no idea what that is," she admitted. "But it sounds cool."

He smiled. "It's basically a boiler fueled with scrap wood, brush, and firewood in a pinch."

She walked over to the solid wood dining set, sturdy enough for even Tack's towering frame to sit in without worry of mishap. Six dark-stained ladder-back chairs sat around a large, family style table. Two matching chairs against the wall had a chess table between them, the board set up for play.

She picked up one of the heavy pewter pieces. "Your dad taught us to play on this set."

"He gave it to me when I finished the cabin, along with the game table as a housewarming gift."

"Not the dining set?"

"Nope. I commissioned that from Granddad. The hutch was his gift to me."

Made of the same dark-stained wood, it was built into the other wall from the chess table. It was beautiful, the workmanship superior to anything that could be found in a factory-stocked furniture store.

"These are lovely," she said of the antique Inuit baskets gracing the top open shelf.

"*Emaa* gave them to me. Her grandmother wove them as part of her wedding dowry."

Caitlin didn't have to ask where the ornate silver tea service on the shelf below came from. She remembered his Scottish grandmother serving them afternoon tea from it at least once a week.

"Your gran used this to teach us company manners and we felt so special she shared it with us, we didn't even mind."

"Gran was smart that way."

"Yes." The expatriate Scottish woman had taught her own son and two hearty Alaskan grandsons polite behavior that wouldn't embarrass them meeting royalty.

And to Caitlin's knowledge, not one of them ever complained.

Tack ran his hand along the back of one of the chairs. "It's a house blessed by family love."

And one day, he would fill it with his own. Tack would make an amazing husband and father, when he met a woman worthy of all that Taqukaq MacKinnon had to offer.

"Can I see the rest?" she asked, not wanting to dwell on those thoughts.

He waved toward the other side of the room. "Well, that's the living room."

A huge brown leather sectional dominated the space, but a matching recliner was set up to also take advantage of the view of the huge plasma screen mounted on the wall opposite the short end of the sectional.

The long side faced a huge stone fireplace, its raised slate hearth jutting a good foot into the room.

The loft was set up as a library/home office, with floor-to-ceiling bookshelves covering the walls. There was a desk off to one side, no doubt one of his father's or grandfather's creations. A sofa in the same brown leather as the sectional downstairs faced a smaller fireplace on the other side of the room. They must share a chimney.

Waist-high bookshelves made up the half-wall that overlooked the great room below.

"Down that hall are two smaller bedrooms that share a bath on the left, and the master suite is on the right." Tack waved to a log-framed arch, centered in the back wall.

She didn't ask to see the bedrooms and he didn't offer, but led her back downstairs where he showed her the dry sauna he'd boasted about. The cedar-lined room housed a hot tub as well.

"Now, this is decadence, Tack," she told him.

"It feels more like a necessity after a week of winter hunting."

"I bet." He'd never talked her into going on an overnight hunt in the winter, much less one that lasted a week.

Beyond the sauna was a utility and mudroom that opened into a heated garage that filled the space under the upstairs bedrooms.

"It's an amazing house, Tack," she said as they came back into the great room. "Everything you ever dreamed of."

A strange expression came over his rugged, masculine features. "Almost, but neither my Scots nor my Inuit ancestors believe in perfection."

She couldn't imagine anything that could improve on the beautiful dwelling and told him so.

"That's funny coming from a woman who lived in a Los Angeles mansion."

"That house was as soulless as the man who bought it." She much preferred Tack's welcoming log and stone home but figured he knew that by her already voluble praise.

They drifted to the kitchen and she leaned against the big center island. "Aunt Elspeth would go into raptures in here."

"She pestered your gran and Miz Alma to put an island in her kitchen for weeks after her first visit."

Of course her aunt had already been here. Life in Cailkirn had gone on without Caitlin's presence.

"How did they talk her out of it?"

"Miz Alma tried to appeal to her practical side, telling her it would be ridiculously expensive to do the remodel."

"You make it sound like that didn't sway Aunt Elspeth." And honestly? Caitlin wasn't surprised.

Practicality wasn't her youngest aunt's strong suit.

"Not even close, but when Miz Moya said they would have to get rid of the kitchen table the Grants had been eating at since their first homestead cabin, Miss Elspeth decided she didn't want the disruption of the remodel anyway."

"Clever gran."

He nodded, his body suddenly closer than it was before, though Caitlin hadn't been aware of him moving. Which was odd, considering how in tune she was to his presence since sitting so closely to him in the diner.

She tilted her head back to look at him, confusion at his nearness in no way masking her desire to pull him even closer. "Tack?"

"Kitty."

"You're very close."

"Observant of you to notice." His big hand tucked under her hair to cup her nape in a move she'd quickly learned to crave.

CHAPTER TWELVE

I don't understand." Her heart sped up from his nearness.

"You didn't eat lunch."

"I wasn't hungry." With him so close, taking up all her senses and concentration, she didn't have anything left over to feel shame or worry about that.

"You haven't been hungry since our hike."

She couldn't deny it. She'd done her best to eat, but she'd skipped more meals than she could afford to.

He nodded, as if she'd confirmed something he was thinking. Only he didn't bother to share it with her.

"I'm trying," she told him, not wanting Tack to think she was more broken than he already believed. "I've done pretty well."

"I lifted you into the truck."

"Yes." Her breathing turned shallow and there was nothing she could do to stop it.

His proximity was wreaking havoc with her equilibrium.
"You've lost weight."

Not much and it could only be a guess on his part, one
she wasn't about to confirm. So she said nothing. Because
she wasn't going to lie either.

"You enjoyed what we did at the overlook."

"You know I did." He was the one who didn't want to repeat the experience again.

Tack shifted so his body pressed hers against the island.
"Enough, I wonder?"

"Enough for what?" she asked, unable to bring her voice
above a whisper.

He just shook his head, his masculine lips tipped in a
barely-there smile.

And then he did the unthinkable. He kissed her. Again.
Right there in his kitchen.

Completely unprepared for this turn of events, Caitlin
had no hope of withholding her response. Her arms wound
around his neck of their own volition, her body maintaining
a rigid posture for all of about three seconds before she
melted into him.

He teased at the seam of her mouth with the tip of his
tongue and she brazenly parted her lips to give him entrance.
He swept inside, taking possession and teasing her with the
need for more at the same time.

He kept the caress of his tongue light, barely there.

She pressed up against him, wanting more contact, but he
dropped one hand to her hip and held her in place.

Frustration overrode pleasure and she pulled away from
the kiss. "Why are you teasing me?"

"You want more, wildcat?"

"*Yes.*"

He dropped both hands away from her and stepped back, his expression firm. "Eat the lunch I make you."

"You want me to eat?" She didn't understand.

"That's the deal, Kitty. You eat and I'll rock your world."

He was aroused; she could see the impressive evidence pushing against the front of his jeans. So why was he talking about eating?

Noticing where she was looking, he gave her a feral smile. "Like what you see?"

"Yes." There was no point trying to deny it. Not to him and not to herself.

"I do too."

"Oh." She wasn't sure why those words were so shocking.

She knew he was turned on, but the idea *she* had done that was a new concept for her. At least lately. She'd been told countless times how pretty she was as a teenager and young adult, but it had been a long time since those days.

His claim that he liked how she looked impacted her deeply, warmth suffusing her physically and emotionally. Sometimes she wanted to be thin again, but she knew that was the anorexia talking. She tried to enjoy breasts that actually filled her bra and a bottom that curved.

It was a lot easier to like her new body when she knew it excited the man in front of her.

Tack tucked his thumbs in the front pocket of his jeans, outlining his obvious erection with his hands. "You want some of this?"

She nodded, her mouth too dry for speech.

"Eat lunch."

Sparks of desire traveled down her body, right to her core, and made her legs squeeze together to try to control the overwhelming sensation. He wasn't just offering her a few kisses; *he was offering sex.*

Real sex. The stuff he said she was too damaged for.

She didn't know what had changed his mind, but she wasn't about to ask. Not beforehand anyway.

She still didn't understand why he was linking sex with her having lunch, but Caitlin wasn't an idiot. If eating would get her access to Tack's body and his big hands on her again, she would eat.

The nerves and nausea that had plagued her earlier were gone, too, making the inner declaration an easy one to make.

"Okay," she agreed.

His smile was both pleased and just a little smug. "Sit over there." He pointed to one of the two bar chairs on the side of the island.

She did as instructed, her stomach clenching with unusual but welcome hunger. "What are you feeding me?"

"Leftovers. I've got chicken and vegetable rice from last night." He pulled a couple of containers out of the refrigerator and then poured a glass of the chocolate drink he'd given her on the hike.

He handed it to her. "Drink up."

While he plated and microwaved the food, she sipped at the chocolaty goodness. "You sure you won't give me this recipe?"

He just gave her a look she'd known well a long time ago. The one that said, *Yeah, not in this lifetime.*

"Do you cook like that for yourself all the time?"

He shrugged. "I eat at the Homestead several nights a week with the family."

Just like the Grants, the MacKinnons had built their current large dwelling on their original homestead. It always passed down to the eldest son in the family and was the traditional gathering place for the entire MacKinnon clan living in or near Cailkirn.

"But yeah, I like to cook. It's relaxing. I usually make enough for two meals anyway, so it's not so much effort for one person."

"Was that supposed to be your dinner tonight?" she asked, nodding toward the microwave that had just beeped.

"Nope. We're eating with the family tonight, remember?"

When he put the plate in front of her, there was a chicken breast and at least a cup of the rice-vegetable mixture.

Her heart sank. Even hungry, there was no way she could finish that amount of food. "This is too much."

"So, do your thing. Divide it in half."

It didn't surprise her that he'd noticed her ritual. Tack always saw what others didn't.

His easy acceptance of it was a little startling, though. "You don't mind?"

"No." He winked at her. "I'm not going to withhold sex if you eat half of what I served you."

She nodded, as if she understood, but really? She didn't. This whole sex-for-food thing was still proving problematic to her sense of logic.

However, the food ritual was something she was very familiar with. So, it should just be a matter of doing what she'd done hundreds of times before, but she couldn't seem to act on what her brain was telling her to do.

She was reeling from his acceptance. She was used to odd looks, even from her aunts, but Tack acted like it was perfectly normal for a woman to meticulously separate her food and only eat half.

"Need some help there?" he asked, a devilish light in his dark eyes.

She wanted to say yes, just to see what he'd do. Only that would be silly. It was one thing for him to play her quirks off like they didn't matter and another for her to pull him into them.

With a shake of his head, but no condemnation that she could see, he picked up the fork and table knife he'd placed beside her plate. Then Tack proceeded to cut the chicken breast in half lengthwise, careful to make the portions equal. He diced one side into small, bite-size pieces.

This man was going to make the most wonderful father someday. She found the fact that he was doing this for her, a grown woman, touching instead of embarrassing. Go figure.

He separated the rice, again making sure the two portions were equal. "There you go, wildcat. Have at."

Emotion choked her, but she discovered it didn't impact her ability to take the first bite. Or the second, or even the third.

"You're a good cook," she complimented him eventually.

He snagged the extra half of the chicken with his fingers and started to eat it. "Thanks."

"You're still hungry?" she asked with surprise.

He grinned. "I wasn't finished with my lunch when we left."

"Oh." She hadn't noticed. "I'm sorry."

"No reason to be. *Aana* didn't mean to upset you with her fussing, but you weren't going to eat that salad with dressing all over it."

"I could have refused it."

"You'll get there." There wasn't an ounce of censure in his voice. "Just remember, *Aana* and your family don't want

to tear you down like Barston did. They want to help you get
well, but they don't know how."

"Why are you so good at it?" she asked without meaning to.

His easy acceptance meant too much, but no way would
she turn away from it.

"You'll find your feet with your family and the town
again." Which wasn't an answer, but she understood it was
the only one she was getting. "You're slowing down. Do you
need a little more incentive?"

"What?" She had no idea what he was talking about.

Until he moved in, swiveling her chair around so he could
kiss her, a soft caress of his lips against hers. Nothing more
than that, but it blew her away. This easy intimacy.

She'd never experienced it before, couldn't imagine it
with anyone but him.

Then he fed her a bite of chicken with his fingers. She got
a little taste of him with the meat. When she finished chewing, he kissed her again, another simple bussing of lips, and
Caitlin thought she would never hesitate to eat if doing so
was always so pleasurable.

She was finished with her lunch before she even realized
she was close. That hadn't happened in a very long time.
There was still way too much *have to* with eating, but like
Tack said, she'd get better.

Dr. Hart had believed it and on her good days, Caitlin did
too.

She stood up to put her plate in the dishwasher, but before
she got the chance, Tack swept her up in his arms and
headed out of the kitchen.

One of her shoes clattered as it landed on the hardwood
floor.

"What are you doing?" She was breathless and not even a little embarrassed about it.

"I thought you knew what came next," he answered in a voice richer than gourmet chocolate.

"But the dishes..."

"I've waited long enough, wildcat." His low, masculine voice went through her like a caress. "You aren't the only one who wants this."

Which she'd known, but it hadn't sunk in completely. Even with the evidence before her eyes. That he would admit it was outside her experience too.

But that he was impatient to make love? That was better than a hot fudge sundae on a summer day and a lot less stressful.

He took the stairs two at a time, the burden of carrying her not slowing him down at all. Her second shoe made a noisy descent down the stairs as they went up. The loft library went by in a blur, the hallway barely registering.

She didn't know if it was because he was moving so fast or simply because nothing but his big body registered with her.

Nuzzling into the spot where his neck and shoulder met, she inhaled his scent. It had always meant safety to her, but right now? The manly fragrance filling her senses caused a visceral reaction in her, beading her nipples, sending a blush of desire to wash her body with heat, causing prickles of excitement to spark down her nape and spine, right to her inner thighs, making her vaginal walls contract almost painfully with the need to be filled.

She'd never responded this way to Nevin, not even in the early days.

And that was the last comparison she was going to make.

There was no place for even the tinge of those memories in the present.

She'd never craved making love as she did right now, had never responded to another man's touch, much less his presence, like she did to Tack's. Everything felt new and different. And that was all that mattered.

He laid her in the center of the huge bed and then stepped back, yanking his Henley off as he went. Then he sat on the edge of the bed and took off his boots and socks, the sound of them thumping to the floor in quick succession making her smile.

She knew there was probably something she should be doing. However, she was too entranced watching the play of afternoon light over his dusky skin as his muscles rippled with every movement.

He stood up to yank off his jeans, revealing thighs heavy with muscle, long masculine legs sprinkled with black hair. His dark blue knit boxers stretched obscenely in front, making his erection look bigger than it was.

Right? Of course he wasn't *that* big. Just because he was six and a half feet tall and as broad as a door didn't mean he was proportional everywhere. Did it?

Filled with fascinated trepidation, she watched him shuck the boxers and turn to face the bed.

She let out a sound between a gasp and a squeak at her first sighting of the club between his legs. Rigid and dark with blood, the thick hardness rose toward his flat stomach, its tip crowned with pearls of viscous fluid.

"You look like you're staring at the Eighth Wonder of the World there, wildcat." Aroused humor infused his tone.

"I think maybe I am."

He gave a strangled laugh. "Nope. Just a man."

Or rather a very particular part of a man, because she couldn't pretend to be looking at anything but his extremely impressive erection.

With effort, she shifted her gaze up to his face, meeting dark eyes filled with pure sexual desire. "There's nothing *just* about you, Taqukaq MacKinnon."

"Glad you think so."

He joined her on the bed, his movements predatory as he crawled over her. "This would go a lot easier if you were naked, wildcat."

"Yes." She nodded, only vaguely aware of the decided *lack* of stress she felt at getting naked with this man.

That was something of a miracle, and a welcome one.

He grinned, the expression feral. "You going to take your clothes off, then?"

"Can't."

"Am I in your way?"

"Yes. No. Don't move." She liked him right where he was.

He caressed her breast through her sweater. "This is soft, sweetheart, but not as smooth as your skin."

She didn't reply, her voice lost to the sensation of his hand on her. He gently pinched her turgid nipple through the layers of fabric.

"Oh!" Pleasure radiated out from her peak, sending goose bumps skating along her skin.

He squeezed again and then cupped her breast, gently kneading the swell of flesh. "Does that feel good?"

"Yes."

"It will feel even better naked, wildcat."

Her thighs pressed tightly together in involuntary reaction to the dark promise in his voice.

"N-naked would be good," she choked out with a stutter.

He sat up, keeping his weight off her as he straddled her hips. "Let's start with this."

By *this* he meant her black cashmere Hermès sweater, the T-shirt she wore beneath it, and her bra. He never hesitated, removing each article of clothing with single-minded determination until they had all been stripped from her and thrown aside, landing on the floor somewhere.

Tack didn't give her a chance to worry he found her thin-side-of-normal figure wanting, but mapped every inch of her skin, his eyes as hot on her as his big, calloused hands.

He cupped her breasts, his thumbs brushing back and forth over already distended nipples so very eager for his touch. "So pretty."

"I have freckles." Just a smattering over her shoulders and breasts, but enough they couldn't be ignored. "And I don't tan."

Not even a little. Her skin was so pale she swore it glowed in the dark.

He shook his head. "You think there's some bad there?"

"You don't?" Okay, so a few insecurities *had* surfaced.

"Your freckles are like cinnamon sprinkled over whipped cream. They make me want to lick each one and see if you taste as sweet as you look."

"Oh?" she asked on a gasp.

"And I tan enough for both of us."

She giggled. "You do."

His skin wasn't as dark as his mother's, but in the summertime, Tack took on color in a way that Caitlin had always envied and made his Inuit heritage a lot more obvious.

"Does that bother you?" he asked.

Her brows drew together. "What? Why would you ask that?"

He was by far the sexiest man she'd ever seen, but she wasn't going to say so, pretty sure his ego didn't need that stroking. Still, how could he worry he was *too* dark?

"It's the same as you worrying you don't measure up to the California golden crowd you're not even a part of anymore."

"I didn't mean…" But that *was* where her uncertainty came from.

Years of living among perfectly tanned bodies, where her natural brassy red hair stuck out as much as her pale skin, had convinced her she was lacking. She'd highlighted and color-toned her hair, gone weekly for spray tans, worn the latest size-two fashions, and had *still* felt like a Holly Hobbie among Barbie dolls.

"You do remember the first couple of years at USC?"

"Um, yes?" She did, but she wasn't sure what part of that he was referring to.

His eyes challenged her. "Did I ever date a single beach bunny or Rodeo Drive diva?"

"No."

"I want *you* exactly as you are, Kitty Grant." His dark chocolate eyes burned with a hunger she couldn't mistake.

"I'm very glad." Her body was burning with how *glad* she was.

Tack leaned down and kissed her, the slide of his lips against hers not as devouring as his expression, but far from chaste. His tongue sampled her flavor but didn't dwell there. Moving his mouth down her neck, he pressed tasting kisses along the path of her freckles like he'd said he wanted to, leaving a trail of sparking nerve endings in his wake.

She'd never had someone trace her collarbone this way, drawing forth a response she wouldn't have guessed possible from a spot she'd never considered an erogenous zone.

"So good," she said on the tail end of a moan.

He hummed. "Delicious."

Changing tactics with her breasts, he rubbed his soft, short whiskers against her skin until her skin was so sensitive each brush sent a thousand nerve endings screaming with pleasure.

"Tack! What are you doing?"

He looked up at her, his expression wicked. "Playing."

His answer was so unexpected, she gaped at him for several seconds. "I thought we were going to make love."

"We are. Haven't you played in bed before?"

"No."

His smile was one hundred percent wicked. "I told you, I'm going to rock your world."

"Consider it rocked."

He shook his head. "Not even close, Kitty. We've got a long way to go before mind-blowing pleasure."

"Speak for yourself," she gasped out, her breathing ragged already.

He dipped his head, his mouth closing over one nipple, and he bit down just enough that she felt the edges of his teeth and no pressure. It was the most exquisite sensation, and she didn't move even a centimeter so it wouldn't stop.

Then he started to suck.

She keened. Her pelvis thrust upward, her body bowing with an involuntary contraction of muscles. Sexual ecstasy coiled tight inside her. Did other people experience this every time they had sex?

His mouth pulled off her now-aching peak.

She whimpered, wanting him to keep doing what he'd been doing. "No, don't stop."

She was ready to beg in a way that none of Nevin's bullying could have elicited.

CHAPTER THIRTEEN

Y ou react as if you've never been touched before." Tack sounded like he was trying to work something out in his head.

She couldn't help him. How could she respond to the implied question in his observation without bringing the past where she didn't want it to be?

That sexy, feral smile showed itself again. "I like it."

"I'm glad." *More than thrilled* might describe it better.

Caitlin didn't know what she'd do if he wanted her to react with blasé sophistication in bed. She just didn't have it in her. Never had and never could with this man.

"I used to fantasize about taking your virginity," he admitted in a tone that made her shiver. "I feel like that's what I'm doing right now."

She swallowed and then decided his admission deserved equal honesty. "I feel like you are too. Nothing has ever been like this. My body *is* a virgin to this kind of pleasure."

How could a modern man look so primitively pleased? But Tack's expression would have been more typical on one of his ancient ancestors.

She reached up and cupped his cheek. "You're happy."

"Yes," he said gutturally.

"Good." She mock glared at him. "Now, more touching."

"Demanding little spitfire, aren't you?"

"Never have been before."

"Must be the man in your bed, then." Oh, that tone was smug.

And she couldn't argue his right to sound that way. "Technically, it's *your* bed."

A strange expression turned his dark gaze remote for a couple of seconds, but then he was bending down to give equal attention to the other breast and there was no room for speculation in Caitlin's brain.

She was fully occupied with carnal delight.

She nearly cried when he stopped again, but it was only to show her how much sensation there was to be had with him using his mouth on her stomach of all things, an area she'd *never* considered sexy. He seemed to find it endlessly fascinating.

When he stopped and moved away, she didn't care that it was to take the rest of her clothes off.

"Want. Want. Want," she chanted, trying to pull him back.

He chuckled darkly. "Don't worry, wildcat, I'm not leaving you hanging, but it's time to get a little more intimate."

"What was that?" she demanded. "A handshake?"

He laughed out loud, the warm sound cascading through her, leaving behind a whole other type of pleasure.

"Always figured you'd be a handful like this, but damn,

sweetheart." He shook his head as he tossed her slacks over his shoulder.

"I'm a Grant; it's in the genes."

He didn't smile; he was too busy staring at her nearly naked body, and from his expression, the fact that she could still stand to gain ten pounds didn't bother him one little bit.

He hadn't found the waiflike figures so popular in Southern California attractive when they'd attended USC, but there was no doubt *she* turned him on.

He hooked his fingertips onto the elastic of her panties' waistband. "You ready to lose these?"

She loved that he asked, especially considering his hard-on had to be painful at this point. Nevin used to whine if she made him wait a couple of minutes to use lubricant to make entry easier.

"Yes, more than ready."

Tack didn't wait for further encouragement but slipped the panties right down her legs, exposing the last bit of her body to him and taking any lingering modesty with them.

He gently brushed his fingertips along the ends of the hair at the apex of her thighs, barely touching and sending shivers of delight through her. Who would have known that could be so stimulating?

"I like this." He ruffled the red curls, sending a different kind of delight through her.

She'd vowed never to wax again but wasn't sure she would have kept that promise to herself if he evinced a preference for smooth skin. "Yes?"

"Mmm-hmmm. Pretty." He slipped a finger between her folds, gently rubbing along the soaking flesh.

Getting so wet was new with him, too, and she liked it. A lot. Not only did it make his touching her more pleasurable, but it was also physical evidence she wasn't a defective woman.

"Aaaah...feels so good, Tack."

"Yes, it does." He dipped into her swollen channel. "You're so wet, wildcat."

"You're surprised?" she teased with a seductive tone she'd never used before.

Probably all his partners got wet like this. He was just too good at sex.

Lust flared in his dark gaze. "Let's see what we can do about getting you ready for me."

"I am ready," she promised.

But that didn't stop him from touching her intimately, spreading her moisture around her labia and up to her clitoris.

She jumped when he touched the highly concentrated bundle of nerve endings. Pleasure shivered through her as he alternated between pinching the swollen flesh and caressing it in small circles with the pad of his thumb. Carnal bliss centered there and then exploded through her, taking her closer and closer to a climax she wasn't ready to have.

Not until he was inside her.

"Want you, Tack. Inside me."

"Not yet," he gritted, his savage expression implying the delay was as hard for him as it was for her.

"Yes. I need you *now*. Please. I'm going to come."

"So, come."

"No," she pleaded. "Not until you're in me."

He stared down at her. "I'll make sure you come with me inside you too."

"Not the same." She didn't know why it was so important to her, but she desperately needed the intimacy of this orgasm happening when she was as connected to him as possible.

He jumped off the bed.

"No!" The word was torn from her.

"I need a condom," he said in a barely discernable tone.

"Hurry!"

He was back seconds later, ripping a foil packet open.

She reached out to help, but he brushed her hands aside with a shake of his head. "If you touch me, I'm going to blow."

Those words were the most exciting touch he'd given her yet. Though they affected her heart and not her body, the impact couldn't have been more intense.

There was no keeping the moan of pleasure inside her, no way to stop herself from writhing on the bed like a wanton.

"You are so damn sexy, wildcat." His gaze burned as he finished rolling the condom over at least nine hard, very thick inches.

She parted her thighs, lifting her knees in blatant invitation. "Come inside me."

Suddenly he was all explosive, primitive movement as he leaped onto the bed and moved between her legs. His erection pressed against the entrance to her body, like he was kissing her in a supremely intimate caress.

"Now," he said gutturally.

"Now," she pleaded without any sense of shame.

The certainty that she could ask this man for what she needed without worrying he would use it against her created a warm, steady glow deep inside her even as the fires of desire raged around it.

He surged inside of her in one smooth, inexorable thrust. While it lacked the pain, tearing, blood, and tears of losing her virginity, it was no less profound. Maybe even more so.

She wasn't sure if she was imagining it, but it felt like she experienced every centimeter of the stretch necessary in her most intimate flesh to accommodate his heavy girth.

He bumped against her cervix, sending a whole new type of pleasure through her. She'd never been invaded this deeply. Never known a connection that seemed to reach to the very depths of her soul.

He cursed like it was a prayer and stilled, embedded inside her. "You're so tight."

She had no words. Couldn't believe he'd managed speech.

Then he started to move and even rational thought became impossible.

It was all sensation. Burning pleasure. Sparking nerve endings. Hot breath catching in her chest. The slick slide of engorged flesh against tender tissues. A rapid heartbeat pounding in her chest. Ecstasy pushing against every particle of awareness.

Until rapture crashed over her in a tsunami that devastated everything in its wake.

The sound of her name shouted in his deep tones sent another peak washing through her, her body going rigid to the point of pain before melting bonelessly back into the bed.

They lay together in the aftermath, his body a welcome weight on hers, their breathing harsh in the stillness of the room.

Her throat was raw, like she'd screamed, but she couldn't remember doing it.

She didn't know how long they lay there either, but eventually, he pulled out of her, his fingertips holding the condom in place. Even with him softened, she felt the retreat along her inner walls and it sent residual pleasure through her.

Reaching across her, his big body emanating heat, he grabbed a tissue from the box beside the bed. He took care of the condom, tossing it in a trashcan next to the nightstand.

Then he moved to sit on the side of the bed, his breath shuddering like he'd just climbed the highest peak in the Kenai Mountains. "That is worth doing again."

Tension she hadn't been aware of holding in her body released. "Agreed."

He turned his head, his gaze trapping hers. "Yeah?"

"You need to ask?"

"You want more sex, no more skipping meals."

"Are you serious?" She wasn't sure if she should be offended or touched like she'd never been touched before.

"As a grizzly hunting food."

"Why, Tack? Why is this so important to you?"

He shifted so he was sitting sideways, facing her, his nearest leg bent at the knee and resting on the bed. "How can you ask that?"

"I'm not your responsibility."

He reached out and placed his big hand in the middle of her naked stomach, his thumb tracing over one hip bone. "You've been my responsibility since we were six years old."

Unlike so many times in the past when she was even remotely this vulnerable, she felt no urge to scoot under the covers or leave. Which was really strange, because he drew forth more real emotion than anyone else could these days.

She should be terrified of him, but she just wanted to lay her hand over his. So she did.

But she couldn't agree with his assessment either. "I abdicated your care and protection eight years ago."

"It's not something you get to decide."

"I never realized how arrogant you can be."

"Kitty, you used to yell at me for being too bossy and stubborn all the time."

"It's not the same thing."

He shrugged, like it wasn't worth arguing about, especially since he clearly thought he was right.

Definitely arrogant.

Why didn't that irritate her?

Maybe because his confidence was well earned. Taqukaq MacKinnon hadn't made her mistakes and he'd built exactly the life he'd always said he would.

That didn't mean he was always right, but she wasn't going to dismiss his opinion without consideration either.

"You want me to be healthy." Enough to offer his body as incentive for her to eat.

It would be funny to the point of ridiculousness if it didn't hit her straight in the heart. This man who said he didn't want anything emotional with her was offering security unlike anything she'd known since leaving Alaska for college. And he seemed determined to make her believe she was beautiful just as she was.

She'd found inner strength she'd thought she'd lost, but she dared any woman to be strong enough to turn this man down.

Tack gave her a serious look. "I'm not the only one."

"No one else has ever cared enough to look for a way to help." Her therapist didn't count, since Dr. Hart had been paid to teach Caitlin tools to overcome her eating disorder.

Tack frowned, the first flicker of criticism showing in his expression. "Your gran came down to California when you were in the hospital."

"And left as soon as I was out of danger."

"She wanted you to come back with her." His tone said he thought Caitlin should have done just that.

But she'd still been taking intravenous nourishment in the hospital as she worked back up to being able to eat normally for almost a full week after Gran had flown back to her beloved Cailkirn. "It wasn't an option."

"There's always an option."

"You think I should have ripped out my IV and checked out against medical advice when I could barely stand without help, much less walk? I'd only managed to hold down broth and baby cereal at that point."

A frown of confusion creased Tack's features. "She stayed until you were better."

"I was no longer in danger of sliding into a coma or any of my organs shutting down. I was eating by mouth." If in a very limited fashion.

"She left you alone to face that bastard you'd married when you were still so weak?" Tack demanded, clearly furious.

Caitlin did her best to forget how abandoned she'd felt. She'd known when she made a life in the Lower 48 that her grandmother wouldn't be coming for yearly visits. The fact that Gran had come to the hospital was huge.

"It wouldn't have made any difference if she'd waited another week."

No way had Caitlin been willing to put Gran between her and Nevin. If she was honest with herself, and she tried really hard to be nowadays, Caitlin hadn't been willing to return to Cailkirn before she'd gained enough weight to no longer look like a walking skeleton.

She hadn't been able to stand the thought of the town,

and this man in particular, seeing the evidence of her idiocy. She'd been ashamed enough that her grandmother had witnessed how far Caitlin had fallen.

"It would have for that week," he insisted.

She couldn't argue that particular truth, so Caitlin focused on what she could. "I was a grown woman. It wasn't Gran's responsibility to hold my hand."

"Bullshit. Family takes care of family."

"She hated being out of Alaska, Tack. You know she doesn't even like getting as far away from Cailkirn as Anchorage."

"She could have asked someone else to come."

Caitlin just shook her head.

"You needed her."

"I needed to do exactly what I did." Caitlin had taken back control of her life, bit by bit. "I got better."

It hadn't been easy and leaving Nevin hadn't even been the hardest part of it, but Caitlin *had* made it.

"You ready for a shower, wildcat?" he asked, startling her.

She would have thought he'd want to keep hashing out Caitlin's past until he was satisfied. However, showing yet again that he knew when to stop pushing, Tack was offering her something much nicer than a discussion that ultimately couldn't change anything.

"Sure." She'd rather stay in bed with him, but she realized that wouldn't be the wisest move at this point.

They couldn't afford to miss the MacKinnon family dinner. Neither of them would ever hear the end of it. She wasn't keen on sharing this newfound *whatever this was* with their families yet either.

Besides, she'd been so overwhelmed by Tack's lovemaking, Caitlin had done very little touching of her own. A shower seemed like the ideal place to rectify that oversight.

* * *

Tack tugged Kitty across the bed and lifted her onto his lap; despite the disparity in their sizes, she fit perfectly against him. "We need to leave for the Homestead in ninety minutes, unless you want me to drop you by the Knit and Pearl beforehand."

"You don't mind taking me home after?"

"Of course not." The stuff she worried about kept surprising him.

"Okay. I'll just ride over with you, then."

"Good." No one would question it this time, but they'd have to be careful that their families didn't get the wrong idea.

"You ready for that shower now?" she asked with a heated look.

His postorgasmic relaxation disappeared just like that and his dick sat right up at the thought of naked Kitty Grant under hot streaming water.

He couldn't count the number of times he'd jacked off to that particular daydream.

"Yeah." But he burrowed his nose into the joint between her neck and shoulder, inhaling the fragrance of her recent climax and regretting they had to wash away the scent of their combined pleasure.

He could easily spend the rest of the day and night in a sexual marathon with this woman.

Tack had set out to rock Kitty's world and ended up shaking his own foundations like a California earthquake.

That knowledge, more than anything, had him standing with her in his arms and heading to the master bath.

"You're carrying me again," she observed, sounding bemused.

He shrugged, making the side of her body slide up and down his torso. *Nice.*

"I *can* walk, you know."

"I've seen you," he said without cracking a smile.

"Is this a thing with you?" she asked as he put her down inside the bathroom.

"What?"

"Carrying women around."

"No." In fact, he'd never carried another lover.

"So, I'm special?"

She always had been, but he wasn't about to say that out loud. The time for those kinds of declarations was almost a decade in the past.

Instead of answering, he focused on starting the shower, turning on all the jets, and adjusting the temperature.

"It can't be good for your back."

That had him shaking his head and turning to face her. "Really? You barely weigh more than my winter camping pack and I carry that for miles across frozen tundra."

She stood up straighter, as if her five-foot-five inches were going to appear taller. "I'm not a shrimp."

"Never said you were."

She glared up at him.

He let out an impatient breath. "I *like* carrying you, okay?"

"Sometimes."

A smile twitched at the corners of his mouth. "Noted."

The genuine and clearly happy smile she gave him took

his breath away and sent renewed desire surging through him.

She flicked her blue gaze down to his cock and then back to his face. "Keep that thought."

Then she turned around and grabbed a towel to wrap her hair in. He would have told her he had shower caps, but watching her bend over to get her hair into the towel wrap was better than porn.

She straightened, deftly twisting the towel and tucking it in the back. "That should do it."

"Very resourceful of you."

She cocked her head to one side, her sky eyes going narrow. "You've got shower caps, don't you?"

"What do you think?" he asked, indicating his thick, shoulder-length hair.

There were occasions in the winter when he didn't have the time or inclination to dry it before leaving the house, but walking outside with a wet head would be bottom-of-the-barrel tourist stupid.

"I think it's time to get wet."

Damn. Did she do sexy well.

He pulled her into the oversized shower, turning their bodies so the highest stream was directed at his head. They pressed together, her breasts pillowed against his torso, his rapidly hardening dick brushing her stomach.

Tipping her head back, Kitty smiled up at him sweetly, undulating against him with an unconscious sensuality.

"Is the temperature okay?" he forced himself to ask.

"It's delicious." Her voice was pure sex.

Making him wonder if her sensuality had been so unconscious after all. When she started running her hands over his back and down his buttocks while pressing forward against his semi-erection, he was damn sure of it.

She reached for something behind him and then he felt the natural bath sponge against his skin, lather and water making it glide easily. Though the rough surface brought him more pleasure than washing himself ever did.

He went to grab the bar of homemade soap, but she pushed his hand away. "Let me do it."

"Okay."

"Turn around."

He obeyed without asking why. If she wanted to wash him, he'd let her. He had every intention of returning the favor, in great detail.

He spent long minutes in bliss as she gave careful attention to washing every inch of the back of his body. After she bathed him with the soapy sponge, she rinsed him with her hands. Those caresses felt distinctly sexual, though it had been more fun having her wash him with her body pressed against his.

He felt her move back a step. "Turn back," she instructed.

Only too glad to face her again, he did so with alacrity.

"Tip your head back, get your hair wet."

"You want to wash my hair?"

"Yes."

"I don't think that's going to work."

"Oh ye of little faith." She climbed up on the cedar bench that ran along one side of the tiled shower stall.

He'd included it for his future wife to sit on and shave her legs and do the other stuff women did in the shower. Then Tack had discovered he enjoyed sitting on the bench and letting the water pour down on him sometimes.

He'd never pictured Kitty Grant standing on it so she could wash his hair, though.

He put one hand out to steady her. "Careful there, wildcat."

"I am not now, nor have I ever been the klutz I told the ER staff I was." The lack of bitterness in her tone felt like a personal victory for Tack.

"Impetuous and headstrong yes. Klutz, no," he affirmed.

CHAPTER FOURTEEN

Tack hadn't had his hair washed since he was a little boy, and he'd had no inkling it could be the pleasurable and sensual experience that Kitty was making it.

The thought that she might have done this for her ex sent irrational jealousy rolling through Tack. However, he was determined not to give voice to it.

"You're good at this, Kitty."

"Aunt Elspeth taught me how to give a scalp massage while washing someone's hair." Which did not answer the question of whether Kitty had offered this delight to another man.

"This doesn't feel like a Miss Elspeth–style massage."

Kitty laughed, the sound so beautiful he savored it as more precious than summer sunshine and twice as warming. "The sounds you're making aren't anything like the ones she does either," Kitty offered in a voice laced with amusement-tinged desire.

"Maybe it's different with a man."

"Maybe it's different with you."

"Could be."

"I used to love when she washed my hair for me." Kitty went quiet for a minute, her fingers kneading his scalp and sending chills of bliss through him. "I never wanted to do it for anyone else, though."

"I'm glad you decided to experiment on me."

"Me too." Her hands slid down to massage the tension from his shoulders.

"I'm going to be a puddle of goo you'll never get out of the shower at this rate."

"We'll see." There was both promise and challenge in her voice. "Okay, time to rinse."

She stayed on the bench while he let the water wash the shampoo lather away.

"You like being tall?" he asked when he was done.

"I figure I'm just the right height for a kiss," she said with a playful wink.

"Shit, sweetheart, it isn't kissing I'm thinking about when your naked body is on display like this, but I'll take it."

"Glad to hear it."

She didn't wait for him to initiate the kiss, pressing forward to mold her mouth to his. Her small tongue came out to flirt against his lips.

With an animalistic growl he would have been embarrassed by with another woman, he yanked Kitty's body against his and deepened the kiss until their tongues were tangling.

He didn't like it when she pulled her head back, but she avoided his questing mouth. "Time for me to wash your front."

That was not an offer he was going to refuse, not considering how desperate a certain appendage in his front was for some attention.

The little tease started with his shoulders and worked her way down his chest, giving more attention than any other lover had to the brown discs of his male nipples. She rubbed them with the sponge and then rinsed them with her fingers, squeezing the tiny nubs gently and making him gasp with unexpected pleasure.

Just when he was ready to push her up against the wall and bury his cock inside her tight channel, she stopped and stepped down off the bench.

When she dropped to her knees, precum just about gushed out of his cock as it bobbed with an infusion of lust-driven blood.

She didn't touch him there, though. Instead, Kitty started at his feet, giving them and his legs the same attention as everything else.

When she finished with his thighs, she peeked up at him through her lashes. "I feel like I forgot something. Is there a part of you that doesn't feel clean?"

He pressed his dick forward so the head brushed along her lips. "I've got something that needs attention."

Her little pink tongue flicked out and tasted the pearls of pre-ejaculate oozing from his slit. "Mmm...I like that."

"Me too." So much he didn't think it would take long before he came all over her face.

Pretty certain she wasn't looking for that reaction, he ruthlessly clamped down on his growing need to come.

Both her hands curled around his cock, the fingertips not quite touching, but his dick didn't care. It felt incredible, and when she jacked him slowly, he couldn't hold back a deep-throated groan.

"You like that too."

"Oh yeah."

She smiled and then put her mouth right over his weeping cock head, her tongue caressing him even as her hands continued their slow pistoning of his length. When she started to suck, his knees nearly buckled.

She pulled off, her expression pure seduction. "Maybe it's your turn to use the bench now, hmm?"

His pride no match for his sexual need, he sat down with alacrity and spread his legs to give her room between them.

She moved forward, her hands sliding along his thighs as she knelt between them. "You're so gorgeous, Taqukaq."

"What I am is horny, wildcat."

She didn't laugh. She didn't even smile, the intensity in her blue gaze like an all-over body caress. "It's my turn to rock your world, Tack. I hope you're ready."

This was the Kitty Grant he remembered, ready to challenge him head-on, no matter the circumstance.

"More than," he promised her.

Her bathing him had been some of the most prolonged foreplay he'd ever experienced directed at *his* pleasure and it had left him primed and ready to shoot.

She didn't make him wait but dropped her head to lave him from head to root and back again, her tongue bathing him with even more care than her hands had taken with the rest of his body. When she took his head back into her mouth, she started sucking right away, her tongue busy while her hands stimulated his length.

It took about thirty seconds of this stimulation before he was warning her of his imminent climax. "I'm going to shoot, wildcat!"

She popped her mouth off but kept her face right there, rubbing her cheek over his sensitive head.

"I mean it, wildcat."

She looked up, her expression fierce. "Come, then. Right now if you can," she challenged.

He did and she let his pearly white jizz land on her cheeks and over her throat.

It was one of his deepest held fantasies, and seeing his cum on Kitty Grant's face because *she* wanted it there made him shoot again, less semen coming out but the pleasure no less intense.

His head fell back against the tiled wall, his body like a rag doll on the bench.

This woman was going to kill him.

* * *

Wearing her bra, T-shirt, and panties, Caitlin blow-dried her hair while Tack dressed in the other room. Her towel wrap hadn't been equal to their fun in the shower and she couldn't make herself care.

His climax had been one of the most amazing experiences of her life. The one he'd given her afterward with his hands while he alternated suckling each of her nipples had rivaled it, though.

She had *loved* the way he got so hot from climaxing on her face. She'd wanted it, but couldn't have told him why and was glad he hadn't asked.

She had a few questions for him now, though. Things she realized she couldn't ignore, even for the sake of more mind-numbing physical pleasure.

Because once her brain came back online, too many thoughts vied for resolution.

He came in, a huge grin creasing his face. "That's a different look for you, wildcat."

"Shut it. I can't help that your bathroom is woefully understocked."

"I have a blow-dryer. What more did you want?"

"Oh, I don't know. A little hair product? A diffuser for this ancient piece of...equipment." The man's blow-dryer needed to take a train back to the nineties where it belonged.

"What's the matter with my dryer?"

"Other than the fact that it doesn't have any adjustable settings and is heavier than Aunt Alma's ledgers, nothing."

"It *is* almost as big as your arm."

She bared her teeth in the facsimile of a smile. "I know."

"Well, it sure puffed your hair up." Laughter danced in his eyes.

"I know." She grimaced. "I'll have to braid it." The process was tedious, but she'd need the tight French braid to hide her puffball hair.

Tack frowned. "My mom will notice the change in your hairstyle. We'll need to stop by the B and B so you can change your clothes too. She'll think you just changed for dinner with the family."

His words couldn't have been clearer. "You don't want them to know about us." Which she agreed with, especially when she wasn't sure what exactly *us* meant.

However, hearing his absolute dedication to making sure there was no chance they'd get sussed out bothered her.

He leaned against the doorjamb, filling the opening. "I don't make it a habit of introducing my casual sex partners to my family."

"But I'm already a friend."

"Exactly."

"So, we have to hide that we're having sex." She spelled it out, needing to know exactly where she stood.

Tack looked relieved she got it. "Right."

"You said you didn't do sex with locals."

"For exactly this reason. I don't like subterfuge, but I won't have my family thinking they've practically gotten me married off either."

Because sex wasn't love. It wasn't even a relationship.

"Why break your rules?" She hadn't forgotten he said he didn't do friends with benefits either.

"I wanted you." He leered at her, the expression both funny and unexpectedly arousing. "I still want you."

"A few days ago, you were telling me I was too damaged for sex."

"With strangers."

"Or you." Or maybe the *no sex with him* thing had been about his rules.

Caitlin didn't like the confusion clouding her brain.

"Look, we established that I had my reasons for not want-ing to do this." He waved his hand between them.

"But you set those reasons aside. Why?" She might well regret asking, but she didn't hide anymore.

At least not from herself.

"I didn't think it through."

"What does that mean? You didn't think of this sex-for-eating thing?" She could believe that all too easily. It was a little weird and she wasn't sure she bought that he wasn't us-ing it as an excuse to do something he wanted. She liked that explanation better anyway.

"No. That works for me and you, too, if lunch was any indication."

She frowned, but didn't comment.

"Back at the Skilak trail, we started something."

Oh, yes, they had. "Something you said you didn't want to do again."

"I was wrong."

"So, you want me?" She started braiding her hair, aware of how provocative the stance with both arms above her head was.

His focus went to her breasts, his eyes darkening. "If that's not obvious, I've been doing something wrong."

"No. I get it." She smiled, enjoying the way his attention never wavered from her. "What I don't get is how I went from too damaged to have sex to you offering your kisses and body as incentive for me to eat."

"You're overthinking it, Kitty."

"Maybe, but that's what I do." For good or ill. And maybe she was just trying to get him to admit that there was more to it than his strange deal. "You're using sex to take care of me."

"I didn't think it through up on the trail."

"Think what through? Rejecting me?"

"Exactly. I didn't see it as rejecting you."

"Just sticking by your rules." And protecting her from herself, even if he wasn't going to admit that part now.

"Right. Only it turned out be some kind of trigger for you."

"You noticed." Of course he'd noticed; he offered her kisses in exchange for eating lunch only a couple of hours ago.

"I figured if saying no kisses caused the problem…"

"Offering them would fix it." Caitlin wasn't sure how she felt about being seen as a problem. *A project.* Something he had to fix.

Refused to accept that was all she was capable of being.

There was one thing she could give him that no one else could. Closure on the past, even if it opened up her present to feelings she didn't want to deal with.

Oh, he clearly didn't think he needed it, but just look around. Here Tack was, living in his dream home, the one he'd built for his future family with no concrete plans to share it with someone else. Sure, he said he'd get married someday, but he wasn't looking. Not even a little.

He was working insanely long hours, building a business that anyone else would consider firmly established.

Tack had shut part of himself off. She wondered if anyone else had noticed. His family didn't act like they did. Maybe they were too close to him to see it.

Caitlin wasn't vain enough to believe her rejection was the only cause, but the death of his grandfather had come after and with it the loss of any chance for Tack to prove his value to the old man.

Tack deserved to be happy. He deserved all of his dreams coming to fruition.

He needed a friend like her, someone who saw beyond the confident exterior he presented to the rest of the world. And if having a sexual relationship with her helped him to get past her rejection of him, she wanted that too.

Even if all she could give him was *amazing* sex and companionship he enjoyed, that wasn't nothing. It was something besides his business to focus on every minute of every day. He smiled, shamelessly adjusting himself. "Exactly."

Or maybe just unconsciously. He liked the idea of kissing her, that was for sure.

"And the sex?" she taunted.

"If it'll help you heal, no way am I letting you go to a stranger until you're in a better place."

Well, that made sense, even if it was borderline insulting. The man had a protection streak wider than a glacier and just as solid. She finished her braid and realized she had nothing to hold it. "Do you have a hair tie?"

He sometimes wore his hair pulled back in a ponytail.

"Sure." He opened a drawer in the double vanity, pulled out a black one, and handed it to her.

She took it, her mind reeling. "Do you mean to be patronizing, or is it just a side effect of your certainty you know what is best?"

He frowned. "I saw a problem—"

That problem being *her*. "And you wanted to fix it."

"Right." His tone implied he saw nothing wrong with that.

"And if I don't want to be seen as a *problem* to fix?"

"Don't kid yourself. No way can sex be that good if I see you as anything but a drop-dead desirable woman."

Okay, that made no sense and flew in the face of what he'd been saying. Only the absolute certainty in his voice brought her spiraling thoughts to a screeching halt. Not only did he believe what he said, but also he was right.

That sex had not been the result of pity; it hadn't been *medicinal*. It had been earth-shattering.

And it was something else only she could give him right now. His rules meant no other locals could and he was going to be too busy with MacKinnon Bros. Tours to go into Anchorage anytime soon.

"So, what was the shower?" she mocked, wanting to push and reveling in the fact that with this man she *could*. "Payment on account so I'm obligated to eat dinner tonight?"

"The shower was a fantasy lived out in three-D Techni-color."

Yeah, she'd kind of gotten that impression. "You liked it."

"Not sure *like* is the right word for something that burned every rational thought from my mind and turned my legs into jelly."

Okay, so she was a project. But she was also a woman who could give him pleasure he didn't expect or know how to control.

Caitlin could work with that.

He moved in until she was pressed between him and the counter. "Look at me."

He waited until she met his gaze.

All she saw in his chocolate brown depths was sincerity.

"I'm going to take care of you, Kitty. You can trust me not to lie to you, not to promise things I can't or won't give, and I make this promise: I won't break you like he did."

"O—" She cleared her throat and tried again. "Okay, but just so you know. I wouldn't let you."

His smile was almost too bright to look at. "Good." He turned to go back into the bedroom, but stopped. "Kitty?"

"Yes?"

"You'll eat tonight because you're hungry, but if thinking about what we're going to do later helps, then fantasize away."

She threw the towel on the counter at him. "Arrogant jerk comes to mind."

"If it makes you feel better, I'll be thinking about it too. Don't make me have to come home and jack off."

Sexy arrogant jerk.

* * *

Tack watched Kitty greet Gran MacKinnon, thanking her for the invitation to dinner. Though the invite had come from his mom via Tack, the Homestead was still technically Gran and Granddad MacKinnon's. Kitty's recognition of his gran's status was just the right thing to do.

She fit in Cailkirn better than she thought she did. Always had.

When she turned and hugged his Inuit grandmother and greeted her with equal deference, something dormant came to life inside of Tack.

He turned away from the tableau that caused the strange feelings, determined not to let them take root.

It didn't help that when Kitty had changed, she'd put on a pretty, figure-hugging blue dress. And her shoes were a good two inches higher than the more sensible heels she'd worn earlier, making her legs look about a mile long.

She'd done something with her eyes, too, making them seem bigger and the blue even brighter than usual. Her freckles weren't as pronounced, like she'd put powder over them or something. Having her hair back in a braid enhanced the perfect oval of her face but took her from Kitty-sweet to Caitlin-chic.

He preferred her natural beauty, wild red hair, freckles, and all.

His fingers itched to undo her hair, letting the wild mass fluff around her face. If he could, he'd strip the dress off and reveal his wildcat underneath too. He was sure she hadn't done anything to disguise the sweet cinnamon sprinkles over the upper swell of her breasts.

Contemplating her nakedness and what he'd like to do with it sent a montage of X-rated images through his mind.

"She looks better than she did at lunch," *Aana* observed.

Tack nodded, trying not to choke on his thoughts. "She was a little stressed."

Aana frowned, concern darkening her eyes. "I didn't mean to upset her."

"I know, *Aana*, and so does she." He reached down and put his arm around his diminutive mom's shoulders. "Kitty's just adjusting to being home. Cailkirn doesn't offer the anonymity of the big city."

"But surely that helps her to feel more protected and cared for."

"Or smothered." Hell, sometimes even he felt smothered and he loved their small town.

Aana looked unconvinced. "Considering how badly that anonymous life in LA went for her, I'd think she would be glad to be home, surrounded by people who know and love her."

"I am," Kitty said, having heard at least part of their conversation.

She gave his mom a more genuine smile than anything she'd offered earlier.

As long as he didn't let himself start thinking about things better left in the broken dreams of the past, having a casual sexual relationship with Kitty could be good for both of them.

He craved her body with an intensity he would have found impossible to ignore forever. Better to give into the desire while he still had some level of control. He would work through longings that needed to be relegated to the past and she could reconnect to the feisty, sensual woman who lived inside her.

Kitty pulled his *aana* from him and into a full body hug. "I'm so sorry for behaving like an idiot at lunch today. You are and have always been one of my very favorite people."

Aana blushed with pleasure. "Thank you, Caitlin. The feeling is mutual."

Kitty let his mom go but didn't try to establish a city-sized bubble of personal space around her. "Even after today?"

"Of course. Tack has reminded me that you need to get used to having people around who care about you."

"I'm sure he's right." Kitty's tone wasn't as confident as her words.

She'd never really enjoyed the intrusive nature of small-town life, but she'd been more resigned to it in the past. She'd get there again. It was an adjustment for anyone used to the anonymity of city life. While the benefits of living in Cailkirn outweighed the faults, they still existed.

His mom didn't seem to notice Kitty's iffy sincerity. "I would like time to catch up with you away from all this hub-bub."

"I'd like that too." Kitty didn't even wince when she agreed.

Had her attitude changed so much, or was she hiding her real reaction?

"Good." *Aana* was all smiles and motherly approval.

Kitty took a step back, an unconscious bid for distance he doubted *Aana* noticed either. "Gran and my aunts would be delighted if you'd join us for lunch Friday."

That explained Kitty's change of heart about sharing a meal with his mom. The Grant sisters would make a good buffer, more than willing to answer questions Kitty found difficult. Not only that, but they would also stop his mom from grilling her too intensely.

They were a wily group of women. And though they might not completely understand Kitty's recovery needs, they were fiercely loyal and protective of their chick.

"I told Gran how poorly I'd behaved and that I wanted to invite you over to make up for it."

Tack had chalked the half hour Kitty had taken to change her clothes up to her extra efforts with makeup and such. Apparently, she'd taken some time to speak with her gran, who had not joined him and Miss Elspeth in the parlor until just before Kitty came downstairs.

When Kitty had taken Miss Elspeth aside to talk quietly to before leaving with Tack, he'd assumed she was reminding the elderly woman about the dinner plans with his family.

A completely irrational urge to horn in on Friday's lunch hit Tack. What if her family didn't notice how stressed his mother's probing made Kitty? What if they didn't run interference like she so clearly believed they would?

He realized he'd gotten lost in his head when both *Aana* and Kitty stared at him expectantly.

"Sorry I missed that. What did you ask?" he directed his inquiry in their general direction, not knowing which woman had done the asking.

"I wondered if we should just invite you to join us right off, rather than have you come up with some excuse to stop by the Knit and Pearl at lunchtime on Friday." His mother's expression was too knowing.

The question was way too close to the thoughts running through his head. And there could be only one reason for that.

No. No way in hell was she going to start thinking he and Kitty were headed toward being a couple. He had to nip this line of hopeful speculation in the bud.

"No," he said louder than he'd meant to. "That won't be necessary. I don't usually forget my lunch."

Both women appeared taken aback at his vehemence.

"I thought you'd jump at a chance to have Miss Elspeth's cooking," his mom said with a perplexed frown.

Oh. Oh shit. She hadn't been thinking about him and Kitty at all.

"Even her cooking isn't worth sitting through one of your gabfests." He winked at Kitty. "I'm warning you, once those three get started solving the town's problems, both real and imagined, even Miz Alma takes herself off. If *Aana* brings *Emaa*, it'll be even worse."

"I'll take that under consideration." Kitty's joking tone and smile was more forced than before.

His mom slapped his arm. "That's enough out of you."

"You know it's true."

"Just for that I'm going to call Miss Elspeth tonight and ask if she won't defrost some of her venison stew for our lunch," *Aana* threatened.

"That's fighting dirty."

His mom put on her most innocent face. "I don't know what you mean."

Kitty laughed at them both, the sound too natural not to be sincere. "I'm sorry to mess with your revenge plans, Miss Malina, but I already asked Aunt Elspeth to make her summer vegetable soup."

"It's not summer yet."

"Frozen vegetables work almost as well, though she won't approve of me telling you that." Kitty winked at his mom.

She was going to be just fine on Friday.

CHAPTER FIFTEEN

When it came time to sit down to the table, Tack avoided the open spot beside Kitty. He was illogically sensitive to how things looked after his mix-up about what his mom might be thinking about him and Kitty. So, Tack elected to sit to the right of his cousin Cian.

Then Tack spent all of dinner regretting his cowardly move.

Him sitting next to the woman who used to be his best friend wouldn't make his family start wondering if something was going on between them.

If he was going to manage a secret casual sexual relationship with Kitty Grant, he would have to work on the paranoid.

Thankfully, his *emaa's* grilled salmon was perfect. Flaky and moist with the hint of the special herb rub she used and the smoke from the fire, it teased his appetite despite his frustrating thoughts.

Tack was happy to note that Kitty had divided her food and was eating steadily between bouts of conversation. She sat between his uncle, who didn't add much more than a grunt here and there, and Shila.

Tack's sister kept up a steady stream of conversation and Kitty didn't seem to mind.

"Why aren't you eating your dinner?" his mom asked Kitty when there was a lull in the competing voices at the table.

Wishing again that he'd taken that seat beside Kitty, Tack frowned at his mother warningly. "She's eating just fine."

Hadn't his *aana* learned anything at lunch today?

"But she's barely touched her food."

"That will be enough, Malina. I'm sure your mother raised you better than to embarrass a guest at our table." His gran nodded toward *Emaa* while chastising her daughter-in-law in a tone Tack had never had the courage to ignore.

"I did," *Emaa* backed Gran up with a gently chiding look for his mom.

"I didn't mean…" *Aana's* voice trailed off.

He felt bad for her, but sometimes she took her fussing too far. She just always thought she knew what was best for everyone and had a tendency to act on that belief.

He'd been told he shared that particular trait.

"I just took too much food," Kitty offered, and Tack hated that she felt the need to lie.

Gran winked at Kitty and exaggerated her Scots accent. "Dinna worry yourself, lass. We'll put up your leftovers and you can have them for lunch tomorrow."

Now that was his practical gran.

"Oh, that would be so kind," Kitty said, sounding more emotional than the offer warranted.

Gran nodded as if that was the end of it, and Tack had no

doubts it would be. There wasn't a person at the table who would defy his gran when she had that expression on her face, not even Tack's mom.

They had strawberry shortcake for dessert, made with his gran's scones and berries frozen last summer. It had always been one of Kitty's favorites.

Tack wondered which of the women who shared the Homestead's kitchen had remembered that. He wasn't surprised when he learned it had been his mother.

Her concern tilted toward consideration more often than intrusiveness.

Shila offered to split one of the desserts with Kitty, claiming she was too full for a whole one. Considering that his teenaged sister was self-conscious about her body, the offer might have been genuine. Tack was pretty sure she'd made it for Kitty's sake, too, though.

"You don't mind sharing?" Kitty asked.

"No way. It'll keep me out of trouble with Gran." Shila gave Gran a suitably cowed expression, which earned her a mock glower. "She hates when the food from her garden goes to waste, much less her scones."

Kitty smiled and accepted.

Shila allowed Kitty to divide the dessert in the bowl without comment and Tack knew his sister had seen Kitty's food ritual for what it was. He wasn't surprised. Not after what he'd learned about eating disorders.

A whopping eighty percent of people suffering from an eating disorder were teens. His sister had probably witnessed behavior like Kitty's firsthand.

Tack's eyes skimmed around the table to see how the rest of his family was taking the additional evidence that Kitty had a compulsive need to divide her food.

Most of the clan were too busy with their own dessert and conversation to even notice, but he saw a look of comprehension dawn over his mother's sweet face. His gran didn't appear surprised or critical. *Emaa* was nodding with approval.

Tack wasn't sure of what, whether it was her granddaughter's obvious sensitivity, her daughter's belated discretion, or even Kitty's food ritual.

* * *

When it came time to leave, Cian stepped up to Kitty. "You came in with Tack, yeah?"

"Yes?" Kitty asked rather than stated.

"I've got a mended nightstand to return to Miz Alma for the B and B," Cian said like that was all that needed saying.

Used to his cousin's more taciturn nature, Tack explained to Kitty, "He's offering you a ride home so I don't have to drive the opposite direction before heading home."

"Oh, I…" Kitty looked up at Tack, uncertainty in her expression.

He shrugged. "Thanks, Cian. I appreciate it."

Kitty's eyes darkened with disappointment before she masked it, but there was nothing Tack could do about that. He didn't see any way of going ahead with their plans to go back to his place without causing speculation among his family.

And if he took her aside to talk when they'd be seeing each other at work tomorrow morning, it would be just as suspect. He only hoped she realized that.

"Yes, thank you, Cian," Kitty said in soft tones. "I didn't mean to be an inconvenience for Tack. If I'd brought my tennis shoes, I could have walked back to the B and B. It's only a few miles. I probably should have driven myself in the first place."

Well, crap.

From anyone else, he'd know she was being overly polite and expected to be contradicted. Kitty, however, had always been stubborn. She *would* have walked the six miles between the MacKinnon Homestead and the Knit & Pearl rather than put anyone out.

Her claim she should have just driven herself was a direct reprimand to Tack. He knew her well enough to know she was implying that if it was so inconvenient to take her back to her home after they had sex, he shouldn't have made plans to do it in the first place.

He spit an epithet out under his breath.

Kitty ignored him.

"My truck's the dark blue F150 with a hard-shell." Cian turned and went out the front door.

The fact that he'd given Tack and Kitty a minute alone indicated Cian had felt the underlying tension in Kitty's words, even if he didn't know what it meant. He'd probably heard his cousin swear too.

"I'd better get my leftovers. See you tomorrow, Tack." Kitty pivoted and headed toward the kitchen without another word.

And then she was gone, leaving Tack standing there feeling like an idiot for more than one reason.

First, he'd pissed Kitty off, which meant he'd hurt her. That made him feel like a pile of steaming moose dung. Second, he craved her body with the desperation of an addict. He'd been sporting wood all night because of what he knew was coming later. He'd never been so grateful for the cover of a table.

And he'd given up his chance for satisfaction without a second thought. *Before* accepting Cian's offer on Kitty's behalf.

He *was* an idiot.

"Something wrong, brother dear?" Shila smirked up at him knowingly.

He frowned down at her. "Why would you ask that?"

"Um, because you look like a grizzly with a sore paw."

"What is it with my family always comparing me to a bear?" So his name meant grizzly bear; they didn't need to harp on it all the time.

"Maybe because you act like one?" Shila asked sweetly.

And there was only one way his mood was going to improve. Making a decision that had nothing to do with his sister's teasing, Tack spun on his heel and headed out the front door.

He didn't bother saying good-bye to Shila or take time to wish his family good night. He'd catch hell from his mom and grandmothers for it later, maybe even his da, but Tack had something he needed to do.

* * *

Caitlin went out the back door in search of Cian's truck, equal parts irritated and hurt. She'd thought Tack was looking forward to making love again later as much as she was.

Discovering he couldn't even be bothered to turn down his cousin's offer of a ride for Caitlin was more than a little demoralizing. Seriously, how hard could that have been?

She came to a stop in the leveled gravel parking area next to the old family home; no sign of a dark blue truck with a hard-shell was in evidence. While the sky was cloudy as usual, the sun wouldn't set until after ten. So there was plenty of light to see by.

The F150 and Cian were both gone.

Nonplussed, Caitlin turned in a circle as if that would somehow reveal her ride home. Had he pulled around to the front of the house, thinking she'd leave through the "company" door?

"I sent him on his way," Tack said as he stepped out from behind his truck, his dark gaze fixed on her.

She kept her distance, not taking anything for granted. "Why?"

"We had plans."

"They didn't seem all that important to you inside."

"Cian's offer blindsided me."

"He wasn't asking for your left kidney. He didn't even actually offer me the ride home. You did that for him." She did nothing to hide her irritation at that fact.

"He told you he was taking a delivery to your aunt."

"So?"

Tack sighed. "If I turned him down, everyone would wonder why."

"They didn't used to." Tack and she had been inseparable right up until she pushed him away. "No one cared."

Neither of their families had made a big deal of it back then. But then, they'd been best friends for a long time.

"You really believe that?"

She frowned. "Yes."

He shook his head. Like she was deluded.

Maybe she had been.

"My family, and yours, too, thought you'd get your wanderlust out of your system going to college in California. They figured we'd come back to Cailkirn, get married, and have lots of Grant-MacKinnon babies."

"They did?" Her gran and aunts had never even hinted at that. "No, they couldn't have."

She'd been so adamant she wasn't spending the rest of her life in the small backwater town of Cailkirn, Alaska.

He nodded with a harsh jerk of his head. "We all had dreams we had to let go of, Kitty. The loss of that dream hurt my family. It hurt your gran and your aunts, though I'm not sure Miss Elspeth ever gave up hope of you coming home."

"I'm sorry."

"Don't be. You weren't responsible for the hopes of other people. It wasn't your fault you didn't love me. It took me a while to realize that, but you can't dictate feelings."

He'd be surprised how false his belief was. Caitlin had refused to let herself love Tack and she'd managed to marry another man.

"You don't want to build up their hopes again," she surmised, realizing at the same time that neither did she.

The knowledge she'd hurt others more than she'd ever been aware didn't sit well with Caitlin and she had no desire to do so again.

"There's no reason to allow false expectations to develop. They will only end up hurting the ones who indulge in them."

Was he warning her? Telling her if she got her hopes up, they were bound to be dashed?

"But you sent Cian away."

"He's not just my cousin. Cian's one of my closest friends. I trust him."

Like Tack no longer trusted Caitlin.

"You don't think he'll mention that he didn't end up driving me home after all?"

"I asked him not to."

"Oh." Which meant what?

"I explained about our arrangement."

"You told him you're having sex with me so I'll eat?" Did Cian find that as strange as Caitlin did?

"Of course not."

Relief coursed through Caitlin. She hadn't really liked the idea of Tack telling Cian about that. She was healing, darn it. She'd like to be seen as the competent woman she'd worked so hard to become again. "What *did* you tell him?"

"That we're both adults. You're divorced, not some innocent. He knows I'm not ready to settle down. The sexual attraction between us isn't going anywhere. For right now we're enjoying it."

"He was okay with that?"

"Why wouldn't he be? This may be small-town Alaska, but casual sex happens here too."

"So you told me." And she didn't like thinking about that in relation to Taqukaq MacKinnon.

"Cian was worried I was setting myself up for a fall like eight years ago," Tack added in a tone that said how ludicrous such a concern was.

"I'm sure you set him straight."

"Yeah."

"So, you're taking me home?"

"After."

The banked embers of desire burst into flame inside her just like that. "After."

* * *

Caitlin pulled up in front of Nik Vasov's restored Victorian home at the north of town. She'd come to Cailkirn determined to get her own life together and avoid complications, even friendship.

After accepting that she wanted to be Tack's friend again, Caitlin had recognized the truth that avoiding relationships wasn't going to get her where she wanted to be anyway.

A strong and healthy woman with a normal life.

It hadn't taken her long to realize someone else needed a friend and that was Savannah Vasov. Whatever was going on between her and Nik, she could do with a friendly face.

And Caitlin was going to offer that.

She climbed out of her gran's ten-year-old Subaru, the dark green paint as pristine as when it had been driven off the lot. Of course, gran kept the little hatchback garaged and had had it repainted twice.

Caitlin rang the doorbell and waited on the veranda for someone to answer.

Someone fumbled with the lock and then the door swung wide. Joey grinned up at her, his eyes round with surprise. "Hi, Miss Grant." He yelled over his shoulder. "Mama, it's the nice lady from the plane."

Savannah came rushing up, a look of panic on her face. "Joey! You know you aren't supposed to answer the door."

"But, Mama, I thought it was my new friend."

"It doesn't matter, young man."

"Yes, ma'am." Joey looked down at the floor. "May I go upstairs?"

Savannah sighed and ruffled her son's hair. "Sure, sweetie. I'm sorry I yelled."

"You didn't, Mama. Not really."

"I did and I'm sorry." Savannah offered a strained smile to Caitlin. "Come on in. I've just made a pitcher of sweet tea if you'd like a glass."

"I know I stopped by unannounced. If this is a bad time…" Caitlin let her voice trail off, offering the other woman an easy out.

"Oh no. Not at all. I get a little testy when Joey answers the door, but I'm really happy you came by."

"You know Cailkirn isn't like the city. He's probably fine opening the door on his own."

"I'm not sure, what with the cruise ships docking now and so many strangers in town."

"Strangers who probably aren't going to hike two miles north to come knocking on your door."

"You never know."

Caitlin didn't have children, so she didn't know if Savannah's level of concern was normal or not, but she never remembered her gran being upset when Caitlin answered the door as a girl. Still, times *were* different.

Savannah led the way into a beautifully remodeled kitchen. The mix of modern and traditional was too perfect not to be the result of a professional designer and she said so.

Savannah looked around, as if seeing the kitchen for the first time. "I suppose so. I never really noticed, but if I'd thought about it, I *wouldn't* have assumed Nik did the decorating."

"Not his thing?"

"From what I can tell, work is pretty much his only thing."

"So, you're on your own a lot?"

"Well, me and Joey. Sometimes just me." The other woman grimaced. "Joey is fascinated by Nik."

"And he doesn't mind having your son around?"

"No. I should be grateful. I *am* grateful. It's just…"

"You get lonely."

Savannah sighed, but smiled too. "Yes. I should be used to it."

"But in the city, there was more to keep you occupied and you had all of Joey's attention."

"You're pretty insightful." Savannah opened a cabinet that turned out to be a façade for the fridge. "Sweet tea or juice?"

"I'll just have water."

Savannah nodded and pulled two glasses from the cupboard. She gave Caitlin her water first and then poured herself a glass of what she called sweet tea, but the clear amber liquid did not look like the treacle a lot of restaurants served by that name. "Would you like to sit in the parlor?"

"I'm happy here." Caitlin made good on her words by taking a seat at the kitchen table. "I actually came by to see if you and Joey would like to go on a hike with me. I'm not a professional guide, but we could do one of the simpler trails close to Cailkirn. What do you say?"

"You have time? I thought everyone was incredibly busy now that the cruise ships are in the harbor."

"Gran and my aunts insisted I take the afternoon off." Again. But since it had been her first free afternoon since the ships came in, Caitlin didn't argue.

"I thought Nik said you worked at MacKinnon Bros. Tours?"

Caitlin smiled. "So, you and Nik *do* talk. At least a little."

Savannah's smile wasn't big, but it was genuine. "Yes, I suppose we do."

"Anyway, I only work there in the mornings."

"And you want to go on a hike with us this afternoon? Aren't you tired?"

"Nope." When her gran told her to take the afternoon off,

Caitlin had thought of the hike and planned to go alone if Savannah didn't want to go with her.

So, she'd driven to work and from work directly to Nik's house.

"I'd love to go, but Joey is supposed to spend the night with one of Nik's cousins. She has a son the same age and another one two years older. Joey adores them."

The doorbell rang. "Speaking of, I bet that's them now."

Caitlin waited in the kitchen while Savannah answered the door and waited through the sounds of Joey leaving.

When she stepped back into the kitchen, the Southern woman looked a little lost. "He's off."

"I'm sure he'll enjoy himself."

"Yes." Savannah gave Caitlin a warm smile tinged with gratitude. "I'm really glad you decided to take pity on me and spend your afternoon off showing a tenderfoot one of the local hikes."

"No pity involved. I've been away from Cailkirn for a long time and haven't had the time to renew old friendships." Or the inclination, but Caitlin left that unsaid. "We better get going, though. The days are getting longer, but it's not summer yet."

"I'll just go change."

"Wear layers. It's still pretty chilly in the shade."

Savannah didn't take long changing into her hiking clothes and they were on their way only a few minutes later. Caitlin drove back through town on her way to the trail she'd picked for their hike. It went up through a meadow behind town, into the forest, and circled back around to come out at the other end of the boardwalk.

She and Savannah could do some shopping after the hike if they wanted, on the way back to the car.

"It's so beautiful here," Savannah said as they crossed the meadow, and then she gasped and stopped. "Did you see that? It was a deer."

"I'm sure you've seen some around your place." Caitlin knew guests at the B&B often spotted wildlife in the backyard because it butted up to the forest.

"Yes, but we're in town."

"Not really."

Savannah pointed over her shoulder to the houses that populated the streets behind the boardwalk. "Looks like town to me."

"The deer consider the meadow their stomping ground."

"They'll have to share today," Savannah said with a cheeky smile.

Caitlin grinned and nodded. "I'm not sure the bears will agree, though."

"Bears? There are bears?"

Caitlin laughed. "Tenderfoot. Bears almost never come this close to town."

"What about the forest?" Savannah gave the trees ahead an askance look.

"Don't worry. We aren't going deep enough to be concerned about running into any predatory wildlife."

"Well, that's good to know."

Savannah was quiet when they walked the trail through the forest. Caitlin told her about the local flora and fauna, keeping her voice low. Not because she was afraid of drawing a predator's attention, but because she didn't want to disturb the wildlife around them.

She'd always found this particular hike peaceful and enjoyed the fact that Savannah didn't try to fill the quiet space around them with chatter.

"Why did you leave?" Savannah asked as they got to the deepest part of the forest for this particular path. "It's so incredible here."

"I wanted to see something different." *Wanted to be someone different.*

"You came back."

"It's home." It was as simple and as complicated as that.

"It's my home now, too, but it doesn't feel like it yet," Savannah confided.

"Give it time." That's what Caitlin's gran always said.

Savannah nodded.

They spent the next few minutes talking about life in Cailkirn. Savannah didn't ask Caitlin any probing personal questions and she appreciated that enough to keep her own curiosity to herself about why a woman would enter into a proxy marriage.

They were approaching where the trail exited the forest when a loud snuffling grunt to Caitlin's left caught her attention. A small brown bear laid waste to someone's picnic that had been stored in a Day-Glo green nylon backpack.

"Where'd you leave the food? I told you we shouldn't have gone swimming." A teenager's voice got louder as the sound of stomping feet drew nearer.

"It wasn't that cold. You're a wuss."

"Am not."

The sound of a scuffle ensued. Unfortunately, Caitlin wasn't the only one who noticed. The bear lifted its head.

Savannah squeaked beside Caitlin.

"Shhh...," Caitlin admonished.

"You said there weren't any bears," Savannah hissed.

"There aren't usually, but then most people are smart enough not to leave food where they can sniff it out."

"He did more than sniff. He tore that backpack apart."

"He's a bear. He's not going to use the zipper."

Their conversation was held in tight whispers, but Caitlin knew if they didn't start backing away, the bear was going to notice them. The only problem was, he was definitely going to notice the teens too.

"Back away slowly and as quietly as you can. We're almost back to the boardwalk. Go to the tour office. Hopefully one of the guides will be there."

"I have my phone. I'll call."

"You need to go, Savannah."

"The bear—"

"Is going to notice us any second."

"Then you need to go too."

"You heard the kids."

"But—"

"They're probably tourists." A local wouldn't have left their picnic in a backpack on the trail to take a swim in the still frigid waters of Poppy Pond. "They won't know how to handle a bear."

"So, what are you going to do?"

"Whatever I can. Now go, Savannah."

Savannah shook her head, but Caitlin gave her a gentle shove and finally the other woman started her quiet and slow retreat.

"Dude, I'm serious. Where's the food?" the one teen demanded plaintively. "I'm hungry."

"I left it right here."

"Someone took it? But this is Alaska, man!"

The bear seemed undecided between his interest in the approaching teens and the lunch they'd inadvertently supplied for him. Caitlin started moving in an arc to intercept the teens if possible before the bear decided he was more in-terested in them than the food and they did something dumb, like run.

She caught sight of two boys, lips a little blue from the cold pond and shivering in their damp clothes. The idiots really hadn't prepared for their impromptu dip. The sun might be shining, but temperatures weren't high enough for them to dry anytime soon.

She waved at them to get their attention.

The taller one noticed her first. "Hey, did you steal our food?" he demanded loudly.

She made a shushing sign with her finger to her lips.

"What? Lady, if you took our food—"

The other boy bumped the taller one's shoulder. "Chill, dude. Do you *see* our backpack?"

"No, but where is it, then?"

"The bear has it." She tried to project her whisper without gaining said bear's attention.

"Bear?" the shorter one demanded, looking around fran-tically. "Where?"

"Shhh," she hissed, glaring at him and then pointing to-ward where the bear was devouring a sub sandwich, paper wrapper and all.

Both boys looked and then froze. She could see them planning to run even as she said, "Don't run. He'll chase you."

"But, lady, it's a bear."

"And right now he's more interested in your lunch than you. Walk over here slowly and then we'll head out of the forest." When neither moved, she said, "Come on."

It took them longer than it would have taken her, mostly because she made them stop every few feet and get quiet because they were so noisy. But the bear didn't come after them and eventually they reached the end of the forest trail.

One of the teens whooped as they broke from the trees.

Caitlin shook her head. "The bear can still hear you."

"But he's not gonna come out of the forest, right?" the taller teen demanded.

"He's not a vampire. The unfiltered sun isn't going to stop him."

Apparently that was too much for the boys because they broke into a run, heading back toward the boardwalk and the cruise ships.

They passed Tack as he headed toward Caitlin at a fast clip. He was right up to her when he asked in a suitably quiet voice, "Are you okay? Savannah Marie said there was a bear and some kids."

"Those were the kids and the bear is *hopefully* still in the forest enjoying their lunch and the remains of their backpack."

"I hope you're kidding."

"About the lunch? No. The backpack. Maybe."

"I'll have to get it. We can't leave that kind of litter there."

"Are you kidding me?" No, of course he wasn't. "Where's Savannah?"

"She's with Nik at the café. She's a little freaked."

"I told her how rare it is to see a bear."

"Well, you didn't count on the bear finding his lunch."

"Right."

He headed toward the forest but stopped and turned around, coming back to her. Tack cupped her shoulders with his big hands and gave her a thorough once-over. "Are you okay?"

"Yes. I was more worried about the boys."

"Did they even thank you?"

She shook her head.

He said something not very complimentary about the teens and she pretended not to hear it.

"I have to get the garbage."

"I know."

"Will you go to the café and wait for me?"

"Will you promise to leave the garbage if the bear is still snacking on it?"

He looked like he didn't want to but he finally nodded.

"Then I'll wait for you at the café. I'll even order lunch."

"Good." Tack placed a firm but brief kiss on her lips and then turned away.

Nik and Savannah were at a table for four in the back of the crowded café. The other woman jumped up and raced to Caitlin when she came in. "Are you okay? I was terrified that bear was going to eat you."

"I'm not as appetizing as a sub sandwich, believe me."

Savannah laughed, the sound strained but clearly relieved. "I called Nik. I didn't know what else to do. He said he'd call Tack and then ordered me to come to the café."

From the disgruntled sound of her friend's voice, Caitlin didn't think Savannah had liked being ordered to do anything. "You did the right thing. Please believe me."

"I admire you for staying to help the teens," Nik said.

Savannah frowned. "I wanted to stay."

Nik put up his hand. "That was not meant as a criticism of you, Savannah Marie. I imagine it was difficult enough for Caitlin to lead the teenagers out of the forest without having to worry about you too."

"And I suppose you didn't mean that as a criticism either?" Savannah asked, her voice laced with hurt.

"I didn't." Nik grimaced. "I can't say anything right with you."

Thankfully, the waiter came up to their table right then. "Would you like to order anything, ma'am?"

Caitlin nodded. "A shaved chicken breast sandwich à la carte, no mayo, and an onion burger with fries and salad." She knew Tack's schedule and he hadn't had time for lunch yet either.

"We already ordered," Savannah offered before Caitlin could ask.

"Do you want me to bring all the food out at once?" the waiter asked.

"That will be fine," Nik answered for all of them.

Silence descended on the table and Caitlin cast about for a safe topic to break it. Savannah was looking down at her lap, so she didn't notice the looks being cast her way by her husband, who clearly was still very much a stranger to her.

"Have you heard anything about the movie they're making in town?" Caitlin asked Nik.

"They are filming at Jepsom Acres."

"Oh?" That would explain why she hadn't seen any film trucks in town.

"I don't know how Carey talked Rock into that one," Tack said as he slid into the booth beside Caitlin.

Caitlin reveled in Tack's nearness and did her best not to show it. "I wonder. I don't remember him having much of a sense of humor or adventure for that matter."

Rock had been four years ahead of her and Tack in school, but he'd never really been a kid. It seemed like he was always watching out for his little brother and sister. His parents had been pretty absent from the picture long before the plane crash that killed them both.

"Who's Rock?" Savannah asked.

"A self-made millionaire who lives south of town."

Savannah's brow furrowed. "Then who is Carey?"

"His baby brother," Nik answered.

"Rock's got the patience of a saint to put up with him," Tack grumbled.

"Glad your parents gave you Egan?" Caitlin teased as the server put their food on the table.

Despite the undercurrent of tension between Savannah and Nik, lunch was surprisingly pleasant and Caitlin was sorry to see both men leave—Tack to lead an afternoon tour and Nik to return to work.

"As long as we're here, want to do some shopping?" Caitlin asked Savannah.

Savannah's eyes lit up. Oh, ho. Her new friend liked to shop. "You bet I do."

They managed to spend three hours on the boardwalk and Caitlin was so exhausted by the time she got back to the B&B that she took a nap before Tack was supposed to pick her up and take her back to his house.

* * *

Tack dropped a photo on Kitty's desk on his way into his office.

It was a purple wild iris, one of the earliest blooming wildflowers in the area. He'd taken the picture the day before while leading a group of hikers up one of the steeper trails on the peninsula. Irises usually grew in clumps, but this one had stood beautiful and proud alone.

It had reminded him of Kitty.

He could have given the print to her the night before.

She'd been at his house for dinner and a hell of a lot of entertainment after. It wouldn't have been the same, though.

He liked the look of surprised pleasure that came over her face each time she found a new picture on her desk. The framed board he'd put up on the wall behind where she sat already had a decent "bouquet" growing from the center outward.

He wasn't the only one providing pictures of Alaskan wildflowers. Once Egan and Bobby saw Kitty's photo board, they'd started looking for the perfect specimens of their own to add.

The other two wilderness guides didn't print the pictures off, though, but sent them to Kitty's phone.

Only Tack got the privilege of seeing her delight as she picked up a new flower to add to her "bouquet."

Which was why he made sure he was in the reception area when she came in.

She saw him and her sky-blue eyes sparked with happy welcome. "Good morning, Tack."

"Hey, wildcat. You sleep good last night?"

Kitty gave him a sultry up-and-down look. "Oh, yeah."

He'd taken her home after midnight, grateful that her gran and great-aunts went to bed by nine, no matter the season.

The Grant sisters' nocturnal habits had made him and Kitty getting together a lot easier. The influx of tourists from the first of the ships also helped keep everyone too occupied to notice Tack and Kitty sneaking around.

Though it was riskier to share dinner, like they'd done the previous night. Tack considered it a calculated risk worth taking when the benefits were so pleasant.

"Shouldn't you be gearing up?" she asked. "Your tour leaves in less than an hour."

"It's a pretty easy hike." He'd taken one of Egan's tours so his brother could drive their mom into Anchorage on a last-minute errand.

Their schedule still wasn't as full as it would be once all the cruise lines had their Alaska routes running.

Tack could have driven *Aana* because he'd planned a day in the office, but he would take a hike over the big city any day. Even an easy one.

He would end up doing the paperwork he couldn't delegate to Kitty at home later.

"Is Bobby at the pier by himself organizing both groups?" Kitty asked, sounding worried.

"He can handle it."

Kitty looked at him askance. "He's got twenty-five people signed up for the Cailkirn Beach Walk."

"I've only got ten cruise passengers going up to the Skilak Lookout Trail with me." Tack and Egan's tours were limited by the number of passengers their two tour vans could hold.

Both had room for eleven passengers and a driver. They capped their tours at ten in case they got a call from a desperate cruise director who needed a spot for a VIP or disgruntled ship passenger.

It happened often enough that Tack planned for it. They either charged the ships three times the usual rate for the last-minute booking or gave it away to cruise directors who sent a lot of business their way. It was a win-win.

"You're going back up to the overlook?" Kitty's tone was wistful.

"You have the schedule."

She turned away, but not before he noticed the tell-tale color on her cheeks. "I didn't pay attention to the fact that *this* was the tour you were taking over for Egan."

He wasn't sure why it mattered to her, but for whatever reason it seemed to. "Do you want to come?"

"I'm working, if you hadn't noticed. You hired me to answer phones and handle your scheduling."

"So, forward the phones to your cell and take my tablet in case you need to refer to the schedule. You're even dressed for it."

She usually looked pretty fashionable in the office, but she'd worn jeans and a sweater today. She'd need her hiking boots, though.

"I've got all the info on my phone." She shook her head. "But I can't just leave the office unattended."

"What do you think we did before you started working here? The phone doesn't stop ringing when you leave in the afternoons either." And he hated that moment when he had to forward it to his cell.

At least Egan and Bobby took their turns doing that onerous task too.

"But—"

"It'll be a chance to see what you're selling when you're talking to a potential client."

Kitty gave him a look he hadn't seen in a lot of years. It was her *let's do this even if it gets me in trouble* look. The one she gave him before she set about proving that not only could she keep up with him, but she'd also challenge him to keep up with her.

Hell if it didn't send blood surging into his prick. "You in, wildcat?"

"I'm in."

"We'll stop and get your hiking boots on the way out of town."

"The trail's in the other direction."

"So?"

She laughed, the sound so much like her old self he couldn't help yanking her into his arms for a kiss that put arriving at the pier on time in jeopardy.

CHAPTER SIXTEEN

Caitlin couldn't believe she was going back up to the Skilak Lookout Trail with Tack.

Their last time there had been an emotional watershed.

Today she planned on simply enjoying herself. No complicated discussions about the past or feelings. No making
out on the ground, though she might miss that one.

Just watching Tack in his element.

She hadn't told him, but as soon as the customer satisfaction surveys started coming in, she'd started wishing she
could see him in action. His clients loved him.

Egan and Bobby, too, but the kinds of comments that
came in about Tack were different. More *intense*. It was
no surprise that others considered him the epitome of the
Alaskan man, but the way people claimed that he helped
them fall in love with the state?

She wanted to witness that.

It reminded her so much of the friend from her childhood,

the boy who taught her what it meant to belong to Cailkirn, not just live there.

Only, as she listened to Tack give an entertaining and accurate history of the town, accompanied by colorful stories, as they traveled north on Sterling Highway, it wasn't Alaska or the area that Caitlin fell in love with.

It was Tack.

The feeling welling up inside her as she watched him talk into his headset from the front passenger seat of the tour van was as unstoppable as the inlet tides and deeper than the ocean's abyss.

If she'd recognized this *love* during sex, she would have written it off as passion's excess. If she'd acknowledged it when he was helping her, she'd have convinced herself it was the gratitude and loyalty of friendship. Even if she'd gotten an inkling when she found another one of his photo gifts on her desk, she'd be able to dismiss it as sentimentality.

But right here? Right now? Her heart so full that tears tightened her throat, she had no excuses.

The moment was too prosaic *not to be* profound.

She'd been so certain she was inured to adoration of this magnitude, and if it were any other man in the world, she would be. However, the walls Caitlin had built around her emotions had no hope of keeping him out.

Because Tack had been firmly entrenched in her heart since Caitlin was six years old.

His voice washed over her, the words no longer registering as she examined her new knowledge with the exultation and terror of a woman facing true love for the first time in her life. But as certain as the realization that she loved him was the discovery the emotion had always been there.

She just hadn't let herself see it.

Not when they were teens and she never got crushes on other boys at school. Not when they were college students and it had taken her into the middle of their sophomore year before she accepted her first date.

With Nevin Barston.

Not when she'd felt raptor-size claws slash her heart when she pushed Tack away and stopped responding to his calls, texts, or e-mails.

The magnitude of her self-delusion shook her as much as finally accepting the truth of her feelings for Tack, maybe even more.

How long would she have kept hiding from the one emotion she'd denied, the one bigger than all the others combined?

Had the sex opened the cracks in her self-realization? Or had it been day-after-day exposure to this man who was *the man* to her?

Or maybe the layers between Caitlin and the inexorable understanding had been peeled away by the years of pain without him. Nevin had added to that pain, but he hadn't been the deepest source of it.

Oh man. She *really* needed to talk to Dr. Hart.

Caitlin loved Taqukaq MacKinnon and she always had.

She'd never loved Nevin Barston. Caitlin had been bowled over by his sophistication and good looks, but he couldn't occupy a place in her soul that was already full.

He might have done his best to break her spirit, but he could never break her heart. Because he hadn't owned it. Not even a little corner of it.

It had always belonged to Tack, and she suspected it always would. The love of a child for her dearest friend had morphed into something else as they grew into man and woman.

And there had been a time he had loved her too. He'd never said, but she'd known somewhere inside her that she owned his heart too.

She'd ignored that knowledge and followed her plan to outrun the agony of a childhood loss she'd never dealt with.

In some strange way she'd felt like she owed it to her parents to leave Cailkirn too. They'd been so adamant about leaving the town behind. There had been a part of her that thought she had to honor their memory by following their dream and getting out.

Oh man.

Her therapist had been right when Dr. Hart had posited that Caitlin hadn't disliked Cailkirn or Alaska, but the painful grief she identified with living there.

It had caused an obsessive need to leave the small town and she'd known subconsciously she'd never go if she acknowledged the depth and breadth of her feelings for Tack.

So she'd denied them. And him.

Doing it had cost her the one person left in her life she couldn't afford to lose. Tack had been her anchor since she was six and then she'd cut the line and set adrift.

She couldn't deny the horrible awareness that these revelations were coming eight years too late. The damage had been done and this huge feeling inside her had nowhere to go.

Tears tightened her throat to the point it became hard to breathe. Her heart began to pound heavy and rapid in her chest. The first panic attack since Tack had taken her to his house the first time swelled inside her.

"Isn't that right, Kitty?" Tack said loudly through the tour van's speaker system connected to his headset, like he realized she wouldn't have heard him otherwise.

How had he known she was getting lost in her own head again? What sixth sense connected them?

She looked around, but the faces of the other passengers didn't give her any clues as to what he was talking about.

"Excuse me?" she asked, her panic ebbing slightly as she did her best to focus on Tack.

"I was telling these fine people that even our resident ghosts think Cailkirn is something special."

"If they didn't, they'd move on to the afterlife," she said, finally catching up.

Laughter sounded around her and she forced a smile in response, though her words hadn't been meant to be funny. She'd just said the first thing that came to her mind.

"Is it true your grandfather haunts the bed-and-breakfast your family runs?" a woman in the second bench seat back asked.

Caitlin shifted in her seat so she could look back toward the tourists. "I'm not sure he haunts the house as much as he does my gran."

"That's so romantic."

It would have been more romantic if he'd stayed in Cailkirn to take care of his family, Caitlin thought. She kept that particular belief to herself.

Apparently she had her grandfather's abysmal timing. Only he'd died when he left Cailkirn. She hadn't.

Did that mean she'd been given a second chance to win back Tack's love? Could they live out the dreams he'd abandoned when she kicked him out of her life?

Did she want to try?

Caitlin wasn't at all sure she had the mental or emotional reserves to stand up to his rejection if she told him how she felt and Tack shut down any hope of a future between them.

Her heart physically hurt in her chest as she accepted he'd already done that.

Maybe it was for the best.

She wasn't sure she still had it in her to hope, to reach for dreams that could shatter as easily around her feet as the mirror Nevin had once thrown at her.

Needing respite from her heavy thoughts, Caitlin spent the rest of the ride to the trailhead answering questions and sharing her own stories to help Tack entertain the cruise passengers.

Once they'd parked and everyone got out of the van, Tack locked it up and started giving instructions for the hike.

Two young men, one blond with the jock look and the other undeniably Goth with black hair and polish on his nails, broke off from the group. They'd been in the backseat with an older couple that might have been their parents and had spent the entire drive either talking to each other or texting on their phones.

They sidled toward Caitlin, separating her from the others as well.

The blond spoke. "So, my bro here bet me ten bucks you're one of the ship's passengers. He says I've got no skills of observation."

"The only faces he remembers are the ones facing him on a football field," the Goth twentysomething claimed.

Caitlin managed not to roll her eyes. "You lose that bet."

She wasn't impressed with either brother's powers of observation. They had to be the only two people in the van who didn't know she was a Cailkirn resident.

"So, you're a local?" the blond pressed.

"Yes," Caitlin said shortly. "I work for MacKinnon Bros. Tours. You need to listen to Tack right now."

The Goth did roll his eyes. "Don't step off the trail, leave the wildlife alone, don't litter, blah, blah, blah. We've heard it before; this is our third stop on the tour. Mom and Dad insist on doing some kind of *adventure* at each port."

Caitlin recognized the blasé attitude of a college student trying to seem uninterested in anything but clubs and parties. She also noticed he remembered three of the key rules of hiking. At least he had that over the teens who had precipitated Savannah Vasov's first sighting of a bear.

"But other people need to hear what he's saying."

"You don't. You're an expert, I bet," the blond said.

His brother sidled up until he was almost touching Caitlin. "You could be our personal tour guide."

"I'm not a guide. I work in the office." She deftly sidestepped him and tried to put more distance between herself and the young men. "All of our guides are certified wilderness experts."

Even Bobby had his basic certification. Tack had told Bobby that if he wanted to keep working for the business, though, he'd need to get additional certifications in the winter when their tour schedule was light.

The blond moved toward her left and his brother flanked her on the right, stepping close again.

Persistent little brats.

Then, without her having to say a single thing, both young men backed up and started moving away fast.

Caitlin turned around, unsurprised to find Tack approaching. The look on his face? A little less expected.

If she were the boys, she would have retreated too.

"I'm sorry," she said when he reached her. "I tried to get them to stop talking."

"Were they harassing you?"

"No. Just flirting."

"You didn't flirt back." It was a statement.

But she still felt the need to respond. "Not even remotely."

He nodded. "You okay?"

"Sure. It was harmless, Tack."

"Stay close during the hike."

"I'm not helpless."

"But you're on the hike to see what we do, not to have amorous advances from little boys."

At twenty-eight, Tack wasn't exactly ancient, but Caitlin wasn't about to remind him of that fact. He was in full protector mode.

"You're hot when you get all protective like this," she whispered as she passed him to join the others at the trailhead.

It was all she could do not to snicker when she noticed the two brothers standing on the other side of their parents as far from Tack—and her—as they could get.

Tack kept her right beside him as he started the hike, his hand landing in the small of her back.

She stared up at him in shock.

He shrugged. "They'll all be gone tonight."

When their cruise ship sailed. In other words, no one here was a local and it didn't matter if they knew she and Tack were involved in a casual sexual relationship.

Not that it felt all that casual with the looks he was giving the college boys and his hand remaining so possessively on her.

This hike was entirely different from the time before. Tack pointed out the flora and fauna along the way and shared stories of wildlife sightings and information on those they could expect to make.

He told them the history of the trail and about the devastating wildfire burn from twenty-plus years ago.

Caitlin was entranced, listening as closely as any tourist who had never stepped foot on the Kenai Peninsula before.

When they reached the overlook, the cruise passengers took tons of pictures, and so did Caitlin.

She even talked Tack into taking one with her.

Tack had passed out nutrition bars and bottles of water before the hike. It looked like pretty much everyone was taking advantage of both now that they were resting.

"Remember, if you pack it in, you pack it out," Tack told them, and watched closely to make sure none of the hikers from their group left any trash behind.

Suddenly one of them was pointing up at the sky and shouting that it was an eagle.

Everyone went silent, watching the majestic bird circle in the air above. Whether it had eyed prey or was just curious about the group of humans pointing and exclaiming, the eagle flew in dips and swoops, putting on a show no amount of money could have guaranteed.

Caitlin didn't even try to get a picture, she was so enamored of the beautiful bird. Coming upon wildlife, even on hikes like this, was not certain—especially with a noisy group who chattered the whole way up the trail. And eagle sightings were getting rarer each year.

Tack came up close, settling behind her. "This is why I do what I do."

She nodded, understanding in that moment more than she'd ever thought she could. When his arms slid around her, she relaxed against him, letting the security of his presence complete the perfection of the moment.

The eagle finally flew off, breaking the spell holding the group silent.

People started talking and looking ready to make the return hike.

Tack leaned down and kissed her temple. "You're hella hot when you're all spellbound by the beauty of our home state," he said, neatly turning the tables on her from earlier.

* * *

Caitlin's bubble of contentment burst when they got back to town and he dropped her off at the bed-and-breakfast.

"Aunt Elspeth wants to know when you'll be by for dinner again." Caitlin had learned Tack avoided dinner at the Knit & Pearl once tourist season hit and it was filled with guests. "What do you want me to tell her?"

"The first week of October." He didn't sound like he was joking or willing to compromise on that.

Still, she had to try. "Come on, Tack. Even full to capacity, we never have more than a dozen guests."

"I spend all day with tourists. I'm not eating my dinner with them too."

"You didn't seem to mind them today."

"I don't. They're my livelihood, but I don't want my job sharing my dinner table."

Caitlin did her best to hide her disappointment. After his invitation to join him that morning, she thought he was as interested in spending time with her as she was with him. Even if it meant putting up with a few strangers at the table.

Apparently, she'd been wrong.

It was hard to swallow the truth that while she'd finally admitted to a love that was never going away, he still saw her as a *project* and his current casual sex partner. She couldn't forget that one.

"See you later tonight?" he asked, proving her thoughts.

She almost said no, but if this was all she got of Tack, she wasn't giving up a moment of it. "Nine-fifteen like usual."

He'd taken to stopping by to get her after Gran and her aunts were in bed. Last night had been an exception, but one she had a feeling wouldn't happen often.

He brought her home around midnight. They'd gone a little later on a couple of memorable occasions, but sleep was as necessary as food to Caitlin's healthy recovery. And she didn't like the thought of Tack doing challenging and even dangerous hikes with too little sleep.

Come to think of it, now that the tourist season was in full swing, they probably shouldn't meet every night.

She'd have to bring that up later because the van was already disappearing from the bed-and-breakfast's drive.

* * *

"What do you want?" Tack demanded, leaning over her sweaty, flushed nakedness.

Kitty *did not* suggest what he thought she just had.

"It's not what I *want*." She glared at him, her blue eyes sparkling with annoyance despite the vocal orgasm she'd had only moments before. "Some of your tours leave at seven in the morning. That means you're getting up closer to five to prep."

"First, I prep my pack when I get back from a hike, not before going on the next one, so it's always ready. Second, I get up at five-thirty every morning, regardless of what time my tours are."

She winced. "That's even worse. You're not getting enough sleep even now."

"So what?" He could sleep when he was dead.

"We need to limit our late nights to a couple of times a week. You probably already realized it, but it didn't occur to me until earlier today." She bit her lip, her expression thoughtful. "Maybe Friday and Saturday nights because you can sleep in the next day, or at least take a nap."

Yeah, like either of those things were going to happen. He wasn't going to bed in the middle of the day unless she was in there with him.

"And maybe Wednesdays."

He tugged one wild curl. "Wildcat, you're overthinking this."

"No." She shook her head, causing an interesting ripple effect down to her naked breasts. "This *isn't* overthinking. It's me watching out for you. You do it enough in the other direction; it should be a familiar concept."

"You're not getting any more sleep than I am."

"You're wrong. I take a nap before dinner almost every evening."

He was actually relieved to hear that. She was still recovering, even if the strides she'd made in the last year were pretty damn amazing. "What does your family think about that?"

"It's not all about what our families think," she said fiercely. "Anyway, you don't have to worry about it. My gran and aunts think I need a break from the tourists. They each have a time of day when the others cover for them so they can have solitude."

"That's good."

She frowned at him. "For me, but it doesn't help you."

"I need help?"

"You aren't getting enough sleep. Haven't you been listening to me?" she asked peevishly.

"I admit, listening isn't on the top of my priority list when you are lying naked in my bed."

"We're not on the bed."

She was right. They hadn't made it past the sectional in the great room. It was better than the time he hadn't even let her get out of the cab of his pickup.

They'd made out like horny teenagers, and it was a damn good thing he kept condoms under the driver's seat. He'd keep them in the glove box, but then his *aana* might find them when he was giving her a ride somewhere.

"Look, what if we compromise? You could take me home earlier, like ten o'clock."

She was kidding, right? Forty-five minutes with driving time taken out wasn't even going to touch the wildfire of desire between them, much less quench it.

"We might as well just have sex in the truck behind the B and B and then you can go back inside after."

She looked like she was considering it.

"Hell no." He stood up and lifted her into his arms. "I am not...just *hell to the no.*"

"Are we going up to the bedroom now?" she asked, sounding like she thought he was being the unreasonable one.

"No." He was going to sex her ridiculous *compromises* right out of her head.

He carried her down the hall to the hot tub and sauna room.

"You think this is a good idea?" she asked as he stepped into the water with her.

He'd prepped the hot tub earlier in anticipation of what he wanted to do. "Oh yeah."

"The hot water is liable to put us to sleep."

"What is it with you and sleep tonight? Trust me, neither of us is going to be *sleeping*."

Her eyes flared with instant yearning and a sweet curiosity. "What are we going to do?"

"Relax and let me show you, wildcat. I guarantee it will be more informative than any explanation I can make."

"And what am I supposed to do while you're *showing* me?" she demanded.

She got frustrated when she thought she hadn't participated enough. Eventually, Caitlin was going to realize that what mattered was mutual pleasure, not tit-for-tat touching.

"Enjoy yourself and turn me the hell on by letting me touch you any and every way I want to. Think you can do that, sweetheart?" It was a serious question.

After her past, he kept waiting for her to put a stop to the things he wanted to do to her, but she kept showing more and more trust. Trust *he* had a hard time believing in.

"Is that really what you want?" she asked.

"Yes. Very much yes."

"Okay."

He grinned, primitive triumph filling him. She brought out things in his nature no other woman ever had. He felt like a Cro-Magnon man who had just won the right to mate his chosen female.

She sucked in air.

"Kitty?"

"That look on your face."

"What about it?"

"It's really intense."

Was this where she drew the line? "I'm not going to hurt you."

"I know that," she said with a good dose of *duh* in her voice. "It's just really sexy. When you look like that."

He kissed her because he couldn't not, letting his hands roam over her naked skin from her collarbone to her toes and touching everything in between.

He was careful to keep his touch light between her legs. Water wasn't as slick as her natural lubricant and it would be too easy to rub tender tissues raw.

His promise not to hurt her extended to not leaving her too sore for more lovemaking, even when they didn't have the time to indulge.

She squirmed on his lap, moving enough that his semierect cock bobbed up in the water between their bodies. Her hand curled around it, her grip loose like she realized water wasn't the perfect lubricant for a hand job either.

Good thing the waterproof lube he'd ordered online had arrived in his mailbox today. Even better the Amazon box looked like it could just as easily have had books in it as the sex stuff.

After long moments of the leisurely touching, his prick was hard as stone and it was time to move on to the next step in the seduction plan.

CHAPTER SEVENTEEN

He reached over the side of the tub to where he'd put the red oblong flotation device he brought on excursions that took his hikers too close to water.

He dropped it into the water and then stood up with her.

She squeaked, grabbing on to his water-slick shoulders. "What are you doing?"

"Something I've been thinking about for a while."

"Oh," she said, her voice still pretty high pitched.

He laid her back in the water so her head and neck were supported on the float, her pretty red hair floating around her like silk in the water. She stared up at him, her sky blues filled with trust and confusion.

The fact she was feeling both surprised him all over again. She had no idea what he wanted to do, but she was willing to let him try.

"Do you have any idea what a turn-on it is that you're willing to just let me have my way?"

"I know it made Nevin furious that I could never relax with him, not even in the beginning."

"That bastard," he spit out.

"Doesn't matter anymore."

She was right. Barston was back in Los Angeles and he'd screwed up badly enough that Kitty would never go back to him. Tack had a suspicion she wouldn't ever return to California either.

He wasn't convinced she'd stay in Cailkirn, but if she ran again, it wouldn't be to the Golden State. Caitlin had a habit of identifying a place with the emotion she'd experienced there, more than she probably realized.

Dismissing thoughts that were better left for another time, he maneuvered her so she was floating freely, her breasts above the water, her legs open.

He guided her hands to either side of her head on the float. "Curl your fingers around the edge. I don't want it floating away and your head dropping under the water at a crucial time."

She laughed softly, doing as he suggested. "That would be bad."

The reach arched her body, leaving her a bounty laid out before him.

And he planned to feast.

"How does that feel?" he asked her.

She gave a closemouthed smile, the expression mysterious and all woman. "Really free, like my body is weightless."

"Now let's see what we can do to make it feel something *more*." He was going to remind her how much pleasure they got out of each other's bodies and how ludicrous it was to think about limiting that.

He began with his hands on her breasts, the sight of *her*

hands effectively trapped above her head increasing his desire in ways he never would have expected. Oh, he liked control, but the way she *gave* it to him was the real turn-on.

He played with her nipples, greedy for every little sound she made and reveling in how tight the buds got.

He wanted to nibble on them, but it wouldn't work with him still standing. So he dropped to his knees, kneeling to the side of her in the water.

That was much better. In fact, it was perfect.

He put one hand under her back to keep her up and lowered his head and took a rosy peak in his mouth, gently scraping his teeth across before sucking with a lot more force than he usually started with.

But they'd made love once already.

His efforts were rewarded by a soft cry. He wanted more of those needy, out-of-control sounds. Tack set about turning her on to the point of no return.

It only took a few strokes with his fingers coated with the waterproof lube between her nether lips, already swollen and sensitive from earlier, before she was saying his name with choking demand.

"You want something, wildcat?"

"You, Tack." She looked at him with passion-glazed eyes. "I want all of you."

Something in his chest tightened at her words. This was just sex, but she'd sounded...emotional.

Pushing aside what was undoubtedly just his imagination, he got the condom on and then spread the lube over his latex-covered dick.

Pushing inside her was like nothing else on earth and the angle he got because of her buoyancy in the water was fantastic.

His brain shut off as lust took over and he pistoned in and out of her grasping channel.

The water didn't allow her to push back against him, though he could tell she was trying.

He curved his hands on either side of her hips, holding on tightly and increasing the pace of their lovemaking. She moaned out her approval, her entire body flushed with desire.

"I need," she cried out. "Please, Tack!"

She needed just that little bit more of stimulation. The way she reacted, he knew he was touching her G-spot inside, but it wasn't enough. If he let go to touch her clitoris, he would lose his hold for the forceful thrusts they both needed.

But she could let go of one hand and still keep the float under her head.

"Touch yourself," he told her in a guttural tone he knew excited her.

Kitty's mouth parted on a wail. "I can't."

"Sure you can, wildcat. Touch yourself and bring us both off."

When her pale white hand moved over red curls darkened by the water, carnal triumph surged through him. She touched herself hesitantly at first, but pretty soon she was lost to sensation and her hand moved almost as fast as his hips.

They climaxed together, her clamping vaginal walls extending his pleasure, her very vocal cries telling him that the extra hardness he achieved just before climax enhanced her orgasm.

They soaked in the water afterward, him reclined in the water and her sideways on his lap again, her body lax against his.

"Not skipping some nights of this," he vowed.

She didn't answer, just turned her face into his chest.

* * *

Caitlin made an appointment for a Skype session with Dr. Hart, needing help in finding perspective on her love for Tack. She didn't tell her gran or Tack about the planned session.

If it worked, Caitlin planned to continue her therapy because she wanted to be completely well. If Tack was ever going to give her a real chance, and that was a big *if* after their past, he wouldn't do it if he thought she was still broken.

So, she couldn't *be* broken. She had to be fixed and Tack couldn't be the fixer. Caitlin had to do that herself if she wanted an equal relationship with him, even friendship.

"I'm doing better," she told Dr. Hart after their initial greetings, and then the doctor asked about the effect of the move on Caitlin. "A lot better. It's not perfect, but the move home has been good for me." She'd even had a talk with her gran and aunts. They'd been very understanding when she explained about how she needed them to support her and the things that actually backfired.

Surprisingly it was her crusty aunt Alma who had been the most compassionate and least defensive, asking for specific instances and ideas of ways they could help her to feel safe and comfortable in her own home. How to make food not an issue between them.

And it had been going great.

"That's interesting," the lovely honey-blond woman with gentle eyes observed.

"What is?"

"That's the first time I've heard you refer to Cailkirn as

home. It was clear from things you said in our sessions before that is how you see the town, but you never gave it that recognition in your head."

"No, I guess I didn't."

"Why do you think that is?"

"Because it would have been disloyal to my parents. Home was Phoenix."

"Until you were six."

"I had a hard time accepting that." Then Caitlin shared all of the revelations she'd had while riding to the Skilak Lookout Trail.

Including her realization of the love she'd always felt for Tack.

"What does that make you feel about your years married to Nevin?"

"Stupid," Caitlin replied without hesitation. "I should probably feel guilty, but I married him in good faith. He's the one who set about destroying what feelings I did have for him."

"I'm impressed."

"Why?"

"That's a big realization to make. You weren't there before you left California either."

"I never fit the LA mold."

"You never felt you fit the mold your husband and friends made it clear they thought you should. Los Angeles is one of the most diverse cities in the country."

"Not Beverly Hills."

"In your experience."

"You're telling me it wasn't California that was toxic for me but the people in my life."

"That would be my supposition, yes."

"And the anorexia?"

"How are you eating now?"

"I hardly ever skip meals and I haven't come in under calorie goal in a while."

"Since you started having sex with Tack."

"Yes." Did that mean she'd traded one crutch for another?

"You look like something about that bothers you."

"Why did sex make such a difference?"

"Was it just sex?"

"No. I love Tack and I finally opened up to the possibility of being with him." Even though she had denied that vehemently at first.

"So, was it the sex that made it easier to eat or that you were no longer hiding from deep and powerful emotions?"

Understanding washed over Caitlin and she felt a huge grin take over her face.

Dr. Hart gasped.

"What?" Caitlin asked.

"I've never seen you happy, Caitlin. I agree wholeheartedly with you. Moving to Cailkirn, Alaska, was very good for you."

The rest of the session was good, though Dr. Hart pushed Caitlin to dig deeper into her reaction to the town's often voluble curiosity about her. They ended their video session with plans for another one in a week's time.

Hope like Caitlin wasn't sure she'd felt since before her parents' unexpected and tragic deaths filled her with a glowing warmth. The weightlessness of realizing she no longer had to drag the chains that had tied up her emotions, both deep pain and joy, anymore was incredible. Easily as powerful and filled with mental pleasure as her time in the hot tub with Tack had been physically.

* * *

Tack left the cold coffee French press he'd ordered for Kitty on her desk. He'd printed off directions on how to make the best cup of coffee with it. He put them next to it, along with a note that told her it cut the acidic content of the coffee by sixty-five percent.

He knew she missed her coffee. The look of longing she got when she watched him drinking his was enough to limit his caffeine intake in a way *Emaa's* chiding never could.

So, when Nik told Tack he knew a fellow Marine who had to go to cold-press coffee after coming home from his tour in Afghanistan because his stomach couldn't handle the extra acid anymore, Tack had been determined to get one for Kitty.

She wouldn't be here for a couple of hours and he had an excursion that left in thirty minutes. Which was for the best.

The French press wasn't a big deal, not even a gift really. Not when it would make it so Tack could drink *his* coffee without feeling guilty.

But Kitty would get all weird about it. She was like that, treating the least little act of kindness like some kind of mini miracle.

She'd always been sweet about efforts other people made on her behalf. Even as a little girl, she'd been genuinely and honestly appreciative for her gran and aunts taking her in. Kitty'd never taken a gift or a favor for granted, but since moving back to Cailkirn, she took that to a whole other level.

He liked seeing her happy, but he didn't want her making a big deal about this. Especially in front of Egan and Bobby. Tack would never hear the end of it from them.

They already went around calling him *sweet* because of the way she'd responded when Tack bought that little under-the-desk heater.

Kitty was too used to California weather. While Tack had already taken to wearing short sleeves some days, Kitty was still dressing in layers.

When he'd overheard her mention to Egan she didn't like wearing her tennis shoes in the office but that her feet got cold, Tack had known he had to fix that. She was his employee. Her comfort was his responsibility.

Her gratitude had been over the top, and now his brother and cousin teased Tack about being a *pushover* and *sweet as candy.*

But he hadn't minded the way she'd expressed her thanks later that night. Not even one little bit. She'd grown increasingly adventurous the more often they made love and he enjoyed himself immensely because of it.

If he hoped for more of the same tonight … well, it wasn't the reason he'd bought the coffee press, so that was all right.

* * *

Caitlin savored her first cup of coffee in ages. The smooth flavor surprised and delighted her. She'd never been overly fond of the strong underlying bitterness in some coffees; it was as if this method of preparing coffee had been designed just for her taste buds.

It wasn't quick. She'd had to leave the grounds and filtered water cold-steeping at room temperature for twenty-four hours. But if she refreshed the water and grounds each day after she pressed the steeped mixture, she'd have coffee ready for her every morning when she came into work.

Coffee she could drink without stomach upset.

Tack's gift had been so thoughtful, but she hadn't been able to express her appreciation yet. He'd been out on a tour while she was in the office yesterday and they'd had to give up their nightly tryst the night before.

One of the bed-and-breakfast guests had had an asthma attack after spending the day hiking. Apparently the woman's allergies were so intermittent, she'd forgotten to take an inhaler with her, and by the time she'd returned to the Knit & Pearl, she'd been in a bad way.

Her husband had been cranky with worry. Aunt Elspeth had gotten fluttery because of it, which brought out the dourest side of Aunt Alma. Gran had offered to take the woman and her husband to the clinic.

Caitlin didn't want her grandmother sitting in the waiting room for who knew how long since the clinic was inordinately busy during tourist season. So, she'd insisted on taking the couple herself.

There'd been no question of sending them on their own. That wasn't how the Grant sisters handled things.

It had been after ten when Caitlin and the couple had returned to the bed-and-breakfast. She hadn't wanted to leave in case the woman's allergies had a resurgence. Caitlin would be needed, and her gran and aunts would want to know where she was if she wasn't in her room.

However, she had very special plans tonight to show her appreciation to Tack for his very thoughtful and welcome present.

"That's quite the look, wildcat. What are you thinking about?" Tack's deep tone came from the hall to the back door.

Caitlin jerked in shock and nearly spilled her precious

coffee. "I thought all of you were on tours." What was he doing back?

The schedule hadn't changed when she checked that morning.

"My hikers are back at the lodge, getting ready to go."

"I thought you were supposed to leave at eight?"

Tack snorted. "That Carey *James*. Thinks he's too good for his family's name."

She was pretty sure his parents had taken *Jepsom* as a stage name before they'd had their children, but she didn't mention that. Clearly, Tack was irritated with Rock Jepsom's actor brother.

"What does Carey have to do with your tour leaving late?"

"He booked it." Tack leaned against her side of the desk, close to her. "Played the 'Big Dog' and insisted on booking a tour for his *people* with me. I warned him my excursions were more challenging than the Beach Walk or Walking History of Cailkirn tours."

"I take it he wasn't interested in doing them?"

Tack reached out and ran his fingers through her curls. "Said his *people* wanted to experience the real Alaska."

She'd seen the booking. Tack had made it when she was busy helping her gran and aunts at the bed-and-breakfast.

Not that they seemed to need all that much help, which was something Caitlin had been thinking about over the past couple of weeks.

"The excursion you booked isn't beyond the average person's abilities, though." It wasn't one usually on his schedule either, but she knew he and Egan made exceptions when they had a big enough group wanting to book.

"Yeah, as pissed off as Carey made me, I wasn't playing

with my business's reputation by booking him for my All Day Wilderness Experience."

But Tack had wanted to, that was clear.

She fought a smile at his blatant crankiness. "So, what's the problem?"

"Half of them showed up in dress shoes and heels. One woman was wearing a damn dress and Carey, the idiot, had on some kind of duded up kilt no self-respecting Scot would wear."

She tried to hold it back, but Caitlin burst out laughing. "Please tell me he was at least wearing hiking boots with it?"

Tack made a sound of disgust. "You'd think, right? I've worn my colors hiking in the summer, but not with a pair of flip-flops."

Caitlin shivered at the idea of wearing a skirt without leggings and sandals that gave no added warmth in the spring temps. "You told him the dress code for the excursion, didn't you?"

"Yes, I damn well did. I sent it to him in an e-mail too. No open-toed shoes, no heels, and I didn't think we needed to specify to leave the fancy clothes in their suitcases." He tugged her up from her desk, pulling her to stand between his legs.

She went willingly, loving when he got affectionate outside of their sexual trysts, but she wasn't giving up her precious coffee. "Maybe Carey didn't tell the others?"

"You think?" Tack shook his head, his hands caressing her back and bottom. "I felt sorry for his director. I got the impression this production thing is pretty much her responsibility. She was trying to smooth all the ruffled feathers while not telling Carey what an idiot he was. She seemed pretty stressed to begin with."

"Carey was always big on ideas and short on follow-through." Not that Caitlin cared much about the younger man right now.

She was enjoying Tack's nearness too much.

"That's a kind way of putting it. His brother ought to kick his ass."

"What? Why?"

Tack frowned, like he wished he hadn't said anything. "Just saying."

"Come on, Tack." She patted his chest. "I'm not a gossip, but you can't say something like that and not explain it."

"Jackson was at the Homestead for dinner last night."

"What did the mayor have to say?"

"Carey signed a contract for filming in Cailkirn and is using his brother's place for the primary location shoots."

Shock held Caitlin silent for a full ten seconds. "But he doesn't have the authority to agree to either."

"Nope."

"Rock must be livid." Everyone knew how much he despised the industry that had dominated his parents' lives. Not to mention how closely he guarded his privacy.

"Jackson isn't too happy either. Cailkirn is already overrun with tourists in the summer. Bringing a film crew in creates a whole other set of problems he had no chance to prepare for."

Not least of which was town security. "Benji's going nuts, I bet."

The Cailkirn sheriff's department hired additional staff for the tourist season, but even with the "summer deputies" on the schedule, resources were stretched thin.

"I'm pretty sure most of the town leaders of Cailkirn would happily string Carey up right about now."

"You could do them all a favor and let him get *lost* while you all are out today," she teased.

"Kitty Grant, everyone thinks you're so sweet."

"And if you tell 'em different, I'll deny it." She winked at him and took a sip of her yummy, delicious, long-craved-for coffee.

She closed her eyes and savored the flavor, humming a little in her throat.

Tack made a strange sound halfway between a groan and a cough.

Caitlin let her eyes flutter open. "Something the matter?"

"You know I have to leave."

"Uh-huh."

"You're teasing me."

She let a small smile play around her lips. "Maybe."

"That's not very nice."

"I promise to make up for it tonight."

The look he gave her sent shivers right to her toes. "I'll make sure you do."

She puckered her lips to blow him an air kiss, but he swooped in and it became very real, very intense, very fast.

He pulled back from the kiss, set her away from him without spilling her coffee, and stepped out from behind her desk. "See you later, wildcat."

She nodded, speech beyond her, and watched him saunter out the door.

That man was lethal.

* * *

Tack lounged back against the pillows on his bed, naked and unabashedly touching himself. They'd been lovers for three

weeks now, but she still found his open sexuality both irresistible and astonishing.

His willingness to listen to her and try what she wanted
during their intimacy always surprised her too.

True to form, Tack hadn't even gotten a little snarky
when she'd put off any touching until they got upstairs and
then asked him to get naked and get on the bed without
her.

"Are you going to join me sometime soon, Kitty?" His
smile seduced her as thoroughly as his open sexuality.

"Yes."

"You're a little overdressed there, wildcat."

She nodded.

"I'm just saying." His voice dripped with sensual teasing.

He probably thought her *surprise* was going to be her
stripping for him, not what she would reveal by taking her
clothes off. Which got her thinking he might expect her to
be all sexy in how she did that.

"You're overthinking again," he said from the bed, his
deep voice reverberating through her.

She shrugged and then remembered he didn't like when
she did that. "Maybe."

"I've seen you naked before, wildcat."

She nodded. "Many times." She shouldn't feel so self-
conscious.

"I know who you are, wildcat. I'm not expecting anyone
else. Trust me."

"I..." She swallowed. "I want you to enjoy this."

"I promise I will."

"I'm not a stripper," she blurted out.

His expression was so serious. "I want you, Kitty, not
some fantasy woman."

That helped, but her hands still froze on the button of her pants. Why was it so hard to show him what she was wearing under her sweater and jeans?

"You remember when we were teenagers?"

His brow creased like he was trying to figure out where she was going with that. "Sure."

"You said you thought the sexiest thing a woman could wear was a red lace bra and panties."

"I never told you that," he said with certainty.

"No. I heard you talking to Benji Sutherland."

"I was pretending to know what the hell I was talking about so my friend who was older and more experienced would think I was cool. You know how kids are."

"Oh." Disappointment welled.

This was stupid. She'd thought she had something special to give him, a fantasy he could live out.

Because before she left California, Caitlin had bought herself a red lace bustier and thong. She'd purchased it so she could feel more feminine, though she hadn't managed to talk herself into putting the lingerie on before today.

She now realized that old comment she'd filed away in her memory had influenced her purchase. What other man could define sexy and feminine for her?

Only he hadn't meant it.

Well, there was nothing for it. Unless she wanted to undress in the bathroom, Tack was going to see her red lace underthings. And Caitlin wasn't that much of a coward.

It might not be his fantasy, but he'd probably still like seeing her in it. Right?

Might as well get it over with.

She pulled her sweater off over her head and then shucked her jeans without giving herself time to think about it. Caitlin was going to remove the corset-style bra and thong with the same efficiency but stopped herself.

She owed it to herself not to trivialize this moment. Whether or not this was a long-held fantasy for Tack, this was the first time since her wedding night that Caitlin had donned sexy lingerie because she *wanted* to. Not out of the need to placate, but the *desire* to please.

The belief that she could entice her partner with the view of her body encased in red lace.

This moment was as much for her as it was for Tack.

His harsh inhale brought her gaze shooting up to his.

Dark eyes devoured her. "Oh hell," he whispered reverently. "Will you turn around so I can see it from the back too?"

CHAPTER EIGHTEEN

Caitlin nodded, no thought of denying him.

She pivoted in a slow circle, the sensation of his eyes on her as powerful as any caress. A blush climbed her body as she put herself on display, but it excited her too. Knowing he watched her.

"I lied."

"What?" She tried to reconcile his lust-filled expression with his words.

"You in red lace is the perfect sexual fantasy."

She choked out a laugh. "I'm glad you think so."

"Damn, wildcat." He shook his head. "Just damn."

She climbed onto the bed and crawled across to him, watching his expression go from unashamed desire to full-on feral need.

As soon as she was within reaching distance, his hands shot out and grasped her around the waist, the hold possessive and sexily amorous.

He lifted her and maneuvered her body so she straddled his hips, all in one smooth, powerful movement.

Burying his face in her neck, he inhaled deeply and groaned as if her scent was just one stimulation too many. "If I'd known you were wearing this underneath your clothes, we wouldn't have made it out of the truck."

"Really?" she asked breathlessly as she tilted her pelvis forward and rubbed her lace-covered mound against his hard-on.

They moaned in unison.

"Feels so good, wildcat."

"Yes," she groaned out.

His big hands cupped her naked backside and squeezed. "I like this too."

"Yeah?"

"Oh yeah." He caressed her butt, paying each globe special attention so she could not doubt his words.

One fingertip slid down her crease until he touched her dew-drenched opening.

She couldn't stop herself from tilting her hips a little so he dipped inside. "Mmmm…"

"You're so wet and silky here, sweetheart." His thick finger glided along her vaginal walls.

She rocked on the invading digit, needing more, craving the feeling of fullness she'd only ever experienced with his big phallus inside her.

Only she was enjoying this stimulation too much to give it up. And his rigid length rubbed against her clitoris through the lace of her thong, sending explosions of sensation through her with each small movement.

Kissing up his neck and under his chin, she pressed her breasts against his muscled chest. Her nipples were so hard and sensitized, every tiny adjustment of her body against his sent shivers of euphoria through her. The sprinkling of black hair over his pectorals added to the maelstrom of sensation, even through the fabric of her bustier.

She rode him, all timidity gone in this act as she took pleasure from his body and gave it back with confidence born of his unfettered reactions. The man loved whatever she did to him.

There was a lot of sensual assurance in being with a man who held nothing back.

Their movements grew frantic and he dipped his head to take her mouth in a carnal kiss. Tongues tangled, lips ate at each other, their breath mingled. Ecstasy built inside Caitlin, driving her to more desperate caresses, deeper kisses, tighter and more forceful rocking of her hips, only to be met by a matching urgency in Tack.

He tore his lips from hers. "Want to be inside you."

"Yes. Now. Now. Now," she chanted.

A condom came from somewhere, but she had to lean back before he could put it on. It took Herculean effort, but Caitlin managed to move away from the hot, rigid length of his erection. She couldn't stop herself from helping him roll the condom down and then working him with her hand in long, slow strokes.

He moaned, his face twisted in the rictus of sexual plea-sure. "Damn, wildcat, don't do that."

"Then get it inside me."

He laughed, the sound choked with his desire. His big hands wrapped around her hips, fingertips reaching to her backside, and he jerked her body up and aligned her soaked vaginal opening with the tip of his engorged erection.

He lowered her, stopping when his head ran into a barrier. "Move your thong string aside," he ordered gutturally.

She did, feeling too much lust for hesitation or modesty.

He let her down inch by slow inch as her slickness allowed swollen rigidity to stretch her vaginal walls, gravity doing the rest. He'd barely seated himself fully before he started thrusting with his hips, guiding her to ride him with a hold on her hips.

No sexy, slow beginning this time, but all carnal need and urgency.

It felt so good, bliss radiating from her vagina outward. Every thrust, every tilt of her hips added to the growing hunger between them. He encouraged her movements with his hands and words of praise that filled her with as much pleasure as his touch.

"Come with me," he demanded as he increased the power of his thrusts upward, his erection growing impossibly harder and thicker.

With no thought of denying him, she let the cataclysm of delight shatter inside her, her muscles and womb contracting with such power the pleasure bordered on pain. She exalted in the rapture taking over her body, mind, and heart.

This was what she'd been made for. Or rather, he was the man she'd been designed for.

Later, he insisted on being the one to take off her lacy underwear and it led to lovemaking that was both tender and incredibly passionate.

She fell asleep wrapped in his arms, only to be woken later by Tack's hand gently shaking her shoulder. "Come on, wildcat. I need to get you home."

She shook her head and rolled away, burying her head in the pillow. "'M tired."

Exasperated low laughter sounded near her ear, but he

didn't say anything else and she had the fleeting hope he would let her spend the night.

The ache to wake up in his arms was growing by the day.

But strong arms lifted her right from the bed, him carrying her somewhere again, and then she was being lowered into a hot bath. Strong hands washed her body, no words passing between them.

Caitlin couldn't be angry at how well he was taking care of her, but neither could she chase away the disappointment at his clear dedication to keeping their relationship a secret.

* * *

Tack leaned on Kitty's desk. "Nik's bringing his uh…"

"I think the word you're looking for there is *wife*," Kitty said with some asperity.

"Right. Anyway, they're coming for dinner at my place tonight. I thought you might want to come and get to know her a little better."

"You do realize we have gone for groceries in Kenai a couple of times together already?" Besides, he knew all about their aborted hike and bear-sighting excursion.

"Nik mentioned it."

"Did he?"

"Yes. Not sure why you didn't."

"Right. Because we spend so much time talking about anything besides work and sex. And face it, that doesn't require a lot of discussion."

He looked around to make sure no one had overheard her words, even though he knew that Egan and Bobby were out on tours right now. "We see each other almost every day."

"I barely see you here between your tours and we don't

spend our time together at night talking." There was something in her tone that said that bothered her more than a little bit.

Which maybe shouldn't have surprised him, but it did. He thought she was fine with the way things were between them. He was sure as hell enjoying himself.

He wasn't one for skirting a subject. "Are you complaining?"

"No." But something in her sky-blue gaze said that he was right in believing she *wasn't* entirely happy about that reality either. She sighed. "If we got together outside of work and our trysts, we'd have more time to talk."

"You know that's not possible."

"Remind me again why two friends can't just have dinner together once in a while?" she asked, definite snark invading her tone.

"I'm only home for dinner a few nights a week during the season and I spend most of those at the Homestead." She kept the schedule; she knew how many tours of his went into the evening.

"You couldn't give up one night at the Homestead to eat with me?"

Not without raising brows and encouraging speculation. "You could always come to dinner with the family again. It's not always the whole clan, you know."

"But it is always at least your parents and grandparents."

"Sure." But she liked them; he knew she did. And ever since her lunch with his mom and Kitty's gran and aunts, Kitty hadn't shown any reticence to be in *Aana's* company.

"Right."

He didn't understand what her point was. "I'm inviting you to dinner tonight," he reminded her.

"With Nik, Savannah, and Joey."

"Well, yeah, but I thought you were open to being Savannah's friend. And that Joey is one sweet little boy." He reminded Tack why one day *he* wanted a family.

"Aren't you worried that will seem like a coupley thing to do?" she asked, sounding more annoyed than worried.

"Nah." He'd already laid the groundwork with his family, telling his mom that Kitty was Savannah's only friend in Cailkirn so far.

He explained that to Kitty.

The pleased expression that had come over her beautiful face at his initial denial of concern transformed into one of definite irritation.

"What's the matter? You have to get over your aversion to having other people know what's going on in your life," he said, guessing that was what bothered her. "What is the big deal, anyway? Were you planning to hide your friendship with Savannah?"

"No," Kitty all but snapped. "Hiding one friendship is plenty, thanks."

"We don't hide our friendship."

"Really?"

"You know we don't."

"Do I?"

Man, what was her problem? His wildcat wasn't usually cranky like this. Stubborn, yes. Independent? That too. But not bad-tempered.

"Are you getting enough sleep?" he asked.

Her pretty bow lips twisted in cynicism. "Would it matter if I wasn't?"

Right. She definitely needed a full night's sleep, maybe a few of them in a row. Guilt washed over Tack. He'd rejected her attempts to cut down the number of nights they spent together, thinking it was only about him getting enough rest.

And he was fine.

He'd been noticing signs of her tiredness, though; almost every night, she fell asleep after the second time they made love—sometimes even after the first bout of sex. He should have done something about it before this, but he'd been selfish.

Far from assuaging his need for her, their nightly intimacy had only increased his craving.

"We can make dinner with Nik and Savannah another night."

"No. It's fine."

"No, it's not. You need your rest. I'll go call Nik." He left before he gave in to the urge to take back the words.

Even knowing Kitty needed a break, he wanted her in his house that night. Even if no sex was in the offing, but she needed the rest. He'd forgotten how physically fragile she'd been only a year ago.

It was time to man up. He would have to show some restraint and not push to get together every night.

* * *

Fighting irrational jealousy, Caitlin listened to the rise and fall of Tack's and his mom's voices from his office. Malina MacKinnon had complete freedom to come and go in her son's office. He never looked to see who was around to notice them when he hugged her.

She got to see him on most of his free nights for dinner and when she came in, she got all his attention. No matter if it was the only time all week Caitlin and Tack had to see each other outside of sex, he would take his mom back into his office for one of their mother-son *chats*.

He never invited Caitlin to join them and never kept his mom in the reception area so Caitlin could naturally do so.

It hurt in a way Caitlin had been sure she wouldn't with Tack. She felt like he was ashamed of her.

She knew he wasn't exactly proud of their intimate relationship. He couldn't be proud and so obsessively determined to keep it a secret from everyone that mattered in their lives.

At first, the illicit nature of their sexual relationship had been exciting. She'd liked having something that was just hers and Tack's, but the limits on their time together and interactions when other people were around had grown old.

Added to that, over the last week, he'd shown a marked decrease in his interest in getting together even for sex. Sure, she'd been the first one to suggest they cut back the number of nights they met in his bed. But that had been to protect his sleep.

He said that was his reason now (on her behalf, though), but that really didn't fly. Not after the way he'd completely disregarded her concerns when she'd brought them up before.

The dinner with Nik and Savannah hadn't happened yet either.

All of it added up to some very unpalatable truths. Tack did not love Caitlin and he wasn't likely to ever allow himself to either. Or even be tempted.

A man didn't fall in love with his *project*, no matter how consuming.

In Tack's mind, Caitlin was and would forever be the bird with the permanently broken wing he fed and entertained. He wasn't even as committed to fixing her as he had been.

She wasn't sure she could blame him. *Her* commitment to giving him closure had flown out the window. She didn't want to help him shut the door on the past so he could make a relationship with someone else. She wanted a second chance at the love she should never have tried to deny in the first place.

But it was becoming increasingly clear that he didn't share her change of heart.

As her realization of the hopelessness of her love for Tack grew, so did Caitlin's inner stress. Unsurprisingly, she'd fallen into old patterns of skipping meals.

Nothing like as bad as before, and not even as pronounced as after she'd first moved back to Cailkirn. But Dr. Hart had noticed and pointed out that she didn't believe Caitlin's current relationship with Tack was healthy for her patient.

And in her most rational moments, Caitlin had to agree.

She wasn't sure she had the strength to break it off, but she couldn't deny that emotional pain was at a level she would never have anticipated. Worse, it had become a definitive component for her to their association.

The phone interrupted her unhappy thoughts.

She picked it up and gave her usual greeting, pleasantly surprised to find a cruise director she'd worked with already.

"Hello, luv," Stu said in his charming Australian accent. "We'll be in port the day after tomorrow. I'm hoping you will be able to put together something special for a unique group of guests."

"Tell me about them and I'll see what I can do."

It turned out a group of certified climbers, who were also old college friends, were on board and wanted a true Alaskan experience.

Caitlin moved some things around on the schedule and booked the climbers with Tack on one of his excursions that was rare because so few hikers had the skills and experience necessary to make the trek. All the while, she made small talk with the cruise director and encouraged him to avail his other passengers of their less challenging excursions.

"Will that do?" she finally asked.

"Very nicely. Are you part of the MacKinnon in MacKinnon Bros. Tours?" Stu asked.

Ignoring the twinge the question gave her heart, Caitlin replied, "No. I'm only their part-time clerical help and receptionist."

"More than that, I hope. You're far too good at this."

Somehow they got into a discussion of her education and the years she'd spent schmoozing the glitterati in Los Angeles.

"Have you ever considered a career with the cruise lines?" Stu asked. "Your skills are exactly what we need on the hospitality side and you would have the opportunity to see more of the world."

She asked where he'd been and he listed an impressive number of countries he'd visited in his job.

"Look, this is probably presumptuous of me, but we have an opening coming up in our department. You should apply."

Nonplussed, Caitlin tried to process the offer.

Before her realization that she loved Tack and the equal but far less palatable certainty that he did not love her, she would have turned Stu down immediately.

Only, how would she handle living here in Cailkirn either staying in her current no-man's-land of a relationship with Tack or breaking things off, all the while knowing Tack didn't love her?

Worse, how could she watch him eventually fall in love and build a family with someone else? The family *she* could have had if Caitlin hadn't made her colossal mistake eight years ago.

"You're thinking about it, I can tell."

"I've just returned home." And she'd promised not to leave again.

But her gran and aunts didn't need her like she'd thought they did. She'd realized that pretty quickly. They had been doing just fine without her. Gran's insistence that Caitlin should feel free to put more hours into MacKinnon Bros. Tours only underlined how little the elderly women needed her around the Knit & Pearl.

Caitlin had thought if she came home, she'd finally settle into the one place she belonged on this earth. But maybe she just didn't have one?

LA certainly hadn't been it, but she wouldn't figure out if Cailkirn was if she didn't take the time to build a life here. Not the life given to her by others because she was an orphan child with no other options, but an adult life that she'd put her own effort and commitment into.

Stu had to ring off before Caitlin could tell him she wasn't interested, but she wasn't worried about it. His suggestion had probably been a one off thing anyway that he'd forget by the time his ship was in port.

Caitlin's gaze fell to the bottom right of her computer screen and she noticed one o'clock had come and gone five minutes ago. Ruthlessly crushing the impulse to wait around and see if Malina had left so Caitlin would have a few minutes with Tack before he had to leave for his next tour, she got ready to go.

Once she'd changed into her athletic shoes for the walk

back to the bed-and-breakfast, Caitlin grabbed the string backpack she brought into the office instead of a purse. Wearing it made walking briskly easier, especially with the tourists that crowded the main street's walkway.

Tempted to leave without saying anything, Caitlin could not ignore the ingrained polite behavior taught by her gran, and she called out a *good-bye* to both Tack and his mother before going out the front door of MacKinnon Bros. Tours.

* * *

"Why haven't you brought Caitlin to dinner again, Taqukaq?" his *aana* asked him.

"She's not a piece of luggage for me to cart around, *Aana*. If you want her to come to dinner, invite her." *Please.*

Tack was missing Kitty already, and his self-imposed restriction of his time with her was not even a week old. He didn't like what that said about his feelings for her.

"Don't be silly, son."

"What exactly am I being silly about?"

"Caitlin is yours and always has been."

He laughed darkly at words that weren't anywhere near true. "She was never mine, or she would not have married Nevin Barston. And she's certainly not mine now."

Aana's expression went from patient to patently concerned. "How long are you going to keep punishing her for that mistake? Don't you think the pain that man caused her was enough of a price for her to pay?"

"What are you talking about? I'm not punishing Kitty."

"Are you sure about that, son?"

"Of course." But some tiny voice deep inside asked him

the same thing. Was he punishing them both for choices made when they were too young to see the consequences?

Her for walking away and him for allowing it?

"If that's true, then don't you think you need to stop holding her at arm's length?"

"I don't." But he wasn't about to tell his mom just how closely he held the adorable redhead.

Aana made a dismissive sound. "She needs you, Tack, probably now more than ever. And she's always needed you."

He might have argued that at one time, too, but he couldn't anymore. Not that he was convinced Kitty realized it. She seemed oblivious to how much she needed him and denied that he should have pursued their friendship, rather than giving up.

"I'm ready for grandchildren, Taqukaq."

Tack's gut tied itself in a knot, less from any pressure his mom's words might cause and more from how much they resonated inside him.

He fell back on old explanations, though. "You know I'm too busy building the business to think about looking for a woman to marry."

He ignored the voice in his brain that tried to tell him he'd already found her. Kitty Grant had rejected him once. Giving her the starring role in that dream again would be the height of stupidity. Wouldn't it?

"Your business is doing great. Whatever you needed to prove, my son, you have proven, don't you think?"

He shook his head. "I'm just building a life I can be proud of."

"Your father and I are already proud of you. You should be proud of yourself. Now, it is time to build a *family*. And

you don't have to go looking for the woman to build it with."
Aana gave him a wry look. "She's in your reception area five mornings a week."

Six actually, but he wasn't going to bring that up now. "Kitty and I are just friends, *Aana*."

"Whatever you say, Tack. Just please remember that fooling yourself doesn't mean you're fooling anyone else." His mom stood up and put her arms out. "Give me a hug. I need to pick some things up before I go home."

He did as she asked and then walked her to the door, holding it open for her.

She patted his chest as she walked by. "Don't be too stubborn, son. Nothing good ever comes of denying love."

Despite his best efforts, it was clear his mom was getting her hopes up about Tack and Kitty. But this was not the worst realization he had in that moment. No, it was the knowledge that there was too much truth in *Aana's* words for him to ignore.

The love he'd thought long in the past beat in his heart with all the strength of a mature man's emotions.

And what the hell he was going to do about that, he did not know.

CHAPTER NINETEEN

Tack stormed into MacKinnon Bros. Tours, his mood as dark as an Alaskan winter, only to pull up short when he discovered Kitty still at her desk.

"What the hell are you doing here?"

Her head came up with a snap, blue eyes filling with concern. "Working. What's the matter? I thought you'd enjoy this last hike. You got to take experienced clients out on one of your favorite trails. Did something happen?"

"Something besides Stu telling me you plan to apply for a job with his ship?" Tack snarled.

The damned Australian had been all smiles about the idea, too, promising to give her a good reference. For a price, Tack was damn sure. The man wanted Tack's wildcat.

Kitty's shock was either genuine or she was a hell of a lot better actress than he'd ever thought. "What? No, that's not what I—"

"Are you saying he lied to me?" Other than today, Tack had always liked the man and working with him.

"No."

"Then you are leaving." Tack slammed through to his office.

Her promise to stick around had lasted how many weeks? He knew this was going to happen. And still he'd let himself hope. Did that make him a chump or just terminally stupid?

"I'm not leaving!" Man, Kitty could do volume when she wanted.

She stood in his doorway, vibrating with angry indignation. Her cheeks burned with color, her eyes sparking with fury. "How dare you accuse me of breaking my promise without even talking to me?"

"I did talk to you." He indicated the reception area with a jerk of his head. "In there. You said Stu wasn't lying."

"He wasn't lying that he suggested I try for the job." She stepped into his office, slamming the door behind her, though they were alone in the office. "I didn't agree."

"So, you aren't going to apply?" Tack pushed, his fear-fueled anger not nearly abated.

"Do you *want* me to?" she asked with sharp bite.

"No!"

She stomped over to him in a way that shouldn't be possible in her feminine heels and poked him in the sternum. "Listen here, Taqukaq MacKinnon, I'm not saying it's easy. I'm not even saying I never think of leaving, but I am telling you that when I make a promise, I do my very best to keep it."

"Good."

But she wasn't done. "You may not need me here. My gran and aunts may not need me, but maybe *I* need to be here. Did you ever think of that? Well, did you?"

All the damn time, but the words weren't about to come out. "Who said we don't need you?" he asked, his own voice still gravelly with anger-fueled adrenaline.

"I do."

"You're wrong."

"Am I?" she asked, her blue gaze burning with hope.

"You've made a difference here. Egan is thrilled to have your help. We all are." It was a cop-out but he wasn't ready to share emotions he was still coming to terms with.

Hell, when did a man ever want to talk about his feelings? It sure as hell wasn't a MacKinnon family trait. That was for damn sure.

She glared at him. "There's more to me than my ability to talk on the phone and file."

"I know." To prove it, he pulled her into a heated kiss.

Somehow they were tearing each other's clothes off, all that anger and frustration morphing into volcanic passion. He kissed her in a way that said all the things he wasn't going to and she kissed him back, making promises he wasn't sure she realized she was offering.

They ended up on all fours, his body covering hers, his cock buried deep inside her. They mated like that for interminable minutes, but it wasn't enough. He needed to touch her.

Pulling her back, he balanced on his knees so he was kneeling and she was riding astride him facing away. Taking advantage of the position, he touched her everywhere, playing with her breasts and their sensitive peaks, delving between her lips to rub her clitoris the way she liked.

She screamed his name when she climaxed. He shouted incoherent words of love in Chugach Alutiiq, the language of his mother's people, thankful Kitty had never learned these particular terms.

* * *

Deep in thought, Caitlin descended the stairs slowly on her way to the dining room that evening.

Tack had only dropped her off an hour before. She'd wanted to spend the evening together, but he'd refused, citing plans with his family he couldn't get out of without explanations he couldn't make. Didn't want to make, more like.

She just didn't understand him.

He'd been furious at the thought of her applying for a job that would take her out of Cailkirn, but then maybe that was more to do with not wanting to replace her at MacKinnon Bros. Travel.

No, that was ridiculous. Tack would never get that upset over something business related. Would he?

He didn't make any bones about the fact that his life revolved around his family and his business right now, with no room for a relationship or time to even go looking for one. She knew his business meant more to him than money and success. He had a deep-seated need to prove his worth and had chosen MacKinnon Bros. Tours as the vehicle to do it.

So maybe his anger *had* been about her leaving the tour company.

But the passion they'd shared after their short but loud argument? It had been scorching.

Did a man make love like that to a woman he saw as nothing but a casual sexual fling?

The phone rang as Caitlin walked by the reception desk. She picked it up. "Knit and Pearl Bed-and-Breakfast, may I help you?"

"I doubt very much you can help me. You were never very good at doing it the years we were married."

Caitlin's hand froze on the old-fashioned handset at the sound of a voice she'd hoped to never hear again. "Nevin."

"You recognize my voice."

"Apparently."

"You haven't forgotten me."

"What do you want, Nevin?" She tried to control her breathing, but her inhalations were growing more and more shallow as panic tried to claim her.

"Is that any way to talk to your husband?" he asked in the icy tone that had often meant severe unpleasantness for her.

Caitlin started to shake but did her best not to let that show in her voice. "You aren't my husband anymore, Nevin. You never really were."

"The state of California would disagree."

"Whatever the legal documents said, you failed miserably in the husband arena." She couldn't believe she had the temerity to turn words he'd often thrown in her face back on him, but he wasn't her jailer anymore.

And she refused to forget that truth.

She'd broken free and he wouldn't trap her again, not even in her own mind.

"Bold words for such a weak little slut."

"Two things I never was."

"I beg to differ."

"I don't care. You know what? I don't care what you want either. Call my lawyer if you have something to say to me." Not that she expected the law firm to forward anything to her now that Caitlin no longer had them on retainer for the divorce.

She hung up the phone on his protesting voice.

Not surprised in the least when it rang again, she wanted to ignore it but knew if she didn't answer, her gran or one of her aunts would. Caitlin was no more willing to subject them to Nevin than she ever was.

"Say what you have to say and then stop calling, or I'll file a harassment complaint," she said instead of a greeting.

Only after the words left her mouth did she realize how revealing they would be to someone else if it *wasn't* Nevin on the other end of the line.

"Have you forgotten everything I taught you of manners?" Nevin asked condescendingly.

Relief and disgust flowed together inside her in a confusing emotional mixture. "My gran taught me manners."

"That crazy old bat?"

"Do *not* insult my gran, asshole."

His audible inhalation said she'd scored a direct hit with her blatant disrespect.

"You should take care how you talk to me, Caitlin."

"Why is that?" she asked with sarcasm.

"Who do you think is the principal backer in that little movie deal that's going to put Cailkirn on the map?"

He was behind the fiasco movie deal Carey James had brought to town? Oh, that was funny. It really was. "Cailkirn has been on the map for nearly two hundred years."

"Don't pretend ignorance to what I'm talking about. In a small backwater town like that, a movie production coming to town is going to be the fodder of all the important gossip."

"We don't have the same definition of *important* up here as you and your sycophants do."

"Nevertheless, you do not deny knowledge of the movie production?"

"No."

"Good."

"If you say so."

"Don't be flippant."

"Screw yourself, Nevin. You're the only one who would enjoy it."

She actually smiled at the avalanche of invectives her words instigated. Nevin preferred subtle cruelty to swearing. Caitlin had no use for subtlety with the monster she'd once been married to.

When he wound down, she asked almost calmly, "What exactly are you trying to accomplish here, Nevin?"

He didn't need to know about the sweat making her palms slick, creating wet spots on the back of her blouse and under her arms, or the fine tremors in her fingers.

His initial silence indicated her question shocked him more than her crude suggestion and accusation of sexual deficiency. "You need to realize I still have power in your life."

"No, you really don't." That was one thing she was sure about, something she'd had to fight too hard to make true to give up—ever.

"Are you trying to say you don't care if I pull the funding from this movie deal?"

"Not a bit."

"I don't believe you." But his voice didn't carry its usual arrogant certainty.

"And I *definitely* don't care what you believe."

"That stupid little town is too important to you for that to be true."

"You're assuming I think making a movie here is a good thing."

"Of course it is."

"No."

"Your hometown needs this."

"No." With Nevin, it was better to keep it simple.

"The town is dying."

"In whose deluded imaginings?"

"There are barely more than two thousand permanent residents."

"We have towns in Alaska with a tenth of that population." She sighed, thinking maybe if she laid it out for him, he'd realize his little harangue was hopeless. "This town has lasted centuries without Hollywood. I'm pretty sure it can last at least a few more years the same way."

"You think you have all the answers."

"Honestly, Nevin? I don't know what the questions are supposed to be. I left you more than a year ago. Our divorce finalized months ago. It's over."

"You'd like to believe that."

"I do believe that."

"You owe me."

"You're right. I owe you at least three broken ribs, a fractured wrist and clavicle, countless bruises, a boatload of emotional abuse, too many nights of painful and completely unsatisfying sex, but you know what?"

His silence had a stunned quality to it.

Why shouldn't it? She hadn't stood up to him since their first year together. Even then, she'd been so in awe of his wealth, sophistication, and lifestyle that she'd kept silent about most of the things she didn't like.

"You just don't matter enough for me to want to repay you for all that you *gave* me," she said, throwing back in his face more of the words he'd used to denigrate her so many times.

"You wouldn't be so sanguine if the cruise ships stopped coming to your port."

She wasn't surprised he completely disregarded what

she'd said. That would require acknowledging his own unimportance.

"We're the only port on this side of the peninsula. The cruise ships aren't going anywhere."

"That could change."

"It could." But she wasn't worried about it. That threat had as little power over her as his first one. "However, it would take a much bigger player than you to make it happen. You might be something in LA, but up here? You're nothing, Nevin."

"I have connections—" he started to splutter.

"So do the people of this town. We may be small, but as I've pointed out, we've been here a long time. Whoever you think you've got in your pocket won't go against the interests of their home state and relationships that go back generations, not months."

"Anyone can be bought."

"If that were true, I'd still be in California." Nevin had offered her a great deal of money to drop her petition for the divorce, along with promises to change.

Which this phone call proved had as much substance as his honor. None at all.

"You weren't thinking straight. Your disease had wreaked havoc with your rationality."

"My *disease* was the result of irrationality, not the cause of it."

"Was?" he sneered. "You expect me to believe you're well."

"I don't care what you believe." When would that particular truth penetrate his thick skull?

"You probably still look like a skin-covered skeleton," he scorned. "I don't know why I bothered to call you. No man could get an erection if he had to look at you while fucking you."

She winced at his coarse language. Tack didn't have a lily-white tongue, but he had standards for the words he said around women and children.

"You just keep thinking that." She hung up, done with the conversation, even if he wasn't.

She waited a full minute to see if he called back. If he did, she planned to take the phone off the hook and pretend it was an accident if it was discovered before she put it back in the cradle later.

But Nevin didn't call back.

Breathing a sigh of relief, Caitlin turned to head back upstairs. She needed to change into clothes that weren't sweat soaked.

She stopped short at the sight of Aunt Elspeth.

Caitlin opened her mouth, but she didn't know what to say. How much had the elderly woman heard?

She didn't have to figure it out because her aunt rushed forward and enveloped Caitlin in a warm hug and a cloud of Chanel No°5. "Oh, I'm so proud of you, Kitty dear. You were so strong. I'm sure I would have crumpled under whatever that awful man was saying, but you didn't."

Shocked at her aunt's words, Caitlin didn't reply to them; she just relaxed into the very welcome embrace.

Aunt Elspeth finally pulled away and stepped back. "Come, Alma gets so upset when we're late to the table."

"I need to change my shirt," Caitlin admitted, hoping that bringing attention to the proof of her nerves wouldn't diminish her aunt's pride in her.

For some reason, the emotion was extremely important right now.

"Of course, dear. I'll just tell the others you had a disagreeable potential guest whom you had to turn down, so you're collecting yourself."

"Um…"

"It's not a lie, not really. I'm sure that odious man would like to come up here and see you, but you weren't having any of it."

"I doubt very much Nevin Barston would ever suffer the indignities of travel to such a *backwater* town."

"We can only hope, dear."

Caitlin shared that hope but could not be absolutely certain. It was a sobering realization. She'd been stronger on the phone than she'd known she could be, but how would she respond to her tormenter in the flesh?

There was a reason she'd moved out when he was not in the country.

* * *

"Ten bucks says he got her number," Egan said to Bobby as they came through the back entrance to MacKinnon Bros. Tours.

Caitlin closed the drawer in which she'd been filing paperwork from past excursions and turned to face them as they came into the reception area. "What are you betting on now, Egan?"

Egan stopped short, looking like he'd swallowed a fish… whole. "Oh, hey, Kitty. Thought you were gone already."

"Gran told me to put extra hours in here if I wanted to. She and my aunts just don't need the help everyone thinks they do." And she was hoping to see Tack when he came in from his excursion.

"No kidding. They might be past the age of retirement, but those three are not slowing down," Bobby said with admiration.

"Not that I can tell, no." Caitlin gave the two men as natural a smile as she could. She'd been on edge ever since the call from Nevin the night before. "So, what's the bet?"

"Oh, nothing—" Egan started to say.

Bobby butted in. "There was this hottie flirting like crazy with Tack, even before we got the cruise passengers loaded in the vans. And Tack wasn't exactly freezing her out either. Egan thinks Tack is going to get her number, but I figure he'll just hook up with her. He's got a reputation."

Hot and cold washed over Caitlin in quick succession, leaving her feeling faint. There wasn't a chance she was going to let Tack's brother and cousin see her reaction to their words, though.

Funnily enough, Egan didn't look so hot either.

She forced another smile, this one not remotely genuine. "Oh, does he?"

"You bet." Bobby nodded for emphasis, his grin all masculine approval for another successful hunter. "He's seen the inside of so many cruise ship cabins, he should get frequent flyer miles."

Egan smacked the back of his cousin's head. "Dumb shit."

"What was that for?" Bobby demanded.

Caitlin interjected. "Frequent flyer miles are for airlines, not cruise lines."

Bobby rolled his eyes. "Whatever. You know what I meant."

"Yes, I did."

Bobby glared at Egan. "There. See? I'm not dumb."

"That's not…" Egan looked between Caitlin and his cousin and frowned. "Never mind."

"Do you two have your paperwork and customer satis-faction surveys?" Caitlin asked, with no hint she felt like puking at the thought of Tack flirting with another woman.

A *hottie*, according to Bobby. Probably according to Egan too. After all, he hadn't been betting against Tack and the woman getting together, just that his older brother would get the woman's number.

The guides handed over the paperwork and Caitlin got to work on inputting the customer feedback into the computer. She was still working on it when they left an hour later to take out their second tours for the day.

Tack's would end two hours later, so he didn't have an afternoon tour scheduled. Tonight was one of his open evenings as well.

Regardless of her lack of success the last time she'd asked him, she planned to convince Tack to spend it with her.

While they'd spent the very rare full evening together, he had even been the one to suggest it a couple of times. So, he wasn't against it on principle.

One thing had become resoundingly clear to her in the aftermath of Nevin's call. Her relationship with Tack was nothing like the one she'd had with her ex-husband. Partly because Tack was nothing like Nevin and partly because Caitlin *had* grown stronger.

So many of the obscure emotions that had clouded her in-ner motivations for most of her life were clear now. Caitlin could choose to give in to old pain or fight for new joy.

No matter how the past eight years might have painted her, even to herself, the truest color of her soul was that of a fighter.

Caitlin knew what she wanted and if she didn't ask for it? That was on her. How Tack responded to her needs, *that* was on him.

Something else Caitlin had come to terms with.

Bobby and Egan's *bet* only made it more imperative Caitlin talk things out with Tack. She needed answers to questions she'd just realized she had to ask.

However, as the afternoon wore on and the time for Tack's tour to end came and went, Caitlin's mood grew progressively morose. There could be lots of reasons for him not returning to the tour office, but one of them wasn't that he'd gone straight home. He would have exchanged the tour van for his truck.

Which he could have done without coming into the office, she realized. So, she went out the back door to check the parking lot. Tack's bright red four-by-four was in the same spot it had been that morning when she'd arrived for work.

Caitlin walked back to her desk with thoughts chasing themselves through her head. She and Tack hadn't said they were going to be exclusive. He'd never suggested they go without condoms even after she'd informed him she was on birth control to help even out her hormones.

He'd stopped wanting to see her for sex every night. Was the real reason because he was getting it elsewhere, or planning to do so? Did a man share the kind of passion with a woman that Tack did with her and still look for sexual satisfaction elsewhere?

But she was thinking about Tack. Not any man. If Taqukaq MacKinnon planned to see multiple women for sex, wouldn't he have said so? Tack wasn't dishonest. He didn't hide his motives, not like Nevin.

Which made her initial worries that he wanted to cut back on their nights together for any other reason than the one he stated a little irrational, didn't it?

But then she never would have considered Tack capable of cheating. Only, could it be called that when the sexual relationship between them was unequivocally no-strings?

Not really a relationship at all. Not something that could be *cheated* on.

She didn't want to think Tack would do that to her, but would he see it the same way?

They had a sex-for-eating deal that he'd gone to great lengths to make sure she understood was casual and had no hope of being anything else. No emotional commitments. No expectations or hopes of a future together.

Now that she thought about it, was there even a point in having the discussion she'd planned? She'd wanted to talk to Tack about the call from Nevin as well, as a friend, but were they even that?

The potential answers to those questions hurt too much for Caitlin to keep dwelling on them. Though she wasn't sure she could stop.

At least now she had her answer to *where* he got his casual sex partners in the summer when he was too busy to go to Anchorage. Women from the cruise ships.

Her stomach roiled.

The prospect of *her* Taqukaq having sex right that minute with some faceless, nameless woman in her cabin on one of the huge cruise ships in the harbor filled Caitlin with dread. Acid churned with increasing intensity inside her as image after image of Tack with another woman invaded her brain.

It didn't matter that they were just her imagination, that she didn't know if he'd taken the woman up on her obvious intention to offer. Caitlin's stomach rebelled like it hadn't in months and soon she was rushing to the toilet, where she was sick for the first time since coming to Cailkirn.

The uncontrollable nausea scared her more than the prospect of seeing Nevin face-to-face did. Because while she'd still struggled with eating enough, Caitlin *had* managed to control this part of her eating disorder since before coming back to Alaska.

The prospect she was backsliding sent her into a full-blown panic attack, which brought on another bout of dry heaves along with all the other symptoms at debilitating levels.

She didn't know how long it took her to bring herself back under control, but eventually her stomach stopped seizing. Her breathing returned to a semblance of normal, but every muscle in her body ached from involuntary contractions.

She'd managed to get herself into a sitting position against the wall when she heard noises in the outer office. Had Tack come back finally?

Unwilling to be caught in such a state, she pulled herself together. Drawing a mental barrier around emotions too raw to share with a man who showed no interest in revealing his own, she stood up and washed her face with cold water. There was nothing she could do about her pale face or the haunted look in her eyes, though.

The sound of Egan's and Bobby's voices came through the bathroom door. A sense of reprieve mixed with acute disappointment inside her. Regardless of both, she prayed the men would leave without realizing she was still there.

She'd locked the front door and dropped the blinds already, since technically no one was supposed to be in the office to handle walk-ins and she knew she'd get more work done without random interruptions.

From potential clients or locals stopping in to say hello.

The sound of the back door closing indicated her hopes had been answered. Cautiously opening the bathroom door, she looked out to an office cast in shadow by the blind-covered windows and turned out lights.

Caitlin went to her desk and discovered another stack of survey forms filled out along with the paperwork from the afternoon's tours. She might as well take care of them now.

Caitlin wasn't waiting for Tack to come back for his truck.

She wasn't.

She couldn't even pretend to believe the lie an hour later when she'd finished with the input and filed the paperwork.

Collapsing into her chair, she stared at the computer screen. What was she going to do?

Could she keep *seeing* Tack when he was having sex with other people? No. Not even a remote possibility.

She couldn't be sure he *was* seeing other women, though. Part of her simply refused to believe Tack would go from her to another woman, no matter what his reputation was, no matter how many random hookups he usually had with different women during tourist season.

But even if there was a reason for him not to have come back for his truck, other than taking the *hottie* up on the invitation Egan and Bobby were so sure she'd make, that didn't mean he loved, or ever would love, Caitlin.

Needing an answer to at least one question roiling through her mind, Caitlin picked up the phone off her desk and called Tack's cell.

CHAPTER TWENTY

He picked up on the third ring. "What do you need, Egan? I'm busy."

She tried to talk, but nothing came out except air.

"Egan, damn it, I'm with someone."

"It's Caitlin." Her voice came out low, but at least she got the words past her tight throat.

"Kitty? What are you still doing in the office? Do you need a ride home? I'm pretty sure Da's still in town. He was picking up some stuff for Gran."

"I don't need a ride." She didn't comment on the fact that Tack was obviously too busy to pick her up himself.

"Okay."

The silence stretched and she realized he was waiting for her to tell him why she called.

"I called because—"

"Look, it wouldn't be a good idea to get together tonight."

Each word felt like the sharp stab of a stiletto blade,

but she wasn't taking anything for granted, no matter how damning the implications of his conversation so far.

"I need to know the parameters of our *non*relationship," she forced out, not really caring if she was putting him in an awkward situation.

"Right now isn't a good time to talk about this."

"Just answer one thing."

"Kit—"

"Are we having sex with other people?"

"You want to have sex with someone else?" he yelled.

He wouldn't sound so upset if *he* was with another woman, would he? Some men had double standards about that kind of thing. Women, too, she was sure. But not Tack. She wouldn't believe it of him.

She let out a little breath of relief. "That's not what I said."

"Then what the hell is this about?" he demanded.

"Egan and Bobby said there was a hottie after you in your tour group today."

He swore. "Hold on a second, Kitty." She heard muffled words as he spoke to whoever he was with and then he said, "I'm back."

"Okay." She didn't know what else to say.

"I didn't take Lisa up on her very blatant offer."

"Why?"

"Because I would never disrespect you that way."

"But what we're doing, it's just casual, right?"

"Is that what you want?"

"It's what you said it could be. You don't want anyone to know."

"You know why."

"Yes." Because he didn't want their families getting their hopes up for something that would never happen.

Her heart cracked just a little more.

"Listen, even if it's just friends with benefits, we are friends and I wouldn't hook up with another woman before we both knew exactly what to expect in that regard."

"That doesn't make me feel any better," she admitted with more honesty than she wanted to give, but not as much as she could have.

"Look, Kitty, I don't need sex with anyone else."

"But we're not doing it every night now."

"I don't know what my brother told you—"

"Bobby's the one who said you're a cruise ship Casanova."

"Nice. Little shit. Anyway, cruise season is busy as hell and I don't have the inclination or energy to go for more than one hookup a week, if that."

"Oh." Even cutting back, they were having sex significantly more often than that.

"Are we okay on this now?"

"What reason did you give the hottie for not taking her up on her offer?"

"She wasn't that hot, wildcat. Sure as hell didn't turn me on like you do."

"Good." Caitlin waited in silence for him to answer her question.

"I told her maybe some other time," he said in a frustrated tone. "Are you happy now?"

"Not really, no."

"What did you want me to say? That I have a casual sex partner already?"

"No." But what else could he have said? "Never mind, Tack. I need to get to the Knit and Pearl."

"Look, I'll pick you up at the usual time tonight."

For another casual hookup? "No."

"What? Why not?"

"You want to come to dinner with my family?"

"You know I don't come to the B and B for dinner during tourist season; besides, I have plans tonight."

With his family. "Cancel them."

"I don't like ultimatums, Kitty."

"Me neither." But what else had he been giving her since he offered the first kiss if she'd eat lunch? "I'll talk to you later, Tack."

"Wait, Kitty—"

"Just go back to whoever you're with."

He let out a frustrated breath. "We'll talk tomorrow."

"Take care," she said, not agreeing one way or another.

"Get some sleep tonight, sweetheart. You're going to need a clear head for our discussion." He cut the connection before she could reply.

That didn't mean she was going to do what he said. Get sleep—she wasn't sure that was possible, or talk to him tomorrow.

She wasn't ready. When they talked, she was pretty sure she'd have to break off their sexual relationship. And as much as it hurt to be in it, it was going to devastate her to end it.

But it wouldn't destroy her. She didn't think. Caitlin had to step back before she got to a place where it would.

* * *

Tack stomped back into the house where he'd left Cian hanging in his great room. "That was Kitty."

"I figured."

Tack grimaced. "Yeah."

"Bad call?"

"Egan and Bobby opened their big mouths about a woman on my tour today who was looking for another notch in her cruise cabin bedpost."

"Pissed?" Cian asked in that cryptic way he had.

"Kitty was something. She wanted to get together."

"Now."

"Yes."

Cian frowned. "You told her no."

"Yeah. I need to think things through and it's not my big head I'm thinking with when she's around."

"Bullshit."

"What?"

"Your heart, not your dick."

Shit, Cian was right. "She was all about how the sex is just casual."

"Then why call?" Cian's tone implied Tack was stupid.

"I don't know. I told her we could get together later. She refused."

Cian shook his head. "Idiot."

"Hell, I asked you over to talk this out, not have you call me names."

"You want my opinion?"

"Yes."

"You screwed up."

"Thanks, that's helpful," Tack said sarcastically.

"You're welcome."

"How did I screw up?"

"She wanted more, you refused her."

Tack stared at his cousin. The man didn't get verbose unless he was drunk, but the few words he spoke were profound sometimes. This was one of them.

"Well, shit. You're right."

"Often am."

"Don't get cocky."

"When a man's got reason…" Cian let the words trail off, his meaning clear.

Tack managed a laugh despite the tightness in his chest. "I told her we'd talk tomorrow."

"Stupid."

"Yeah, I'm starting to get that. I should just go over to the B and B and talk to her." Only if he was wrong, if the more Kitty wanted wasn't the more Tack needed, he didn't want the whole town knowing she'd rejected him.

Again.

"Kitty's stubborn." Cian took a swig off his longneck.

"You think I should give her time to cool off." She hadn't sounded angry, though.

"No." Cian looked at Tack like he was a few eggs short of an omelet. "She'll dig her heels in deeper."

"She didn't sound mad."

Cian dismissed that with a flip of his hand. "Why'd she call from the office?"

"She never said."

"She waited for you."

Shit. "You're right." She'd waited for him. She'd told him no to sex but made it clear she wanted to see him for dinner.

Even if the more she wanted wasn't everything he needed, it was about more than sex and he'd screwed up, big-time.

"What are you going to do?"

"Go to the Knit and Pearl."

Cian's expression turned smug. "Thought so."

"Don't be a know-it-all shit."

"Wasting time arguing with me."

Tack was still muttering about his cousin's attitude when he started his truck and peeled out of his drive. Cian would close the house up.

Tack arrived at the Knit & Pearl before dinner and went in through the front door, wanting to see Kitty first if possible. Miss Elspeth was sitting at the reception desk.

That was unusual this time of night. She'd normally be in the parlor entertaining the guests before dinner.

"Good evening, Miss Elspeth," Tack said.

She jumped as if startled, then looked at him like he was one of the apparitions the sisters claimed haunted the B&B. "Oh! Well, hello, Tack."

He'd been quiet coming in, not wanting to alert the people in the parlor to his presence until he figured out if Kitty was in there with them. But he hadn't been silent.

"Is everything okay, Miss Elspeth?"

The older woman looked down at the phone like it was a snake and then back up to Tack. "I don't know. I really don't. I was so proud of her. She stood right up to him, but she's not doing well today. I thought standing up to him was good for her, but she said she wasn't hungry...was going to bed early. That's not good, is it? I'm not going to let her answer the phone again. If he calls, he'll get an earful from me."

"Miss Elspeth, who are you talking about?"

"Nevin Barston." She said like his name was a curse.

Tack's jaw locked. "He called?"

"Last night." Miss Elspeth nodded. "She handled it so well."

"But she's not doing as good today?"

"Oh no. I don't understand it. Do you think he called her at MacKinnon Bros. Tours today too?"

"No way for Barston to know she's working for us."

"He's evil."

Tack wasn't going to argue that, but it didn't make the man omniscient. "Where is she?"

"Up in her room."

"You go visit with your guests. I'll make sure Kitty doesn't take any upsetting phone calls."

"If he calls again, you'll tell him what for, won't you?"

"He'll know not to call again."

"Oh, thank you." Miss Elspeth headed to the parlor.

Tack climbed the stairs, knowing Kitty's room would be the same one she'd had as a child. Miz Moya had told him they'd never used it for guests, not in all the years Kitty had been in California.

He knocked firmly on her door but was unsurprised when she didn't answer.

The knob turned easily in his hand, though, and he pushed the door open. "It's me, Kitty."

Her light was off and the sun-blocking shades were over the window, but he could make out the shape of a Kitty-sized lump in the center of the bed.

"Come on, wildcat. I know you're not asleep."

"Go away."

"Not going to happen."

He flipped the wall switch, flooding the room with light from the overhead fixture.

Kitty lay curled around her pillow, glaring up at him, her eyes red from crying, and he felt like the biggest asshole ever.

Then he recognized her nightgown and it wasn't red lace. "You stole one of my shirts?"

"You haven't missed it."

"No, but I've been missing you."

She was up and out of the bed in a flash, stomping right up to him so she could poke him in the chest. She liked doing that. "Don't lie to me, Taqukaq MacKinnon."

"You're not skipping dinner, Kitty."

"You can't tell me what to do." She poked him with every other word.

"We've got a deal."

Her eyes narrowed even farther and Tack wondered why Nevin Barston wasn't scared as hell of this wildcat. "You can take your deal and stick it right up your as—"

He didn't let her finish, grabbing the hand pointing at Tack and using it to yank her to him so he could kiss her. She resisted for about two seconds and then she went up like dry tinder, throwing herself into the kiss with an angry passion that gave him hope.

They were both breathing heavily when he pulled back. "We are going downstairs and having dinner with your gran and aunts. You can wear my shirt or put on some clothes. Either way, you are coming with me."

"Don't you think they'll know there's something between us when I come to the table in your shirt and it's only over your shoulder?" she demanded in a nasty tone that gave him an inexplicable urge to grin.

"They're going to figure it out when I tell them you're coming home with me and not coming back until after work tomorrow."

"What?" Kitty demanded, her voice going high.

"You heard me."

"But we're a big secret."

"Not after tonight we aren't."

"What if I don't go home with you?"

"Won't matter. The secret's already out."

"What do you mean?"

"I called *Aana* on the way here to tell her I wouldn't be coming for dinner at the Homestead."

"So?"

"I told her why."

Kitty's eyes went wide and her pretty mouth parted on a surprised sigh. "So you could come see me?"

"Yep."

"But I don't think I can keep seeing you," she wailed.

"Because Nevin called?" What had that bastard said to her?

"Because I threw up this afternoon."

He tried to process what that meant, but it wasn't coming together. He needed more information. "Why did you get sick?"

"You didn't come back to the office after your tour."

"I was talking to Cian."

"But I thought you might be with *her*."

"Who?"

"The *hottie*!"

Hell, he'd forgotten all about his brother's big mouth when Miss Elspeth told Tack about the phone call from Barston. "I wasn't," he growled out.

"You told her *maybe some other time*."

"It's an easy way to let someone down. She knew we weren't going to ever see each other again."

"You didn't freeze her out, Bobby said."

Bobby and Egan were going to get an earful from Tack, and a punch in the jaw apiece if he didn't get things worked out with Kitty tonight. "She was a client. I don't make it a practice to offend people on my tours."

Kitty shoved herself away from Tack. "Get out."

"I'm not going anywhere." Where the hell had this emotional, all-over-the-place woman come from?

He kind of liked it. Hell, maybe he even loved it. This was Kitty like he'd never seen her.

"Oh, yes, you are." She crossed her arms under her chest, causing him to have completely inappropriate thoughts for the topic at hand. "I don't want to be your pity sex *project* anymore!"

Where the hell did she come up with this stuff? "Pity is the last thing I feel for you."

"But you do see me as a project. Something you need to *fix*," she spat.

"Hell no. You've done a great job of fixing yourself."

"Liar!"

"I'm not. Sure, at first I used that to justify giving in to the desire that's ridden me for a good portion of my life, but, Kitty, you're the one who got you better. Not me."

"I've eaten better since we started having sex," she said like an accusation.

"I *would* be lying if I said that didn't make me happy, but it in no way diminishes what you've done to get yourself better."

"My therapist thinks our relationship is unhealthy for me." Kitty glowered at him triumphantly.

"You're seeing a therapist?"

"Dr. Hart, from California. We Skype."

"Damn, sweetheart, every time I think you can't, you impress me even more."

"You're impressed I'm talking to my therapist again?"

"Hell yes."

"You don't think it means I'm still sick?"

"I think it means you are determined not to be sick any longer."

"You're right," she grumbled, like she didn't want to admit it. "I *don't* want to let the eating disorder rule me ever again."

"And you won't."

"That's why we have to stop this thing between us."

"You're right."

She stared at him like he'd stabbed her. "I am?"

"Yes. No more casual sex."

"Right." She stepped back. "No more sex."

"Like hell."

"What? You're confusing me, Tack."

Welcome to his world. "We'll have plenty of sex, but we're both going to stop lying and pretending it's anything but serious."

"Are you saying you love me?"

"Are you saying you don't love me?" he tossed back at her.

She opened and closed her mouth several times, no words coming out.

"Right. Neither of us is ready for declarations, but we're both ready to stop hiding."

"No."

"No?"

"If we can't say it, we're still hiding." She sounded pretty sure of that.

He grinned. "Well, then I guess we'll have to say it."

"Don't joke about it." Her eyes went misty. "It's too important."

Yeah, it really was. "Who said I was joking?"

She spun around and grabbed a pair of jeans off the floor.

They must have been the ones she'd been wearing earlier. Leaving them on the floor like that showed the emotional state she'd been in.

His wildcat was a neatnik.

She yanked the jeans on. "Let's go eat dinner."

"You going to leave my shirt on?"

She was swimming in it, the collar dipping to reveal one clavicle bone. The soft washed cotton didn't hide the fact she wasn't wearing a bra, but he sure as hell didn't mind.

"Yes." She glared up at him defiantly, daring him to argue with her.

"Okay, then." He swept her up in his arms. "Let's go have some of your gran's award-winning cooking."

"You're carrying me again."

"I like doing it. Besides, you aren't wearing any shoes."

"Aunt Alma's going to have a fit. I'm not supposed to come to the table without shoes."

"She'll forgive you this one time, I'm sure."

"Only if Aunt Elspeth told them about the call from Nevin."

"What did he say?"

"He wanted me to know he still had power in my life," she said with disdain, and then told him about the rest of the call.

"What a tool."

"That's what I thought." She sighed. "I'm worried he might actually come up here to try his intimidation tactics in person."

"I hope he does."

"You can't!"

"Oh, hell yes, I do."

"Why?"

"I owe that man a beatdown that may or may not leave him walking without the aid of a cane."

"No, Tack. That's not the way to handle this."

"Wildcat, you handle things your way and I'll handle them mine."

She smacked him on the chest with the side of her fist. "I mean it, Tack. No fighting."

He wasn't making any promises like that. "What did Miz Moya make for dinner? You know I'm missing Gran's Cock-a-Leekie soup and *Aana's* fry bread to go with it."

"You could have eaten with your family."

"No, Kitty, I couldn't."

She sighed and subsided against him, her head resting against his chest when he carried her into the dining room.

The guests looked up from the long table, different levels of shock or disapproval showing on their faces. The Grant sisters didn't appear surprised in the least, though, or upset by Kitty's state of haphazard dress, her lateness to the table, or that Tack was carrying her.

Miz Alma harrumphed. "Finally."

"You have taken your own sweet time working things out between you." Miss Elspeth giggled.

"Yes, dear. They *do* make a lovely couple," Miz Moya said to her invisible companion, and then she beamed at Tack and Kitty.

There were two open seats together, complete with place settings, between her and her youngest sister-in-law, clearly left for him and Kitty.

He settled his wildcat next to her aunt Elspeth before taking the chair beside her gran. "Dinner smells delicious."

"It's Elspeth's venison stew."

"My favorite."

"We know."

"How did you know I'd be here for dinner?"

"I wasn't just sitting there waiting for a call, Tack," Miss Elspeth said with one of her gentle smiles. "I would have made one of my own if necessary."

"You knew I'd come."

"Of course we did, dear boy," Miss Elspeth replied, including her sister and sister-in-law in the claim. "You didn't really think we didn't know about the nights you came and got our Kitty to take to visit at your house, did you?"

Well, hell. "I shouldn't have. I can see that now."

Miz Alma nodded as if he were finally showing some sense.

Tack smiled at Kitty. "Your family is every bit as meddlesome as my mom."

"Don't say that like it's a bad thing," Miz Moya admonished. "Your mother is an excellent matchmaker."

CHAPTER TWENTY-ONE

Unable to comprehend how she'd gotten here, with plans to spend the night with her gran's approval no less, Caitlin stared into the empty fireplace of Tack's great room. The pristine grate had no answers for the thoughts darting like fireflies around her brain.

"Did you want a fire?" Tack, darn him, lounged on the sectional as if he didn't have a worry in the world.

Maybe he didn't.

She shrugged.

"No."

She turned to face him, her gaze skittering away from his after a brief encounter. "No, what?"

"No shrugs. No this-doesn't-matter shit. Do you want a fire or not, Kitty?"

"Sheesh. Does it really matter?" He chose the strangest things to get upset about.

"Yes, Caitlin Elizabeth, everything about you matters to

me. If you haven't figured that out by now, you're not paying attention."

"Grant," she whispered nonsensically, his words reverberating through her mind, shaking the very foundation of her certainties.

Only, when he used her full name, he always added the *Grant*.

"Not for long."

"What?"

"You're not going to be a Grant for much longer." His tone was so very serious.

All the air whooshed out of her lungs and her knees just went to rubber. Caitlin plopped down on the raised hearth, rubbing the goose bumps on her arms, not sure if they were from chill or shock.

Maybe both.

"Well?" he asked.

She stared at him, every thought in her brain frozen by that claim. Was he asking her for an answer to his proposal? Was it a proposal?

"Do you want a fire?" he clarified.

Relieved the question was back to the mundane, she said, "You'll be too warm."

"I'll strip down to my shorts. It won't be a hardship."

Not for her either. "Okay."

He got up and came across the floor space to where she sat and dropped to his haunches in front of her. "We're going to figure this out, Kitty."

"It sounds like you think you already know what's going to happen."

"I know what I want to happen and I'm going to fight like hell to make sure it does."

It was fair warning, but unnecessary. "I'm not stupid enough to give up everything I could ever want a second time."

"You're not stupid at all."

"I was." She swallowed, trying to hold back the emotion that threatened to spill over.

He cupped her nape and leaned forward so their foreheads touched. "We both have to let the past go, sweetheart."

She nodded against him, her heart so full she couldn't speak.

He squeezed her neck and then leaned back. "Let me get this fire started, Kitty. Then we'll talk."

Words trembled on her lips, but he put his finger against her mouth, like he knew. She nodded in silent agreement to wait.

He lifted the lid on the wood-box built into the stone base of the raised hearth and pulled out everything he needed to get a cheery blaze going. When he was finished, the heat warming her faster than she expected, he stood and stripped his shirt and jeans like he'd said he would.

His body naked but for the dark knit boxers inspired lust, but the love pouring through her was about a million times stronger.

He put his hand out to her. "Come on, we'll sit on the couch, okay?"

She let him lead her to the sectional, where they ended up cuddled and facing the fire, her own jeans gone along the way. His shirt and her panties her only clothing. And somehow that was just right.

Like this was where she belonged every night before joining him in the big bed upstairs.

"I didn't want to love you," she admitted.

He went stiff beside her. So, not so relaxed, then. "Then or now?"

"Both, but for different reasons." She laced her fingers into his, needing the additional contact.

He rubbed his thumb over the top of her hand. "You loved me anyway."

She stared up at him. "How did you know?"

"I didn't, but I guessed. Once I realized why you really left Cailkirn, a lot of things started making sense. They still hurt like hell, but I understood better."

She didn't tell him she hadn't meant to hurt him. He knew and it didn't matter, because she had. She'd hurt them both so much. "Everything was muddled in my head."

"You wanted to live out your parents' dreams for them."

He understood her like no one else ever had, or ever could. "They were gone. Somebody had to."

"No, Kitty. They already did it. They moved to Arizona. They built a life. They had you. They got their dreams. It's time you got yours."

"That's what Dr. Hart says."

"She's a smart lady."

"Mmm." Kitty nuzzled into Tack's chest. "You scared me. If I didn't let myself love you, you couldn't be taken away."

"But then you pushed me away yourself."

"Like I said, stupid."

"Confused. Hell, Kitty. If only I'd known. If any of us had realized how much you were still hurting, how you made Cailkirn the reason for your pain and not the loss."

"So, I just kept losing because everything... *everyone* I needed was here."

"We still are."

Tears were leaking from her eyes and she let them. "You're the only person I've ever felt safe enough with to cry."

"You're the only woman whose tears don't make me want to run for the hills." He sounded aggrieved by that fact.

She giggled and wiped at her eyes. "Today scared me."

"We almost screwed it up again."

"I'm glad we didn't."

"Me too, sweetheart." He kissed the top of her head. "Me too."

"I didn't think I could do love and marriage."

"I was determined not to consider either with you."

"We were both wrong." She tilted her head back so their gazes met again, his filled with emotion that she realized had always been there. "Right?"

"Yes. I love you, Caitlin Elizabeth."

His words stole her breath, the very ones her heart needed more than anything. "Even after everything?"

"Especially after everything. More now than before. The love I had for you back then was the emotion of a young boy. I wanted the perfect Kitty Grant you showed to the rest of the world."

"And now?"

"Now I want the woman who doesn't always make sense, who gets mad when I don't expect, and who apologizes for things that aren't her fault so my mom won't feel bad, who has messy emotions and turns me inside out with her sensuality."

A band that had constricted her heart for nearly a decade loosened and fresh emotion flowed through, filling her with joy like she'd never known. "You mean that?"

"Every word."

She climbed over his lap, straddling him so they were

face-to-face and then cupped his cheeks with both her hands. "I love you, Taqukaq, with every tiny bit of my heart and I always have. I'll never deny it to myself or to you again. I promise."

"Thank God." And it was a prayer.

The kiss they shared was profound and flavored with tears and commitment. The lovemaking that came after was intense and deeply emotional.

When he was buried deep inside her, their gazes locked, words of love fell from his lips to hers, and she returned them, affirming feelings that had been denied for too many years over and over again until they both came with shouts of love.

* * *

Tack carried a tray with breakfast into his bedroom, the sight of Kitty in his bed glowing in the morning light so amazing, he had to concentrate to keep breathing.

She rolled onto her back, her eyes opening, their blue so bright they looked like a reflection of the summer sky.

The most beautiful smile he had ever seen took over her features. "Good morning, Tack."

"Morning, sweetheart." He set the tray on the table beside the bed, picked up the ring sitting between their coffee cups, and climbed in beside her.

He loved the way she rolled right into his body and rubbed against him with the affection of the kitten she'd been nicknamed. "This is so wonderful. I wanted it so bad."

"Me too, even if I wouldn't let myself think about it."

She grinned up at him. "I'm not the only one who was a little too good at denying my feelings."

"No, you aren't."

"We have to talk about them sometimes. You do realize that, right?"

"Yes. But only with you."

"Our children may want to come to you sometimes for emotional advice or support."

"Our children?" he asked, wondering if she realized what she was offering.

"I'll have to gain a few more pounds, but the doctors said there should be no problem with conception or carrying to term. At least no more trouble than any other woman might have."

Relief flooded through him. "I didn't know."

The information he'd read on eating disorders and pregnancy was varied, not that he'd admitted a personal interest in the issue himself at the time.

Kitty grinned, offering her heart and her future right there for him to share, to shelter and to protect, even if she didn't realize it. "How many do you want?"

"Before I answer that question, I have one for you." He shouldn't be nervous. Not after last night, but he was.

"Yes?" she asked, her expression so guileless, he got the feeling she really didn't know what he was about to ask.

Of course, they'd been talking like it was a done deal since last night. And it was mostly his doing, but they were doing this right. From start to finish.

He rolled onto his side so they were looking right into each other's eyes. "My gran always told me she believed every soul has its mate, but not everyone is blessed enough to meet theirs."

"She and your granddad fit like two parts of one whole," Kitty agreed.

"So do we."

Kitty's eyes misted and he didn't think he'd ever get used to her showing this vulnerability to him. "We do. We always have."

"Since we were six years old."

"The first time I thought of being your wife, I think I was eight and someone had just gotten married in town. You were the only person I could imagine sharing my room with." She laughed. "My concept of sharing was very different back then."

"You never said."

She nodded. "If you'll remember, talking about the future wasn't something I did a lot of, not as a child, not as a teenager, not as a young woman."

He'd noticed back then, but he'd just chalked that up to being Kitty. Now he understood that she hadn't trusted the future enough to talk about it.

"We're going to be doing a lot of planning for the future."

"Yes, we are."

"Starting with this." He lifted the diamond ring he'd bought ten years ago and never shown another soul. Until this moment. "Will you marry me, Caitlin Elizabeth?"

She gasped, her eyes rounded and watered, and then she was hugging him so hard he could barely breathe. "Of course I will. You're the other half of my soul, Taqukaq. Always and forever."

"I love you, Kitty."

"I love you too. So much," she choked out with a happy laugh as he put the engagement ring on her finger.

They kissed until making love became an inevitability.

Still breathing harshly, he rubbed his hand up and down her back. "Four."

"On a scale of what? Because I'd give it a twelve and a half at least."

He laughed, thrilled he would be sharing his life with a woman who was going to fill his days with emotion and humor and incendiary love. "Four children."

"Are you kidding?" she asked with wide eyes, her voice going into that high register that warned him his emotional wildcat was a second from showing herself.

"Not even a little. Da and *Aana* raised three all right."

"But four? We don't live with your parents like they lived with your grandparents."

"Technically you don't live here yet at all."

"And I won't officially move in until after the wedding. Gran would have a fit." Kitty snuggled closer as if that would take away the sting of her words.

He didn't want to upset her gran, but he wasn't waiting any longer for Kitty to move into the house he'd built for her. "If we fax the application to Anchorage today, we can pick up the marriage license on Monday."

"You have tours on Monday," she said without a word for how fast he wanted to move.

"I'll get someone to cover for me." He had a network of friends in the guide community, and as much as he hated putting his business in someone else's hands, this was worth it.

"I take it you don't want a big wedding?" she asked in a tone that said she didn't mind that one bit.

"If you mean big production?" He shuddered in revulsion. "No. If you mean a lot of guests, I figure we can say our vows on the back porch of the Homestead. The clearing will hold a good five hundred easy."

She gasped, her face paling. "Five hundred?"

"Sure. We don't have to invite the whole town."

"Just most of it."

"Don't exaggerate."

She jerked away from him and sat up. "Now, you listen here, Taqukaq MacKinnon. One, we are not having four children until I'm sure I can do a good job parenting the first two. Then we'll talk. Second, we are not inviting *five hundred* people to a last-minute wedding!"

"Deal on the kids." His wildcat would be an amazing mom, but if she wanted to stop at two, hell if she wanted to stop at one, he wasn't going to be a bastard about it.

That wasn't Tack's way, but he was pretty sure they'd end up with four like he wanted. Kitty Grant-almost-MacKinnon had a helluva lot of love to give.

"And the wedding?" she asked suspiciously.

"We'll ask your aunts and my mom and grandmothers."

"That's as good as guaranteeing a thousand guests show up, not just five hundred."

"It'll be fine."

"We won't be able to get married until the end of the season." She didn't sound very happy about that.

Good. Because he wasn't waiting for her to move in for another five months. "No. If it means waiting, we'll elope to Anchorage and come home with the deed done. Our families can throw a reception after the season is over."

"Gran and my aunts would be hurt. So would your family. Every one of the MacKinnons expects to watch you say your vows."

"So, they come with us to Anchorage."

"That's ridiculous."

"Not."

She huffed and crossed her arms over her chest. "You're stubborn."

"Yeah, *I'm* the stubborn one."

"I don't know what to do."

"I think you've forgotten how good our Knit and Pearl Club and the Northern Lights Service Club are at putting on a party. They have social gatherings every month in the fall and winter. They've got this thing down."

"They're not wedding planners."

"They might as well be. Everyone knows their primary function is to see the younger generation married off."

"I don't believe it."

"Trust me." He pushed her back on the bed and hovered over her. "Please, wildcat."

"Okay," she agreed breathlessly.

He didn't expect it always to be this easy, but then if it were, life would be boring.

In love with the most beautiful woman in Alaska, not to mention the most stubborn, Tack was damn sure his never would be.

* * *

There were seven hundred and fifty guests at the Grant-MacKinnon wedding exactly one week after Tack's wildcat agreed to be his wife. Kitty and Tack spoke their vows on the back porch of the MacKinnon Homestead and the Northern Lights Service Club hosted a potluck reception afterward at their hall with the help of the Knit & Pearl Club.

Kitty wore white with her red curls in a mass over her shoulders. Tack wore an Inuit ceremonial necklace and a kilt in the MacKinnon tartan with his nicest hiking boots.

The bride wasn't the only one with tears in her eyes when they spoke their vows, and Tack wasn't the only man wearing a grin that rivaled the brightness of fresh snow under the winter sun.

At the reception, the matchmakers turned their attention to another town son.

Oh, Rock Jepsom's parents might not have originally been from Cailkirn, but the man had the right heart for the town. When he was around that lady movie director, they generated enough electricity to heat the town in the dead of winter too.

The Grant sisters pulled Malina MacKinnon aside and started plotting.

It would only be a matter of time before there was another wedding in Cailkirn, if they had anything to say about it.

And then the babies would come.

When a Hollywood movie crew arrives in
Cailkirn, Alaska, property owner Rock
Jepsom refuses to cooperate—until he meets
the film's star, a hometown beauty
named Deborah Banes...

Look for *Hot Night*,
Book 2 of the Northern Lights
series, in January 2016.

Fall in Love with Forever Romance

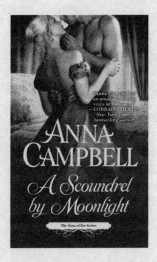

A SCOUNDREL BY MOONLIGHT
by Anna Campbell

Justice. That's all Nell Trim wants—for the countless young women the Marquess of Leath has ruined with his wildly seductive ways. But can she can resist the scoundrel's temptations herself? Check out this fourth sensual historical romance in the Sons of Sin Regency series from bestselling author Anna Campbell!

SINFULLY YOURS
by Cara Elliott

Secret passions are wont to lead a lady into trouble... The second rebellious Sloane sister gets her chance at true love in the next Hellions of High Street Regency romance from bestselling author Cara Elliott.

Fall in Love with Forever Romance

A GOOD ROGUE IS HARD TO FIND
by Kelly Bowen

The rogue's life has been good to William Somerhall, until he moves in with his mother and her paid companion, Miss Jenna Hughes. To keep the eccentric dowager duchess from ruin, he'll have to keep his friends close—and the tempting Miss Hughes closer still. Fans of Sarah MacLean and Tessa Dare will fall in love with the newest book in Kelly Bowen's Lords of Worth series!

WILD HEAT
by Lucy Monroe

The days may be cold, but the nights are red-hot in *USA Today* bestselling author Lucy Monroe's new Northern Fire contemporary romance series. Kitty Grant decides that the best way to heal her broken heart is to come back home. But she gets a shock when she sees how sexy her childhood friend Tack has become. Before she knows it, they're reigniting sparks that could set the whole state of Alaska on fire.

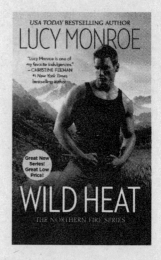

Fall in Love with Forever Romance

SUGAR ON TOP
by Marina Adair

It's about to get even sweeter in Sugar! When scandal forces Glory Mann to co-chair the Miss Sugar Peach Pageant with sexy single dad Cal MacGraw, sparks fly. Fans of Carly Phillips, Rachel Gibson, and Jill Shalvis will love the latest in the Sugar, Georgia series!

A MATCH MADE
ON MAIN STREET
by Olivia Miles

When Anna Madison's high-end restaurant is damaged by a fire, there's only one place she can cook: her sexy ex's diner kitchen. But can they both handle the heat? The second book of the Briar Creek series is "sure to warm any reader's heart" (*RT Book Reviews* on *Mistletoe on Main Street*).

Fall in Love with Forever Romance

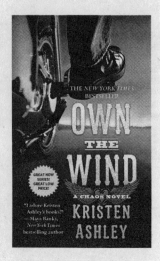

OWN THE WIND
by Kristen Ashley

Only $5.00 for a limited time! Tabitha Allen is everything Shy Cage has ever wanted, but everything he thinks he can't have. When Tabby indicates she wants more—*much* more—than friendship, he feels like the luckiest man alive. But even lucky men can crash and burn...The first book in the Chaos series from *New York Times* bestselling author Kristen Ashley!

FIRE INSIDE
by Kristen Ashley

Only $5.00 for a limited time! When Lanie Heron propositions Hop Kincaid, all she wants is one wild night with the hot-as-hell biker. She gets more than she bargained for, and it's up to Hop to convince Lanie that he's the best thing that's ever happened to her...Fans of Lori Foster and Julie Ann Walker will love this book!